The Game Changer

FINLEY CHUVA

This is a work of fiction. Names, characters, businesses, places, events, locales, and incidents are either the products of the author's imagination or used in a fictitious manner. Any resemblance to actual persons, living or dead, or actual events is purely coincidental.

THE GAME CHANGER. Copyright © 2022 by Finley Chuva. All rights reserved.

First edition: November 2022

Published by Pink Ampersand Press.

Social media icons from flaticon.com.

To my wife, for always believing in me. This book would not exist without you.

CHAPTER ONE

Thwack.

The ball smashed into the upper left corner of the net, but Elena Torres couldn't hear the sound over the roar of the crowd. She whirled around and threw her hands in the air, and the two players closest to her ran forward, palms slapping together with hers.

She'd done it. Elena watched as the giant screen above their heads updated with the new score: 2-1.

"That'll teach 'em to foul you in the box with three minutes left," said Dee, her fellow Denver Defiant forward, moving in close so Elena could hear her. Individual strands of her sweaty blond bangs were stuck to her forehead, and her normally pale cheeks were ruddy with exertion. "Yanking your hair? What a bitch move."

"She can rip it out for all I care right now!" Elena shouted back over the cheers, and Dee laughed. "Let's go to the semifinals!"

"All right, y'all. We've got this!" Joana yelled, rallying the other defenders as they turned to make their way back to the far end of the pitch. "Lock it down!"

Elena moved toward her own spot, muscles aching with fatigue. It had been a long, brutal game, and she was going to have more than a few nasty bruises later. But it would be worth it as long as they could maintain this lead.

It was always worth it. Soccer was what she lived for.

Elena breathed in the scent of grass and fresh air, wiping the sweat out of her eyes, taking a moment to appreciate the cool October breeze against her overheated skin before play resumed.

The Austin goalie kicked off, and the next several minutes passed in a blur of movement. Elena ran like she'd just stepped onto the field, adrenaline fueling her depleted energy stores. She ignored the hot burn of her calves and the way her lungs cried out for oxygen. She was everywhere she needed to be, intercepting a pass, lobbing a beautiful cross over to Dee, keeping the ball anywhere but at the feet of an Austin player.

Finally, two sharp blasts from the referee's whistle pierced the air from a few feet to her left. Elena flinched, a reflex she couldn't stop even after twenty-five years of hearing the sound, but the reaction was more than drowned out by the excitement flooding her body. Today, the whistle blast was the sweet sound of victory.

Elena let out a yell that mingled with the cheers of her teammates and the fans. Subs and technical staff came rushing onto the field to join the celebratory chaos. Elena high-fived Dee and watched as someone's arms were flung around Dee's torso from behind in a surprise victory hug.

"Semifinals, baby!" came a high-pitched squeal from behind Dee's nearly six-foot-tall frame, revealing Mystery Arms to be Annie, the eighteen-year-old forward who had been traded to the team only a month before. Without waiting for a response, she moved away and turned a cartwheel, narrowly missing colliding with Natalie and Min, who were hugging and jumping up and down like they had just won the World Cup.

"Wow. Now that's some enthusiasm," Dee said with a chuckle.

"Hey, if I were going to the semis in my first season, I'd

be doing cartwheels, too."

"Remember what it was like to have that kind of energy?" Elena swatted at her shoulder. "Don't drag me into your whole '*Oh, woe is me, I'm old!*' thing. I'm only thirty-one."

"You're right, my bad. You're in your prime."

"Thank you," Elena answered with mock satisfaction.

"Seriously, though. You are. Your passing game today was even better than usual. And that PK was fantastic."

Elena shrugged. "She was an easy read."

"Still. From captain to future captain—"

"Hey. You know I hate it when you say shit like that." Her excitement dampened at the thought of Dee's impending retirement. She and Dee had been there from the Defiant's inception three years before. Dee was the backbone of the team, and Elena didn't know how they were supposed to manage without her. She also had no idea where Dee had gotten the idea that Elena wanted to be captain, because she most definitely did not.

"*From captain to future captain,*" Dee continued with a pointed look. "Well done. Semifinals, here we come!" She raised her voice on the last sentence, and Natalie and Min echoed her words with shouts of their own.

Elena felt her smile blooming again from watching her teammates celebrate.

"Congrats." Colleen, an Austin defender Elena played with on the National Team, appeared beside her and held out her hand for a quick shake. "That's three wins in a row, right? Think you're ready to go in there and win it all?"

"Hey, we've got the momentum. As long as everyone stays healthy, I think we might actually make it. Knock on wood." Elena mimed the action, and Colleen shot Elena a smile that seemed surprisingly genuine.

"Good luck! I'll be rooting for you."

Elena thanked her and shook a few more hands, then made her way off the field, pausing when she saw a reporter waving her over.

She should have expected this. Elena took a deep breath and mentally ran through some of her go-to lines as she walked toward the woman standing in front of the camera.

"Elena!"

"Hey, Farah." Only a handful of reporters covered their games regularly, and Elena knew all of them by name.

"You have time for a few questions?"

Elena pasted on her interview smile. "Hit me."

Thankfully, it was fairly painless, as far as interviews went. This was the first time in the team's existence that they had finished in the top half of the table, much less made it to the post-season. It made a great story, and Elena was proud to tell it. But she was also glad when the interview was over so she could escape to the locker room.

She was the first player back, and she savored the brief silence that would soon be broken by post-game showers and shouts as everyone fought to get their favorite celebratory jams cued up first. She loved celebrating with her teammates, but she always enjoyed it more if she took a few moments for herself first.

She breathed in for the count of three, then out for the count of four. Just as she finished the count for the second time, she heard the telltale whoops and the sound of cleats on concrete. The door burst open, players poured in, and Min hollered, "Dibs on Spotify duty!"

Elena grinned at their infectious energy. Her parched tongue and jelly-like quads didn't matter. They could do it. She felt it in her bones. They could win it all.

That was, of course, if tonight didn't kill her first.

Four hours, one torturous ice bath, and one glorious nap later, Elena woke to her phone blasting in her ear. The early 2000s Shania Twain ring tone meant it could only be one person. She felt around for the phone, swiped, and held it up to her ear.

"Mar?" Elena's voice was scratchy, and she rubbed sleep out of her eyes as she squinted in the direction of the window, trying to discern the time from the dim orange glow she could just make out along the edges of her curtains. Had she slept through her alarm? "What's up?"

"Don't kill me."

Elena rolled over and stretched, a yawn blurring her first few words. "Wasn't on my agenda for the day, but I can always make an exception if needed."

"I can't go tonight."

"What? No!" The lingering lazy warmth from her nap vanished, replaced by a chill that turned her stomach to ice. Football for All was holding their annual gala tonight. Her agent had made her promise she would be there, and Kit would know if she didn't show up.

"I'm so sorry. But you're not going to believe this. Harvard wants me to head up a medical trial they're doing."

"Holy shit, you're kidding!" Elena forgot about her panic, the rush of surprise jerking her up to a sitting position. "That's amazing."

"I know! It's for the use of gene therapy to treat SCID."

"I have no idea what that means, but if you're happy, I'm happy! It sounds super impressive." Elena paused, frowning. "But wait, what does that have to do with tonight?"

"I'm supposed to start on Monday."

"*This* Monday?"

"The one two days from today. Yeah."

"Jeez, talk about last minute."

"Right? They originally offered another person the position, but it fell through. So they called me, and I said yes, booked my flight, and now here we are."

"That's quite the afternoon. When do you fly out?"

"Tomorrow at 3."

"No wonder you don't have time for little old me and my social anxiety," Elena quipped. "Actually, I think I should skip tonight and help you. You probably have a million things to do."

"I do, and I appreciate the thought, but you know you have to go. Kit will murder you if you skip."

"Listen, yes, she's my agent. Yes, I'm still mildly terrified of her after a decade. But I think she'll understand when I explain that my best friend is a medical god and her alma mater is begging her to return to their hallowed halls to help cure sick children. Clearly, it is my sacred duty to make that happen."

"Yeah, I don't think she's going to go for that. And I'm not a god."

"I love that you only add that as an afterthought."

Elena could practically hear her shrug on the other end of the line. "I know I'm good at my job. What can I say?"

"You can say, 'Elena, I'm gonna need you to fly out here to build me a bigger door. My head won't fit through this one.'"

"Ha ha," Margot deadpanned. "Anyway, I wasn't just calling to bail on you. I also have a proposal."

"For what?"

"To keep you from murdering me."

"I wouldn't murder you. Think of all the sick kids you save."

"Glad I mean so much to you."

"You know you do. But anyway, go on."

"Harper just got back into town yesterday. She doesn't have plans tonight, and she would be happy to go with you."

Elena blinked in confusion. "Harper, as in your little sister, Harper?"

"No, some random guy named Harper I pulled in off the street. In case you're into dudes now."

"You're hilarious," Elena answered in a flat tone as she picked at a loose thread unraveling from the edge of her top sheet. She hadn't seen Harper in probably close to a decade, and they had never been close the way she and Margot were. In all likelihood, they would have nothing in common, and while Margot would have been a comforting presence, Harper would just be another stranger in a room full of them. "It's fine. I'm not holding your sister hostage for the night just so I don't have to talk to people."

"You wouldn't be. She's happy to do it."

Elena gritted her teeth as she heard her therapist's voice in her head. *"Don't say no to sudden changes in plans immediately. Try to think them over objectively first. Give yourself twenty seconds. If you still don't want to do it, then go ahead and say no."*

"Give me a second to think it over. Are you sure she'd be up for it?" Elena took a breath and tried to view things objectively. They could always talk about Margot, at least. It would be better than going alone.

"Seriously, it's no big deal. She was probably just going to be sitting on my couch watching *House Hunters* in her pajamas."

Elena heard a muffled noise that she guessed was a pillow being flung in Margot's direction. She couldn't be certain, of course, but the likelihood was high, given the massive assortment of ugly throw pillows that were strewn atop Margot's living room furniture.

"My apologies," Margot continued, as though she had been interrupted by an assistant providing additional information and not a flying pillow. "She would never watch something so Pinterest-y as *House Hunters*. I meant *Gossip Girl*."

"*Fuck you. I'm literally 28 years old,*" the background voice said, and Elena couldn't hold back a chuckle.

"Well, I hate to take her away from such pressing plans, but if she's up for it, that would be great."

"Consider it done."

"Tell Harper I'll see her at 8?"

"Will do."

Elena hung up the phone and heaved a sigh before she climbed to her feet. It was time to get ready.

CHAPTER TWO

"Really?" Harper hurled mental daggers at her sister across the living room as Margot hung up the phone. They were as ineffectual as the ridiculous, puppy-printed throw pillow she'd tossed at Margot's face a minute earlier. What was with all the throw pillows? The one she was leaning against now looked like it could be in an episode of *My Little Pony*. Her sister may have gone to Harvard, but she didn't have an ounce of artistic sense.

"What?" Margot asked.

Harper pitched her voice up half an octave. "'*Of course she can go with you. She's just a loser who has no friends.*'"

"I did not say that."

"You may as well have."

"It's only Elena. She knows I was just teasing you."

Exactly. It was Elena.

Elena, who had been Harper's teenage bisexual awakening, the object of her secret, soul-crushing affections, which she'd harbored from afar until Elena had moved away to college. (And for more than a few months after, if she were being honest.)

But Margot didn't know about that—which meant she wasn't being purposefully cruel; she was just being an annoying older sister.

"Well, no one watches *Gossip Girl* anymore. You may as well have said *Dawson's Creek*."

"I'll be sure to update my pop culture references." Margot's tone was dry as dust.

"Anyway, the point is, next time, maybe try something like, 'Harper is a successful entrepreneur who's extremely busy opening up her second business, but she's a nice person who is willing to do you this favor.'"

"You can tell her that yourself. It'll give you something to talk about." Margot stood, brushing her blunt bob away from her face. She had inherited their mom's looks, with her stick-straight chestnut hair, soulful brown eyes, and thin, willowy figure. Harper shared her pale skin, but she'd inherited their dad's (lack of) height gene. Her hair was a mass of curls so thick and heavy that her neck ached if she let it grow too long. The color had been described as everything from strawberry blond to "the love child of ketchup and mustard."

That wasn't one you forgot.

"Are you sure you don't need me to help with all this?" Harper waved her hands in a circle, indicating the general insanity that was going to be Margot's next 24 hours. "You're going to be running around like a chicken with your head cut off."

"Your job is to appease my conscience. I feel bad canceling on her so late."

"You're just lucky I brought some of my nice clothes in the car."

The vast majority of her belongings were still sitting in boxes in her old apartment in Colorado Springs, waiting for her new apartment in Denver to open up in two weeks. She was staying with Margot in the interim.

Or, as it turned out, she would be staying alone in Margot's house in the interim.

"Mm." Margot made a noncommittal sound and started climbing the stairs, only to pause halfway up. "Oh! Before you start getting ready, would you mind grabbing my luggage from the garage? It's the hunter green set. Both pieces."

"Sure. No problem."

Harper resisted rolling her eyes as she walked toward the garage. Only Margot would think it was no big deal to get ready for a formal event with barely more than an hour's notice. But that was her sister: brilliant, a little oblivious, and thoroughly content to attend any event in a decade-old dress with nary a swipe of lipstick.

Harper was no fashionista, but she certainly had no desire to face possible photographers *au naturel*.

By the time she located and finagled the luggage out from behind a mountain of camping gear, she was more than ready for a shower. Her favorite Princess Leia t-shirt was smeared with dust, her arms felt like they were covered in grime, and she was fairly certain there were cobwebs in her hair. Why on earth did Margot even have camping gear? She was about as outdoorsy as the wildly expensive espresso machine that sat on her kitchen counter.

Harper grumbled to herself as she kicked a bag of tent stakes back into the corner, then lugged the suitcases up the stairs to Margot's room, where she dumped them unceremoniously on the bed.

"You're welcome," she announced to the empty room, not particularly caring if Margot heard her. "If you need me, I'll be in the shower."

A sound of acknowledgment came from deep within Margot's walk-in closet, and Harper made a beeline for the bathroom to begin her attempt at the world's fastest transformation.

At 8:03 P.M., the doorbell rang, and Harper's stomach jumped. She inhaled deeply and took a last look in the mirror. She was freshly showered, shaved, and perfumed. Her dress had miraculously resisted wrinkling during the drive over this morning, and even her hair was cooperating.

Harper wiped a finger along her bottom lip to remove a tiny lipstick smudge and stepped back to admire her reflection. She looked pretty damn fantastic. Her dove gray dress made her eyes look more gray than green, and it had a sweetheart neckline and a skirt that swirled as she walked. Dresses in her size were often a nightmare, either hanging off her like a potato sack or squishing her boobs so far up she looked like a Regency-era prostitute. She'd finally learned to look for companies that specialized in making plus-size clothes for various body types, rather than treating anyone over a size twelve like one identical giant blob. This particular dress was her favorite. It hugged her curves without being constricting, and the smooth fabric slipped along her skin in a way that made her feel like a goddess.

Harper wanted to look good tonight. She could say it was because of potential photographers, but she knew deep-down that wasn't the truth.

Old habits die hard and all of that.

She called goodbye to Margot and descended the stairs, mentally preparing herself for the sight of Elena. It wasn't as though she didn't know what to expect. Harper had seen her in news articles and the few-and-far-between broadcast National Team games. They were also Facebook friends, although Elena was rarely on any social media. Her Instagram was a ghost town that occasionally spawned a clearly sponsored post featuring some overpriced protein shake.

In short, she knew what Elena looked like, despite the fact that they hadn't seen each other in who knew how many years. (Okay, she knew. It had been five.) Tall. Athletic. Unfairly goddess-esque.

Harper was glad she felt prepared to make a good impression in return, if only because she felt she owed it to her high school self.

Then the door swung open, and it was all she could do not to let her jaw drop like a cartoon villain who had just witnessed the destruction of all her dastardly plans.

Because *holy shit*.

She had tried to mentally prepare, but she hadn't accounted for the fact that she had never seen Elena in anything more formal than a soccer kit or the gray tank tops she had favored back in high school.

Honestly, Harper wasn't sure it would have mattered if she had. There simply was no preparing for Elena Torres in a suit. Her entire outfit was black, from the form-fitting jacket down to the sensibly low-heeled boots. Her black hair was pulled back in a loose French braid, and her golden brown skin practically glowed in the twilight.

The brisk October air bit at Harper's skin and raised goosebumps on her arms, but she still felt strangely overheated.

"Sorry I'm late. I underestimated the traffic."

Harper tried to will her brain back into functioning again. "No worries." She smiled, ignoring the fact that her mouth felt dryer than the Sahara. "Gave me time to finish my lipstick. And besides, I don't think three minutes counts as late."

"Tell that to my coach," Elena said with a wry smile that made Harper's heart do a Simone Biles–level flip inside her chest. Jesus, she needed to chill. "But I'm glad it worked out. You ready? You look really great, by the way."

"Thanks!" Harper's voice sounded way too chirpy, and she held back a wince. She tried again, aiming for a more normal register. "So do you."

It was the understatement of the century, but Harper didn't trust herself to say anything further. Instead, she stepped out and shut the front door, then followed Elena to the small silver car parked in the driveway.

"Where is this event, by the way? Margot told me basically nothing other than the fact that I needed to get out a fancy dress." Harper buckled her seatbelt just before Elena backed out onto the road.

"It's at the downtown Marriott. A fundraiser gala for a soccer nonprofit called Football for All. Have you heard of them?"

"No."

"They establish soccer teams in underserved communities. It's a really cool place, actually. They also do summer camps, and I've partnered with them a few times. But anyway, tonight isn't anything too crazy. First, there's dinner, and some people will talk. Drinks and dancing after if you're into that, but I don't really want to stay too long. I'm not super into the whole, y'know…" Elena paused, and Harper waited for her to finish the thought. "…giant social events thing."

"Sometimes people are just too much."

"You can say that again."

Harper couldn't think of a way to continue that avenue of conversation, mostly because she generally enjoyed being around people, and she sensed Elena didn't feel the same way. She had mostly been a loner in high school, Harper remembered, even though she'd been fairly popular due to her soccer star status. Instead, she just watched the Denver city lights pass by outside the window.

Harper's phone buzzed inside the black clutch she had snagged from Margot's closet. She took out her phone and found a text from Angel, returning her earlier message freaking out about going out with Elena.

Angel (8:11 P.M.): holy shit THE elena???

Angel (8:11 P.M.): like, the one you spent the first two years of our friendship pining after? what the hell happened while i was asleep???

Harper (8:12 P.M.): i didn't pine

Angel (8:13 P.M.): babe. bestie. my heart. you pined so hard your name should have been chris

Harper snorted and tried to turn it into a cough, because

she definitely was not going to be sharing this conversation.

"Nice car." She blurted out the first subject she thought of in order to prevent Elena from asking. Just in case. She wasn't good at lying on the spot.

"Thanks. It's a hybrid. I'd like to go fully electric, but the ones that hold a decent charge are still above my pay grade. Plus, they're not at all practical for road trips."

Harper felt a prickle of intrigue. "Do you go on a lot of road trips?"

"No. Not really, anyway. I just like the idea of them. You?"

"Never been on one. It does sound fun, though," she admitted. "Rolling down the highway, windows down, music blasting. Not sure that would balance out the cheap hotels and constant traffic, though."

"Shh, don't ruin my dream. If you like music, though, there's an aux cord in there." She pointed over toward the glove box. "Anything's fine."

"Great! What kind of music do you like?" A memory suddenly came rushing back. "Wait, you're not still into country, are you?"

"Yeah, why?"

Harper pulled a face. "For shame. Aren't you supposed to be a lesbian?"

Elena's guffaw echoed throughout the interior of the car, and the thought that she was the cause of it made Harper feel a bit light and floaty. "You know, lesbians are allowed to like country music."

"Only the ones with terrible taste."

"There's no such thing. The whole concept is entirely subjective."

"That's something only someone with terrible taste would say."

Elena glanced over at her before looking back at the road. "I'm surprised you remembered that. About the country music, I mean."

"Well, it was hard to concentrate with you and Margot blaring your precious Shania Twain all the time. A girl couldn't even read her Star Wars fanfiction in peace."

"It was not *all* the time. And I can't believe you're judging me in a sentence that contained the words 'Star Wars fanfiction.'"

"Hey, now. Insult Star Wars, and I'll go home and abandon you to a room full of strangers."

"I would never," Elena said, placing a hand over her heart in mock sincerity.

Harper looked down at her phone, trying to keep from smiling too widely as she scrolled through her music. She decided on Brandi Carlile, which was as close to country music as she would allow. Elena approved of the choice, and they were four songs into the album when they arrived at the gala.

They stopped for a photo at the curtained setup right outside the entrance to the ballroom. Harper had a moment where she wasn't sure how to pose, but she just followed Elena's lead and stayed a few inches apart, smiled, and moved on. When they continued inside, Harper's eyes widened. The room was huge, full of people and tables, but it was fairly nondescript, aside from a large, modern chandelier, which hung from the center of the ceiling and immediately captured Harper's attention.

"Wow." It was beautiful, the harsh, intricate angles of it playing with light and shadow in a completely unique way. Her fingers itched for a pencil to capture the effect, but instead she just stared for a few moments, trying to take a mental picture to be able to recreate it later.

"What?" Elena asked.

"The chandelier. It's stunning."

Elena followed her gaze. "It is, isn't it? They have the gala here every year, and I love it."

"So you come every year?" It occurred to her that she could take an actual picture with her phone, but she wanted to look like she belonged, not like she was some gauche hanger-on snapping pics.

"Well, every year since I've been involved with them, so this is my third. I've only been back in Denver for three years. Before that, I was playing in Miami."

"Ah, right," Harper said, like she didn't know that already. "Are you glad to be back in Denver?"

"I am. It's a little weird without my family here, since my folks stayed in Florida. After five years there, they got too spoiled and didn't want to come back to face the Colorado winters."

"Soft," Harper scoffed with a teasing smile, and Elena answered it with one of her own.

"Exactly. But honestly, they sacrificed so much to get me where I am. I was happy to be able to get them a place there. They deserve it. I miss getting to see them as often as I could, but I hated the weather there. Give me mountains over humidity any day of the week."

"I'll drink to that. You do not want to see this hair in the humidity." Harper gestured toward her hair, glad for the easy opportunity to circumnavigate the topic of her relationship with her parents. Now was not the time for that particular can of worms. "Speaking of which…"

"Drinks are this way," Elena said, indicating the far corner. "Then we should head to our table. We're a little late, so dinner should be soon."

"Terrific. I'm so hungry I could eat a cow. And I'm a vegetarian."

Elena laughed and led the way to the bar. "Margot mentioned that. I called here right after she called me, and they said it wouldn't be a problem at all to change it. They must have special meals set aside for people who forget to specify beforehand."

"Thank you." Harper was surprised that Margot had remembered that. Well, not that she had remembered, but that she had cared enough to learn the detail in the first place.

As they passed through the crowd, Harper eyed the outfits of the other people there and breathed out a sigh of relief when she saw that her choice of attire was perfectly appropriate.

They got their drinks—an Old Fashioned for her and a sparkling water for Elena—before they made their way over to their table. There were already four other people there, possibly two couples from the way they were seated.

Harper introduced herself and found out that the two men were a couple, but the man and woman were just business partners. She easily made small talk with them for a few minutes. Elena smiled and contributed occasionally to the conversation, but something about her stiff posture made Harper think she was close to whipping off her suit jacket, tying on some cleats, and running off into the sunset.

"Ooh, here comes the food," Elena said, peering over Harper's shoulder.

A few seconds later, a plate with sweet potatoes, grilled asparagus, and a generous portion of what appeared to be mushroom risotto appeared in front of her. Harper thanked the server and dug in with gusto. The risotto was delicious, a perfect blend of earthy and creamy, and the first bite nearly melted in her mouth.

A tall Black man stepped up to the microphone at the front of the room, and Harper moved her attention to him as she sampled the asparagus.

"Good evening, everyone. Thank you so much for attending. We would not be here tonight if it weren't for the support from each and every one of you."

Harper listened while she ate, happy to listen as the man continued speaking about the things they had accomplished and their goals for the upcoming year.

Elena breathed a sigh of relief when Drew and—Dennis?

Dallas?—left for the dance floor. The speeches had ended fifteen minutes ago, and the other two had gone to do some networking. The room was uncomfortably loud now that the music had started, but at least she didn't have to try to carry on a conversation with strangers. She'd gotten good enough at it over the years, but it still ranked right around getting her teeth cleaned on her list of favorite activities.

A movement near the floor caught her eye, and when she looked, she saw it was Harper's foot tapping to the beat. It was clad in a black, strappy affair with an impressively tall heel.

"Don't worry, I won't make you dance in those shoes."

"What's wrong with my heels?"

Elena felt her cheeks heat as she tried to clarify what she had meant as a funny but friendly statement. "Nothing. They're lovely. Of course. They're just, um, tall."

"Sorry, I was just joking. Don't worry. I promise my shoes' feelings aren't hurt," she said with a wink.

Elena released a breath. "I just know that if I tried to dance in them, I would fall, break both of my legs, and end my career prematurely."

"Good thing you're tall, then. They're kind of a requirement when you're my height. I've danced in heels plenty of times."

"Oh. Uh, did you want to dance?" Elena asked with an attempt at a casual tone. *Please say no.*

"No, I'm good. Just because I can, doesn't mean I want to. My feet would give me hell for it tomorrow, and I have way too much to do to be limping around."

"Want to grab another drink before we go, then?" Elena would have been perfectly content to leave now, but she wanted to make sure Harper had a good time, since she had basically given up a free evening to come be Elena's security blanket.

"Sure."

They found two seats at the long bar that stretched along the far wall. From her new seat in the corner, Elena could see the entire ballroom, and she watched as a few couples took to the dance floor while most stayed in their seats. She always found it much more interesting to observe people's interactions than to actually partake in them herself.

"What are you up to tomorrow, then? Are you helping Margot?"

"Yeah, I'll probably help her with a few things. But I also had plans to go start on some things at Bewitched."

"Bewitched?"

"The Bewitched Bishop. It's the board game café I'm opening."

"Right, Margot mentioned that! Congratulations."

"Thanks."

"How far along are you in the process?" The bartender set their drinks down in front of them, and Elena thanked him before turning back to Harper.

"Well, I have the space leased, but there's still a lot to do to get it ready."

"When do you open?"

"November."

"Soon, then. You must be busy."

"You have no idea. I can't talk about my to-do list right now, though. I'll start breaking out in hives, and they really don't go with this dress."

Elena grimaced. "Sorry, we don't have to talk about business. Just let me know when you're having your grand opening. I'm excited to check it out."

"Definitely. Speaking of other things to discuss, I think you've been spotted by a fan," Harper murmured, indicating with her eyes that Elena should look over her shoulder.

Elena shifted and tried her best to check subtly. She found a woman staring at her and immediately turned away, angling herself in the opposite direction.

"Oh, jeez." She knew that look.

"What's wrong? Do you not do autographs?"

"No, I do." Elena rubbed at her thumb with her middle

finger, willing the woman to stop looking at her. "She just doesn't seem like she wants an autograph."

"How can you tell?"

"Sometimes fans want…more. I'm just not really into that sort of thing."

"That sort of thing?" Harper's forehead wrinkled. She looked like Margot when she did that.

"You know." Elena waved a hand in the air. "One-night stands with fans and stuff. That's Dee's department, not mine."

"Oh. *That* kind of more."

Elena nodded.

"Maybe I was wrong. Maybe she's not a fan. She's just checking you out because you're—" Harper paused, taking a sip of her drink. "She thinks you're hot."

"Mmm." Elena remained noncommittal, sipping at her iced tea.

Harper looked back over Elena's shoulder again. "She seems to have gotten the message, though, so crisis averted."

A wave of relief passed over Elena, and she darted a quick look at Harper's drink to see if she was almost finished. It was something pink and fruity—Elena hadn't been able to understand what she'd said to the bartender over the music—and she still had half a glass left. Damn.

"So, how do you meet women if you don't date your plethora of adoring fans?" Harper asked with a teasing smile.

"Honestly, I really don't."

"Rocking the single life?"

"Divorcée life. Same thing, more baggage."

"Everyone's got baggage. You just get a special sticker." Harper didn't seem surprised, so she must have heard the news through Margot. Besides, it wasn't exactly anything new, her divorce having been finalized two years ago.

"It's just complicated, being out of town as much as I am. Not much time to get to know someone." It was an oversimplification, but this wasn't something she wanted to get into. Harper might have been surprisingly easy to talk to, but Elena didn't like discussing her love life with anyone, much less someone who was barely more than an acquaintance.

"Have you tried Masked?"

"What's that?"

"It's a dating app."

Elena grimaced, but Harper shook her head and cut her off before she could respond. "It's not one of those that's all about hook-ups. It's focused on developing real relationships via openness and being yourself."

"Wait, and it's called Masked?"

Harper nodded, and Elena couldn't help the laughter that bubbled up in her throat. "Oh my god, that's amazing."

Harper looked puzzled, and Elena managed to stop laughing in order to explain. "Sorry. Autism joke."

Harper frowned, and Elena hurried to clarify. "No, I mean, like, it's only funny if you're autistic. Which I am. The term 'masking' means basically the exact opposite, so it's funny."

"Oh, I see." She was probably still confused, but she didn't ask Elena to elaborate. "I just thought of it because it's online, so distance isn't a problem. And you wouldn't have to worry about fans. It's completely anonymous."

"Great, I've always wanted to meet an ax murderer."

Harper snorted. "It's not that bad. You have to put in your phone number when you register, so it's not just a bunch of trolling randos with twenty accounts. But there are no pictures or videos. You just list things you like and what you're looking for, and it matches you to people."

"What, so if I put that I like watching the Discovery channel, it'll match me to someone else who watches it?"

"Something like that."

"Weird." Elena swirled her plastic drink stirrer around, weaving little circular patterns into her iced tea. It was an interesting idea. It would be nice to get to know a woman before having the pressure of a face-to-face interaction. It would also be an excellent way to avoid the insane fans that made her want to hide for a week any time she dared to read the comments on her Instagram. But on the other hand... "But what if, when we do eventually meet, there's no chemistry?"

"Obviously a possibility. But no harm, no foul, right?"

"I guess, but then it just seems like a waste of time."

"Sometimes it is. Someone once told me dating is like a job where you have to put in the work ahead of time because you know the payoff will come eventually. You just don't know when."

"That's a really interesting way of thinking about it. And you agree?"

"I think it makes sense. I want someone to spend the rest of my life with, you know? That's a pretty big ask. You can't just show up your first day on the job and demand a million bucks. I mean, you *can*, but it's not going to work."

Elena laughed. "True enough. So how has that approach worked for you?"

"I'm still doing my time. How do you think I know so much about Masked?" Harper quirked a smile as she held up her phone and wiggled it a couple of times.

Elena slid her own phone out of her pocket and opened the app store. There it was, #2 in the Dating category, featuring a cute little icon of a purple and silver Colombina mask.

Elena thought for a few seconds, then put the phone back away without pressing the download button.

CHAPTER THREE

The next morning, Elena arrived at the Complex early to eat breakfast before the nine A.M. team strategy meeting. The Complex was a small cluster of interconnected buildings that sat alongside the Defiant's practice field. It was her home away from home—made easier by the fact that it was located a mere six-minute drive from her actual home. It housed their team gym, a sauna, a physical therapy room, a large meeting room, the coaches' offices, and even a small dining hall that served coaching staff–approved food at mealtimes.

The weekly menu was chosen based on macronutrients rather than flavor, but Elena ate there for dinner most evenings, anyway. It meant she didn't have to spend twenty minutes deciding what to cook or order every day, and that made bland chicken breast on a bed of oil-free veggies and under-salted wild rice taste like a four-star dish.

The pale blue walls of the dining room echoed as Elena pushed her chair away from the circular table and tossed the empty Greek yogurt container and banana peel into the garbage. The halls were abandoned, as was the meeting room when she arrived, still dark except for the sunlight filtering in from the large windows along the opposite wall. She flipped on the lights and shuffled inside, contemplating what to do while she waited for everyone else to arrive. Then a soccer ball lying alone on the floor caught her attention. She toed it up and starting to juggle the ball with her foot. *One, two, three...*

As she continued juggling, Elena let her mind drift back to the night before. The outing had been different with Harper than it would have been with Margot. Not in a bad way. Just different. Harper hadn't stolen the beets from her salad like Margot would have. She didn't seem to care about people watching, which was how Elena and Margot passed the time at most of the events they attended together. But Harper had laughed more. Margot was harder to please, with a biting wit and a dry sense of humor. Harper was a little goofier, more kind, more open, more...*vibrant* was the word that came to mind.

It was strange how little she knew about Harper, now that she thought about it. Elena knew through Margot that Harper had lived in Colorado Springs since college and owned a board game café there, but Elena had never seen it. The only other facts she could think of had been garnered during the frequent afternoons she'd spent at the Wright household during high school: Harper was into Star Wars and art. Or had been, anyway. Both had been fairly obvious from the assortment of light saber t-shirts she'd worn and the way the walls of her bedroom had been plastered in her own drawings.

Odd, how you could spend so much of your life just one step away from someone but never really know them.

But she was starting to think she would like to know Harper, and not only as a convenient stand-in for Margot. She'd had a good time the night before, which had honestly been a surprise. Elena rarely bonded with people right away. That train of thought brought her to Masked, which she still hadn't downloaded. The little icon kept popping up in her brain, taunting her with the possibility.

Her concentration was interrupted by a huge, jaw-cracking yawn, and the ball went rolling.

"Long night?"

She looked up to find Dee standing in the door frame, dressed in a dark hoodie and sweatpants, a neon yellow ball propped against her hip. She held a large Starbucks cup in the opposite hand, and her closely cropped honey blond hair was in the tousled style she had favored lately.

"Not really. Just a little tired. And distracted."

Dee sauntered forward and flipped Elena's ball up with the tip of her sneaker, then kept it in the air with her knees. *Thwap, thwap, thwap.* It was a familiar rhythm, one Elena had heard thousands of times over the years.

"What was distracting you?"

"Nothing interesting."

Something about her tone must have grabbed Dee's attention, because she let the ball drop to the ground. It rolled away as she stared at Elena, her head cocked to the side, a grin slowly spreading across her face. The sudden intensity of her ice blue gaze made Elena look away, averting her eyes and focusing on the Starbucks cup she held instead. Iced americano, one Splenda. Elena would stake her career on it. When it came to her coffee order, Dee was even more of a creature of habit than Elena.

"Tell me it isn't so."

"What isn't so?"

"After all these years, am I finally going to get to help you with girl trouble?"

"Why do you make it sound like you've been waiting for this day?"

"Because I have. I love giving relationship advice."

Elena scoffed. "Anyone who listens to you is an idiot."

"Hey, now. My advice comes with the standard disclaimer: Do as I say, not as I do." With those words, Dee grabbed a chair and flipped it around, straddling it and then gesturing toward Elena. "Go on, spill."

"There's nothing to spill."

"Tell your big sister."

"You're too white to be my sister."

"Hilarious. I'm still waiting."

"Okay, fine. I was out with a friend last night."

"A friend, huh? *Spicy*."

Elena rolled her eyes. "Not like tha—"

"Wait, it's not Margot, is it? I've always wondered about you two."

"No." Elena paused, debating whether to share the next detail. "Though it was her sister, actually. Harper."

Dee slapped the back of her chair, throwing her head back with a crow of...well, Elena wasn't sure, exactly, but she certainly seemed to be enjoying herself. "Oh my god, you're living in a romantic comedy, and I'm here for it. So, what, are you deep in the forbidden love pining stage? Can't stop thinking about her when you hear those sappy songs on the radio?"

"Oh my god, why are we friends?" Elena rolled her eyes toward the heavens as though actually praying. "Anyway. It's not about her, not like that. She told me about this dating app she likes. Masked."

"Ahh, yeah."

"You know it?"

"I tried it." Dee made a face as she set down her drink and interlaced her fingers behind her head. "Not really my thing."

"Shocking. Since from my impression, it's more for talking to people than sleeping with them."

"A little below the belt, but I'll allow it. You're thinking about dating again, then?"

Elena nodded, then plopped down in a chair across from Dee. "I've been thinking about it for a while, but I wasn't sure how to get started. You know how I am with talking to new people. I like the idea of being able to start behind a screen, you know? Get to know someone without the stress of talking to them face-to-face."

"Sounds like a good idea to me. I mean, a terrible idea *for* me. I'd rather face the Canadian defensive line without shin guards. But a good idea for you."

"I just don't know if I should."

"What, if you should date? Why the hell not?"

"You know."

Dee's brows lifted. "Do I?"

Elena heaved out an annoyed sigh at needing to spell it out. This was why she should have had this conversation with Margot. "Claire?"

"Ah, yes, the Ditching Bitch."

Against her will, Elena snorted out a laugh. "I thought I told you to stop calling her that."

"And I said I would stop calling her that when it stopped being accurate. Which it never will, so." Dee shrugged, like it was simply a fact she couldn't change, not a nonsense nickname for Elena's ex-wife Dee had invented to cheer Elena up right after her divorce was finalized. They'd both been wildly shit-faced at the time, and Elena had a vague recollection of laughing until she cried when Dee came up with it. Two years later, minus the alcohol, she didn't find it nearly as hilarious. At least, she tried not to.

"You could at least abbreviate it or something."

"Nah. Wouldn't have the same ring."

"Anyway, you know why she left."

"Because she's a bitch who decided to leave you due to the fact that you didn't spend your every moment bowing before her and composing psalms about her divinity?"

"She wasn't that bad."

Dee leaned forward, her face suddenly serious. "She absolutely was. Wanting someone to give up their career to be with you is literally the most selfish, stupid thing a person can ask."

"She didn't want me to give up my career."

"Right, my bad. She didn't even give you the chance."

"Whatever." Elena found herself suddenly irritated by the

discussion. "This isn't a session of Bash the Ex. I just wanted to point out the fact that her main reason for leaving still applies. Soccer is still my first priority, and it always will be. At least, until I retire, which won't be for at least another five or six years. Knock on wood."

Dee tapped her knuckles against the back of her chair, which was definitely plastic, but Elena didn't point that out.

"So, you don't want to have another serious relationship until you retire?"

"I think that's the most logical course of action based on previous experience."

"She had completely unreasonable expectations," Dee said.

"She didn't."

"Fine. I'm tired of arguing about this. Assuming the DB—nope, I can't do it, sounds ridiculous. Assuming the Ditching Bitch had a point—which I still don't agree with, for the record—it doesn't mean you can't date at all. Especially since, logic aside, it seems like you want to. I know you're not into the one-night stand thing, but it doesn't have to be The One or The One-and-Done. Find something in between."

Elena frowned. "What do you mean?"

"Just date casually. All the kids are doing it these days. Find someone you enjoy spending time with, like this Harper girl. Go out. See where it takes you. Date. Have a good time. Have sex. But no commitment, no strings. They call it finding The One for Right Now."

"You just made that up so you don't feel bad about sleeping with every pretty woman you meet."

Dee spread her arms wide, looking utterly unapologetic. "Hey, I make sure they feel good. Why shouldn't I feel good about it, too?"

"I really don't know why we're friends."

"Yeah, yeah. Go talk to your other best friend, then. She'll tell you the same thing."

"I highly doubt she'll tell me to go have meaningless sex

with her little sister."

"Good point. Guess you'll just have to decide which of us you want to listen to, then."

"Guess I will."

Obviously, Elena wouldn't jump on Harper like Dee had suggested, but the general idea seemed to make sense.

Min and Natalie entered the room, reminding Elena that it was nearly time for the team meeting.

"Just think about it," was all Dee said before she stood and flipped her chair back around to face the front of the room.

Priti and several others shuffled in together, probably having carpooled from the team-provided apartments. Coach Talia followed right behind them.

"Good morning, everyone," Coach Talia boomed in her deep coach's voice, perpetually a bit rusty from years of shouting from the sidelines.

Elena made a mental note to think about the dating conundrum after the meeting was over. She had semifinals to concentrate on.

Monday's first order of business was simple: get the hell out of bed and over to The Bewitched Bishop.

And while Harper agreed with this idea in theory, it also meant she would have to leave the haven of feather pillows and trillion-count Egyptian cotton sheets that was her sister's bed. Harper was pretty sure the sheets that adorned her own bed were from circa 2012, purchased according to her shopping strategy of that era: buying whatever was cheapest at Walmart. This mattress even had a remote control that could change the firmness level, and she'd found the perfect setting last night. It would be a shame to waste the little time she'd have with it, really. She pulled out her phone as a compromise, so she could stay comfortable and be productive at the same time.

Take that, conscience.

The first thing she saw was a notification from Angel from 2:04 A.M. Her best friend was a freelance graphic design artist and a committed night owl. She swore she was at her most creative from midnight to four A.M., a possible side effect of living in London until her pre-teen years. She claimed to simply have never adjusted to the time change. But of course, creativity also had to take breaks, hence the middle-of-the-night memes that Harper often woke up to.

After chuckling at the Han Solo meme and dashing off a quick **lmao** to Angel, she pulled up her to-do list and skimmed it for things she could do without moving from her cocoon.

She had nailed down an official grand opening date yesterday, after checking that everything was in order with her permits and licenses. She emailed a Save the Date message to her parents and Margot, as well as a few friends from Colorado Springs. She doubted most of them would come, except for Angel, but it was possible.

Next up was her email inbox, and out of habit, she immediately skimmed the subject lines for the automated email that contained the daily closing report for The Playful Pawn, the game café she owned back in Colorado Springs. She skimmed the message, honing in on the important parts. Her brows raised when she saw their bar sales. Must have been a good day for stragglers. Or for drinking. She compared it to their daily pass purchases. Yep, drinking. Probably a bachelorette party or two.

Well, any business was good business. She just hoped it hadn't gotten too rowdy. That was rare, since they weren't a regular bar, but it did happen occasionally. It was one of several reasons she had decided to make one major change from her old business model—Bewitched would not be serving alcohol, only non-alcoholic drinks and food.

She closed the email and then looked for the message from Shawn, her recently promoted general manager. He always sent her a brief recap of the daily happenings when she was away, which wasn't often and until now, had never been for more than a few days at a time. It was still incredibly weird that she wouldn't be there for the day-to-day anymore. She already missed Shawn and the others.

But it wouldn't do to lie around reminiscing. She thought about Bewitched, just sitting there, empty and ready for her to transform it into a living, thriving business, a place for people to come and relax, play, and have fun together. The thought made little butterflies of excitement come to life in her belly. She dashed off a quick reply to Shawn, then hopped out of bed to get on with her morning.

CHAPTER FOUR

An hour later, Harper was standing in the tiny strip of parking spaces in front of The Bewitched Bishop.

It was going to be a success. She could feel it in her bones, the same way she had when she had first started the process for opening the Pawn. Except this time, she didn't feel constantly on the edge of vomiting from nerves.

It was a nice improvement.

Like most of the other buildings in the trendy little historic-style district, this one was constructed entirely from brick. The main parking lot was hidden in the back, which Harper assumed was due to the age of the building. Despite its age, it looked well-maintained and picturesque, with deep hunter green awnings over each of the three storefronts it housed. To the left was a cute little place called Midnight Vegan, which Harper would be partnering with for the food at Bewitched. In the middle was an independent bookstore called The Gay Agenda (And Other Books), which had bizarrely specific opening hours, so she hadn't met the owner during either of her previous visits. She hoped to do so soon, but first on her list today was breakfast.

She crossed over to Midnight Vegan, pushed the door open, and was immediately greeted by the aroma of freshly baked pastries, activating both her salivary glands and her stomach's growl response.

"Welcome to Midnight Vegan," said a girl standing behind the register, without glancing up from her phone.

"Thanks. Is Vivian here?" Harper glanced around for the owner, but she was nowhere to be found. Soft indie music filtered in through the speakers, and Harper admired how the atmosphere was a perfect blend of warm and welcoming with a slightly eccentric flare. Several colorful pieces by local artists hung on the walls, accompanied by minuscule succulents on long, thin display shelves. Vivian either had an exceptional eye for interior design or had hired a professional.

"No, she won't be in until this afternoon." Harper moved her gaze back to the cashier, who asked, "Can I take a message?"

"No thanks, I can come back. I'm opening a business in the building, so I just wanted to talk to her about a few things."

"Oh, *you're* the new owner of the haunted place?"

Harper barely refrained from rolling her eyes. "I mean, I'm pretty sure it's not actually haunted."

The girl, who had skin nearly pale enough to be mistaken for a ghost herself, raised her eyebrows, accentuating the piercings that lined the left one. "Call it what you want, but the past, like, million businesses that went in there went belly up like that." She snapped her fingers.

"Well, I decided to lean into it. Name, theme, the whole shebang. If it is haunted, the ghost and I are going to be besties."

"What are you starting there, anyway?"

"A board game café."

A spark lit up the girl's eyes. "Awesome! I've been dying for one to open up here."

"Well, give me a month or so to get up and running, and you'll be able to join! Friends and family discount is 10 percent off your first visit if you keep this card." Harper whipped out a business card from her purse and scrawled a quick message on the back. "Bring as many friends as you want. They'll all get the discount."

"Wow, thanks!"

"No problem." Harper eyed the menu. It mostly consisted of baked goods, which were clearly the bakery's focus, though it did feature a few main dishes. "Could I please get a breakfast bowl and…do any of those smoothies have caffeine?"

"The Good Morning Green does."

"One of those, please."

The girl rang her up with considerably more cheer than she had greeted Harper with initially.

"For here or to go?"

"To go, please."

Harper was weirdly excited to go plop down in the middle of her empty store space and eat breakfast there.

And that was exactly what she did. Ten minutes later, she was sitting on her yoga mat in the middle of Bewitched, her gaze wandering around the space. In the front room, there was a coffee bar with a small prep kitchen and stock room behind it. The larger back room sat a few steps lower than the front, and it was partitioned off by a full wall with the opening the size of a set of double doors. This would help keep the noise level down a bit, since it could grow to an impressive level with a full house.

Right now, though, the space was cavernous and silent. Harper could practically hear the echoes of her gulps as she finished off her smoothie.

There would be a lot to do.

She let a wide grin unfold as she pressed her hands together and envisioned the way it would look when she was done. It was going to be amazing.

Harper stopped in at Midnight Vegan again a few hours later, and this time, Vivian was there.

The woman was tall with a deep, honey-smooth voice, dark brown skin, and biceps to die for. Maybe it was all the whisking.

They exchanged pleasantries and then slid down into the booth in the back corner. Harper had a preliminary print-out of the menu, which they'd exchanged several emails about.

"I just have to say, the names are so much fun. And those Second Breakfast Potatoes are super addictive. I might have to put them on the menu here, too," Vivian said with a grin.

"They're good, right?"

"They really are! Though I think my favorite is probably Sansa's Lemon Cakes. I can't wait for you to try what I came up with for those."

"Have you run into any problems so far?"

"I finished all the test bakes yesterday, and the only concept I think we'll need to adjust is the Wookie Treats. Making them vegan is pretty time consuming and labor-intensive, which isn't great for me, and they're going to wind up being a lot more expensive. You want to keep them around the same price point, right?"

"If possible. What did you have in mind? These are just a copycat of what I do in my other location, so we can change it up."

They went over the details and settled on two possible solutions, which Vivian promised to test out over the next couple of days.

"I appreciate your willingness to be flexible," Vivian said. "This is going to be really great for us, too."

"Of course! I'm glad we're going to be partners. I don't know if you've tasted your own food, but literally every single thing I've had here has been delicious."

"Also, I noticed something and have to ask…was it an intentional choice to leave off, let's say, one particularly popular fantasy author's works?" Vivian gestured toward the menu.

"It was. I still have them at the Pawn, but I decided to take them all off here."

"Well, as a transgender woman, I appreciate that. Fuck her. Though I would also approve of capitalizing on her popularity to make money that wouldn't go anywhere near her, so. To each their own."

Harper shrugged. "We'll be fine without her."

"Agreed. Speaking of books, though, have you been able to meet Meg yet?"

"Meg?"

"The owner of the bookstore next door."

"Ah! No, not yet. She wasn't in last time I was here."

"She's fantastic. She and her wife have been together for, like, thirty years. And just wait until you meet Sappho."

"Sappho…the poet?"

"Not quite. Meg has a cat that roams around the store. Her name is Sappho."

"Okay, visiting has now officially moved up to number one on my to-do list."

"As it should be." Vivian glanced down at the smart watch that adorned her wrist. "She should be open now, actually. If you like to read, you should definitely stop in. I swear she's part book wizard. You just go in there with an idea of the kind of book you want to read, and twenty seconds later, the perfect one is in your hands."

"I'll keep that in mind for when I have time to read in six months or so."

Vivian gave her a pitying look. "Yeah, I remember that phase. I don't envy you. Good luck, darlin'. And if you need any help, you let me know, okay?"

"Appreciate it."

When she was back inside Bewitched—without having visited Meg and Sappho, because despite the advertised opening time, the store was still dark when she passed by—Harper sat down with her laptop on the floor. She really needed to go thrift store shopping to get a new desk and chair for her tiny office, but for now, her yoga mat would do.

Technically, she could go back to Margot's. The sign wasn't being delivered for another couple of hours, and everything else on her to-do list for the day was digital. But being in her new space brought her joy, and she wanted to stay, even though her back might complain about it later.

A beep from her phone showed a message from Elena, asking about the earrings Harper had accidentally left in her car on Saturday. Her earlobes had been sore, so she'd taken them off and put them in Elena's glove compartment, where she'd promptly forgotten about them until the next morning.

Apparently, Elena was free to bring them over today.

Harper ignored the way her stomach gave a little jump at the thought of seeing her again so soon.

She fired off a reply, brought her laptop up to her knees, and got to work.

Elena swung into the parking lot behind a large brick building with a single, small entrance. She looked down at her phone to double check the message.

Harper (2:21 P.M.): Here's the address. Just look for the best bookstore you've ever seen in your life.

She looked back up at the building again. It didn't look particularly impressive, but his was the rear view. She spotted a few small brass nameplates to the right of the door. When she got closer, she could see that one said *Midnight Vegan* and one said *The Gay Agenda (And Other Books)*—which made her chuckle—with arrows pointing to the right. There was another underneath that said *Amanda's Handcrafted Artisanal Candles* with an arrow pointing to the left.

That had to be the bookstore Harper had mentioned in her text, so she was in the right place. She stepped inside and found herself in a corridor with three glass doors. The one a few feet to her right her clearly opened into the bookstore, and the one farther down showed a few tables with people sitting at them. Apparently Amanda and her artisanal candles hadn't fared so well. She headed to the left and knocked, and Harper appeared on the other side of the door within a few seconds.

"Hey!" she greeted with a smile, pulling open the door.

"Hello. I come bearing gifts." Elena dug into her pocket and pulled out the silver, dangling earrings. They felt solid and heavy in her palm. No wonder Harper had taken them off as soon as possible; Elena couldn't imagine walking around with these things hanging from her ears.

Harper took the earrings back carefully, and Elena noticed idly how soft her fingers were as they brushed against her own.

"Thank you! My friend gave these to me, and she would kill me if I lost them." She paused, smiling a little. "Plus I just like them."

"No problem at all. I'm free for the day, so I had plenty of time."

Harper propped the door open wider. "Want to come inside? I just got my new banner. It's fresh from the printer. Come see!"

Elena followed her inside, immediately noticing a pungent, acidic sort of smell, almost like hot plastic. The source became clear when Harper led her to the huge, professionally printed vinyl banner spread out on the floor next to a bright purple yoga mat.

It said *The Bewitched Bishop* in a large font that made her think of a fantasy novel. Then, smaller, was *Board Game Café*, written underneath. It pictured a close-up of some chess pieces, surrounded by an indigo magical field. It somehow managed to avoid looking kitschy and overly busy and instead looked professional, modern, and fun all at once.

"Oh, wow. That's so good!"

"Right? The delivery guy dropped it off right before you got here, and I've just been standing here staring at it for like five minutes." Harper pulled a face. "I realize that makes me sound like a total loser, but I'm just excited."

"Not at all. You should be excited! Opening your own business is a huge deal."

Harper shrugged, leaning down to fiddle with the banner. "Anyone can start a business."

"That doesn't mean it will be successful, though. You've already done it once, and you're here doing it again. I admire you. I don't know if I'd have those kinds of guts."

"Well, as long as you do your research first, it's not so bad."

"Maybe I'll pick your brain about it someday. I need to start thinking about what to do after retirement."

Harper stood upright again, her eyes wide. "Are you thinking of retiring soon?"

"No, not for a long time. But I just want to have an idea of what I want to do after that. I can't imagine my life without soccer." Elena bit down on her tongue. She was over sharing. "Anyway, if you have time, you should come see us play on Saturday. We're in the semifinals for the league cup."

"Really? That's amazing! I hope it isn't sold out."

"Ha!" Elena laughed, then realized from Harper's expression that she hadn't been joking. "Oh, sorry. You were serious."

"Yes?"

"I mean, we have above-average attendance at our games, and we have a lot of fans, but…well, let's just say it's still a league-level women's soccer game. Getting a ticket isn't going to be a problem. Though, to be fair, you wouldn't need to worry about it anyway, because there's already a seat in the VIP section with your name on it."

Harper frowned. "What?"

"Well, technically, it's in Margot's name at the moment, but I can easily have it changed to yours."

"Ah, I see."

"I mean, if you even want to go, of course," she added, the thought just occurring to her. "Sorry, I didn't mean to just assume. Do you even like soccer?"

"Of course! I'm terrible and never watch anything besides the big national team tournaments, though," Harper said, abashed. "Time to support my local club, right?"

"I'm certainly partial to them," Elena said with a smile.

"Well, no time like the present!"

"I probably won't be able to get you behind the scenes or anything crazy, though. Just warning you."

Harper snapped her fingers. "Damn. And here I thought knowing a celebrity was going to get me into all the cool places."

"Well, if you knew me better, you'd know just how incredibly unlikely it is that I would be deemed 'cool.'"

"Yeah, but you could introduce me to people who are."

"Fair point. There are definitely some more trendy players on the team. I, however, am much more inclined to stay home like a premature octogenarian. Or be on the pitch. Definitely one or the other."

"Well, I'm more inclined to never emerge from my business, even when it means writing emails from a yoga mat, so...I do feel you on the last one."

"Workaholics for the win?" Elena asked, holding her hand up for a high five, and Harper smacked it, laughing.

"What's with the name, by the way? Is there a story?" Elena asked, indicating the banner on the floor.

"Well, chess was the first game I totally fell in love with, so I named my first place The Playful Pawn. I thought about keeping the same name here, but then I found out that this place is haunted, and I just went with it."

"Haunted?"

"By a ghost. The owner wasn't really clear on the details. The long and short of it is that every business that goes in here fails."

"Oh. Uh." Elena wasn't sure what to say to that. "Wow."

"Yeah, I know. You're probably going, 'Why the hell did she go with this place, then?' Well, I don't believe in ghosts, for one. And for another, the owner gave me a really good deal because he's been having such a difficult time leasing the spot. I thought it would be fun to lean into the concept. That way if there is a ghost, they'll know that I'm on their side, you know? Plus, it just works, and it's a fun theme. And for graphics, it winds up feeling very D and D, so it works out great."

"D and D?"

"Dungeons and Dragons. Surprisingly, RPG players are a really big part of my clientele. They come to use the tables while they play, and they always order a bunch of food and drinks. It's part of why I wanted a bigger location, like this one. It's really fun, actually. You should try it sometime."

"What makes you think I haven't?"

"You said you didn't do cool things."

"Hate to break it to you, but I'm fairly certain Dungeons and Dragons isn't cool."

"Twenty years ago, maybe. Now it's all the rage."

"Seriously?"

Harper nodded. "What's not to like? You get to make up your own characters and do magic and go on adventures."

"Wow."

"What?"

"I don't think I ever realized you were such a nerd." Elena threw in a wink so that Harper would know that she was joking. She second guessed the action as soon as she did it. It felt awkward, like something she would never do with Dee or Margot. Dee would start fake-flirting, and Margot would just stare at her or ask if she'd developed an eye twitch.

But Harper seemed to take it in stride, just grinning. "Guilty. One doesn't get into the board game café business without being at least eighty percent nerd. It's basically a career requirement."

"Lucky for you. The main career requirement for being a soccer player is harboring an intense fear of ACL tears. Being a nerd seems like much more fun."

"I have a good time. Plus, I get to do all the decorating, which makes my creative side happy. It's a win-win. Though it does also mean I'll spend this entire week painting. So if you decide you want a sore arm, feel free to come join me."

Elena started backing out slowly. "Aaand on that note, I need to head out now. Have fun nerding it up in here. Say hello to your candle ghost for me if you see them."

Harper's laugh echoed in the empty room. "Will do."

CHAPTER FIVE

Elena lounged on the couch in the middle of her living room and watched as Masked downloaded and then installed itself on her phone.

Tomorrow was the big game, and she needed something to distract herself. She'd had several days to think it over, and she'd decided that Dee's idea of casual dating made sense. But even though she was sort of excited, the thought of dating again made her stomach tense up.

She took a deep breath. She didn't have to do anything she didn't want to. For now, she would just investigate and see what all the fuss was about.

She powered through creating an account, verifying her identity by holding the camera up to her face for an uncomfortable amount of time. Finally, her phone buzzed, telling her she was approved, and she had no idea what the hell kind of AI or database was responsible for this kind of authentication, but it made her want to go off the grid and build her own cabin in Montana.

Then came the painstaking decision of what icon to choose. Since Masked was completely anonymous, you didn't get a profile picture. Instead, you had to choose one of the hundreds of possible icons. Which icon would encompass her as a human? A soccer ball was too on-the-nose, and while woodworking was her favorite hobby, they probably didn't have a lathe or a piece of sandpaper. A tree made her look too much like an annoying environmental activist who would rant at anyone brave enough to chat with her. One of the abstract, artsy ones? God, this was too much pressure.

After taking a break to grab a water bottle and lecture herself for overthinking everything, she finally landed on a nature trail with a sunset background. She enjoyed hiking through the mountains, especially during the off-season, and she loved the freedom and beauty of the concept.

Okay, problem solved.

Now came the matches.

Elena clicked over to the tab and was immediately overwhelmed. After reading through for a few minutes, it seemed to her that the profiles revealed too much and not enough at the same time. Yes, this woman had similar political ideals, but what about the smaller, everyday things? Did she like sleeping in or early mornings? Horror or comedy?

She backed out of the profile and moved on to the next.

It was a bit odd not having any pictures to look at, but Elena was rarely attracted to people upon first seeing them, anyway. So really, it didn't make much of a difference.

At least she was able to browse without every third woman actually being a couple looking for a "unicorn," which was more than she could say for her very short-lived foray into Tinder.

Still, a few profiles in, she was annoyed. But even so, her finger hovered over the app, not closing it. There was still that tiny little voice deep inside her, reminding her she was lonely and that this would be a good thing for her.

"You're never going to find someone if you don't try," she said out loud, immediately feeling slightly foolish at the sound of her own voice.

Okay, time to set achievable goals. Two profiles. She would find two profiles that looked promising and send a casual message to each.

In the end, it took her less than five minutes. She found **willknitfortacos**, who was 33, had mutual interests, and no crazy red flags. After a few more misses, she found **trailrunner22**, age 32, who actually made Elena chuckle out loud while reading her profile. She sent off the same simple greeting she had used for **willknitfortacos** and closed the app, somehow nervous but also satisfied.

Well. That was one hour down, but it was still only 9:30 A.M. Normally she would think of going out to her workshop, but it wasn't what she wanted right now. She knew she would just stare at the wood and think about soccer.

Then a thought occurred to her, and she grabbed for her phone again, quickly scrolling down the (very short) distance to her thread of texts with Harper. She chewed her lip indecisively for a few seconds, then shot off a text, hoping it wasn't too early and that the message wasn't too random.

Elena (9:33 A.M.): Hey!

Her phone dinged with a reply almost immediately.

Harper (9:33 A.M.): hey! what's up?

Elena (9:34 A.M.): I was wondering how serious you were about that painting thing. Are you still in need of some assistance?

Harper (9:35 A.M.): I mean, lol, yeah, I'm still painting. but you don't need to help, don't worry! I was only teasing you.

Elena (9:36 A.M.): I know. But I'm stressed about the game tomorrow and need a distraction, and I thought I might help you out at the same time.

Elena (9:36 A.M.): So, what do you say? Let me give you a hand?

Harper (9:37 A.M.): hell yeah

Harper (9:37 A.M.): you can give me your whole arm if you're so inclined

Harper (9:38 A.M.): in, like, a non-cannibal way, of course

Elena (9:39 A.M.): Why in god's name would I think it would be in a cannibal way???

Elena (9:40 A.M.): You've been spending too much time in those old candle fumes. Or is the ghost messing with your brain?

Harper (9:40 A.M.): (ghost emoji)(eyes emoji)

Elena (9:41 A.M.): I will be over in an hour, along with both of my arms (attached to my body, as I expect them to remain for the full duration of my visit, up to and including my departure)

Harper (9:41 A.M.): no promises.

"This is amazing." Elena stood with her jaw dropped, staring at the mural opposite the coffee bar in the front room of Bewitched. She stepped backward a bit, careful to avoid any fresh paint on the huge drop cloth that stretched across the floor.

She recognized lots of things from Star Wars and Lord of the Rings, and there were others she didn't know. But each one was colorful and vibrant and alive, and it almost felt like they were about to jump out of the wall at any minute.

"Thank you."

"No, seriously. Holy shit. I can't believe you painted this. You did all this yourself? By hand?"

Harper nodded, her cheeks flushed a rosy pink. "I have adopted the 'If I never leave, I never have to stop working,' approach."

"Sounds a little extreme."

"Possibly. I've basically eaten nothing but vegan muffins since Monday. But it's worth it, because I'm almost done! Just this little bit left. And the bathrooms. And another coat on the entire back room. But this is the one that's been a little bitch to finish. So. In short, thank you for coming here and saving my sanity. I've never been so excited to paint a bathroom."

"Don't mention it. I still owe you for the other night. Plus, you're helping me out, too. I was going stir-crazy, but I needed to get out and do something not soccer-related."

"Why no soccer?"

"The last time I was going to the semifinals was my second year in Miami. I got injured the day before, doing a normal warm-up routine. I couldn't play the next day, and we lost. I needed to make certain that didn't happen again. I need to be there tomorrow. I need to make sure we win."

"Well, I'm glad to be of service. Even if it's you who will actually be doing the service, so on second thought, I guess that doesn't really work. Let's just get to painting?"

"Wait, I have a question." Elena pointed to a particularly fierce-looking creature. "What's that?"

"Oh, it's a thing from Magic."

"I mean, most of them are magic, aren't they?"

"No, like Magic the Gathering."

Elena was still mystified, which Harper must have found hilarious, because she burst out laughing.

"Oh my god, you're such a jock!"

Elena chuckled. "Guilty." She turned back toward the wall. "Moving on from that assessment, I honestly can't even believe how good you are at this. You could do it professionally, sell paintings and stuff."

"Thanks. I appreciate the thought, but I don't really want to."

Elena couldn't imagine not wanting to do the thing you loved all the time. "Why not, if you don't mind my asking? You're definitely good enough."

"Thanks. But I tried doing the graphic design thing while I was in school, to help pay the bills. Turns out, I hate having to be constantly creative. It just sucks all the joy out, you know? I love doing big projects like this every once in a while." She gestured at the mural. "But not constantly. I had to quit after about six months, and I decided I just wanted to keep my art for myself. As a hobby, just something I do because I love it."

"I get it." And she did, now that Harper had explained. It was similar to how she felt about woodworking. She knew pursuing it after her eventual retirement was a possibility, but she didn't know if she wanted to, or if it was something she would keep just for herself.

"But you still do your passion for a living, though."

Elena nodded. "True. But I've been lucky. One of my teammates from Stanford went pro right when I did, but she left after only a few years. She was stuck on a toxic team, and it stole all her love of the game. Of course, a lot of players don't do it for love, at least after a while. It's just a job to them."

"But you do?"

"Absolutely. Of course I have days where I'd rather stay in bed than get up and go to a game, but I still fully intend to play in whatever league will have me until I'm old and gray and they have to ship me down to the Florida retirement home league."

Harper laughed. "Well, I'm glad you've found your place."

"It seems like you've found yours, too. After all, you found a way to paint all your nerdy things and play games and get paid for it."

"I'll have you know that this decoration scheme is thoroughly researched to correspond to the target market of this particular business model."

Elena raised her eyebrows, and Harper caved. "Okay, so maybe I didn't have to do a lot of research into that market."

Elena chuckled.

"Anyway, speaking of painting, I believe you volunteered?"

"I did. Let's do it." Elena popped open the buttons of her dark blue flannel and set it over on the coffee bar. "Mind if I leave this here? I don't want to get paint on it."

Harper seemed to be looking at something on Elena's shirt, and she shifted self-consciously. "I know, it's kind of holey. But I keep it around to sleep in, and I wanted something I didn't care about getting paint on."

Harper cleared her throat. "No, no, that's great. I was just about to mock you for wearing a tank top. It's not July anymore, you know."

Elena shrugged, following Harper toward the back room. "I get hot. Was this here before?" she asked, gesturing at the ramp that now took up the right half of the opening between the front and back rooms.

"The ramp? No, they came in yesterday to install it. It was one of the conditions I asked for when I rented. The whole 'old buildings don't have to follow the ADA' thing is absolute bullshit."

"Is that really a thing?"

"Yeah. Like, the bathrooms here were literally one hundred percent inaccessible to anyone in a wheelchair. But somehow that's okay because the building is old? Like, what the hell."

"That makes no sense."

"Agreed. Thankfully, the owner thought so, too, and he said he'd been meaning to get around to it for a long time. Otherwise, I don't think I could have convinced him, because it's not exactly like I was in a position to bargain. Anyway, here we are! Bathroom number one."

It was fairly large for an individual bathroom, with plenty of space for both of them, but the walls were all painted a disgusting shade of brownish green.

"I genuinely can't believe anyone thought this color was a good choice."

"I know, right?"

"Like, who looked at this and went, 'Wow, this looks like mashed peas. I should paint my bathroom this color.'"

"Don't be disgusting," Harper replied, wrinkling her nose. "But it really is just about the worst color you could possibly pick."

"I can't believe Amanda the candle maker allowed this.

Maybe she covered them with unicorn decals or something."

"They did tell us in business school that unicorns are the best strategy for a thriving business." Harper tossed over her shoulder just before she disappeared, then returned, balancing an aluminum tray of primer. "Rollers are in the other bathroom if you want to grab one."

Elena did, and as she grabbed it, she had an idea. "What do you say about making this a good, old-fashioned competition?"

Harper looked doubtful. "I say that your arms are fresh while I've been painting a mural for the past four days."

"So you've been building your strength and endurance."

"So my arms are basically noodles at this point."

"Okay, fine. I'll give you a three-minute head start."

Harper scoffed. "I don't need your pity minutes. Just let me get my stuff set up."

Elena couldn't help the smile that spread across her face. "Yes! It's on."

She pulled the painting goggles over her eyes, adjusting them a bit so that she could see without the plastic fogging up. Even with the tiny upper window propped open, the primer fumes on top of the scent of paint from the other room were strong, and she was glad for the painting mask Harper handed her. They worked together to lay large plastic drop cloths over everything and tape over some of the fixtures. Finally, they were ready.

Some pop music she didn't recognize started playing from tinny phone speakers from the room outside, and Elena adjusted her grip on her paint roller.

"Okay, on my mark." Harper hollered from the next room. "One…two…three…Go!"

Despite the fact that this was all for fun, Elena felt the wave of adrenaline that rushed through her any time a soccer game started. She dipped her paint roller into the primer and rolled it up the wall at full speed. She immediately halted with a gasp, paint spattering her shirt, goggles, and—a quick glance in the mirror over the sink confirmed—hair with a hefty spatter of white goo. She grabbed a couple of paper towels from the dispenser and wiped off the goggles, leaving everything else alone. She could deal with the rest later.

"Everything okay in there?" Harper's voice came from the next room.

"All good!"

"Are you sure? If you need, I can come help—"

"Never reveal weakness in front of your opponent!"

She heard Harper's laugh and was grinning herself as she bent to dip her roller once again, this time carefully letting some drip off back into the pan before she lifted it again. Less spatter, but now it was too slow. She needed to refine the process.

Elena adjusted her strategy a few times, and by her tenth dip-and-roll, she had landed on a process that was efficient, quick, and effective. She was leaving large, smooth stripes up the wall that weren't horrendously sloppy and too-wet like her first few.

"How much do you have left?" she called, in what she hoped was a completely casual fashion.

"Just starting the fourth wall now!"

"Really?" Elena had just started the third. How the hell was Harper so much faster?

"Nope. Never reveal your secrets to your opponent!"

Elena chuckled at Harper throwing her own words back at her.

"You're learning."

"I make a career on games, you know. You're not the only one who can strategize."

"Fair point," she responded meekly, and she couldn't seem to stop grinning. There was a bounce in her step that one wouldn't normally associate with the process of painting a bathroom.

Her shoulder was burning, but she kept going through the pain.

Three walls down, and one to go.

She painted on, and she could see the finish line in front of her with only about a fourth of the wall to go. Then came Harper's voice.

"Done! Ha!"

"No!" Elena couldn't help the involuntary shout.

"I win! Victory!" Harper's voice was elated and immediately crushed the teeny-tiny part of Elena that had been annoyed at losing. She walked to the next room over and stuck her head in, inspecting the walls. All four walls were covered in white primer, and her first wall didn't even look sloppy like Elena's had. "I concede defeat."

She held out her paint-covered hand for a shake, and Harper grasped it, her pale skin covered in even more paint than Elena's.

Elena held her hand for a beat and then released it. "Well played."

Harper grinned. "Thank you, thank you. And I even had the height disadvantage, I would like to point out."

"Clearly your painting skills are simply superior to mine."

"What do I get as the winner?"

"My admiration and envy? A date with some paint thinner later?"

Harper giggled. "I think we could both use a bit of that."

"You're not wrong."

"So, how long are you planning on staying?"

"However long you need. Was that the only coat?"

"That's the only coat of primer, but then we need to go over it with the color I'll actually be using. It's like aqua meets navy but in a chill way."

"So...blue?"

Harper nodded.

"Sounds great! I'm sure it will look fantastic."

"That's the hope! I'm thinking it'll probably need two coats, and it needs about an hour between coats."

"Okay, then how about we hang out here for a bit, do the first coat, and then I can take you out to get some actual lunch. You shouldn't survive entirely on vegan baked goods."

"There's actually all kinds of healthy things in there. I asked Vivian."

"Okay, but are they as good as pizza?"

"Nothing is as good as pizza."

"Good. It's settled, then. Plus, I like this whole three rounds idea. Best two out of three, and the loser buys the pizza?"

"You're on."

Thanks to Elena's help, Harper was able to get out of Bewitched earlier than she had all week. Even though Harper had also won the second round, Elena had still come back after lunch to help with the third coat. She'd left as soon as it was done, though, and the space had seemed a little emptier without her.

Harper went to bed early, exhausted, shoulders aching, but happy. She felt refreshed when she woke on Saturday morning, ready for the drive back to Colorado Springs.

She walked into the Pawn an hour before opening and breathed in the scent of cardboard and coffee.

It was admittedly an odd combination, but she loved it.

She was the first one here, and she looked around and imagined the building as she had first seen it: walls painted the primary colors of the daycare it had been before. Smelling of play dough and glue, just waiting for her to transform it. And transform it she had, after months of work and planning and fundraising. She had poured every ounce of her soul into it.

And it had thrived. She'd taken the community college business degree her parents had turned up their noses at, and she'd made something amazing. Something she could be proud of.

Harper had always loved chess, but she still remembered when she'd discovered board games could be so much more than just Monopoly. She'd just moved in with Angel, having just started her first year of business classes. Angel had introduced her to games like Betrayal at House on the Hill and Pandemic.

Then they'd found out about a local board game café. Two steps inside, it had clicked. She had known what she wanted to do with her future.

She and Angel had spent eight hours there, and Harper had started her business plan the following Monday morning.

And the rest was history.

A clunking noise behind her signaled Shawn's arrival, and Harper quickly moved into action, taking chairs off of tables.

"Hey, boss. I didn't know you'd be here today." He was dressed in a canary yellow polo that would have made Harper look like a chicken, but somehow, with his darker complexion, he pulled it off.

"Good surprise or bad surprise?"

"You know it's always good to see you." He moved in for a quick side hug. She pulled him in, always surprised by the petiteness of his frame. He was the only friend Harper had who was shorter than she was.

"How's the new place? Sorry for abandoning us yet?"

"I miss you all every day, but you know I'm not abandoning you."

"Sure, sure. Go tell that to your new favorite child. Soon enough, you'll have a whole brood of them."

"No, thanks. Two is plenty."

"That's what my mom said after me. Yet somehow I wound up with two little sisters."

"No, but I mean it. Two is a lot, but I can handle it. I don't want more. I'd turn into a Larry, and that's literally my nightmare."

"A Larry?" Shawn frowned at her, his thick eyebrows meeting over the top of his rectangular glasses.

"When I was a waitress, that was the name of our District Manager. He came in like once a month and basically did nothing except fuck everything up and make people nervous. He was totally clueless about how things actually worked day-to-day. He would change things, then get pissed when they failed like we told him they would. So, yeah. Nightmare. Never let me become a Larry. Promise me."

"Pinkie promise."

She held out her pinkie and curled it around Shawn's. "Thank you."

Shawn disappeared into the back room, and Elena finished taking the chairs off the tables before she went to her office. She opened the system for the day, counted the money in the safe, and checked off her initials next to Shawn's from the night before.

Soon enough, it was time to open, and Harper was glad to see Sal and his group of fellow retirees waiting outside the door. They'd been coming every week for six months, after originally coming in out of curiosity. They came back week after week and now had a list of the Top 50 Strategy Games that they were working through.

"Hey, Sal. How's the list going?"

"Good, good."

"What's the selection this week?"

"We're onto Forbidden Desert."

"Ah, a terrific choice."

"The review on that game website made it seem like it might be a little easy, but we're giving it a shot, anyway."

Harper smiled.

It was good to be back. She looked down at her watch. She had about two hours before she would leave so she could make it in time for Elena's game.

Her stomach gave a little happy flutter, and she pretended

she was excited to watch soccer. Anything else would be ridiculous.

That was all.

Just soccer.

CHAPTER SIX

Atlanta was ruthless.

Elena climbed slowly to her feet, staying bent over with her hands on her knees for a few seconds before she stood fully upright. The player who had gone in for the tackle was getting a reprimand from the ref, but she wouldn't get a yellow card. Not this time.

This was how it had gone all game. Unnecessarily physical with the refs turning a blind eye in favor of the opposite team. Min had already been subbed out on concussion protocol after a nasty head collision with an Atlanta midfielder. The whole game had been difficult, exhausting, and completely fruitless. They were still tied 0-0, with less than fifteen minutes left of regulation time.

Elena took the free kick, but the defenders didn't let it near the goal. Their defense was rock solid, an impenetrable force. She tried to find a hole, a sliver of space, so much as a crack. Nothing she did was working.

Now, without Min, the front line was struggling to form any sense of cohesion as a whole. Coach Talia had subbed on Annie instead of Clarice, which Elena hadn't expected and was still questioning. Annie had only been traded to them a month ago. She was excellent during practice, but she had barely a handful of meaningful minutes on the field. Simply put, Elena didn't trust her.

But Elena still had Dee, and she had herself.

Elena stayed vigilant, reading her teammates and watching for her next move. The ball was heading her direction, and Dee shimmied a few inches further toward the goal and signaled to show that she was open. Joana passed Elena the ball from midfield, and she crossed it to Dee.

Dee took the shot, but the keeper punched it away.

Elena gritted her teeth.

The next few minutes passed too quickly, with the ball on the other end of the field more often than not. She could see the Defiant defenders flagging. Elena winced when an Atlanta forward dribbled around Meredith with ease. She sent a ball flying toward another player, who was positioned perfectly for a header into the corner.

Avery saw the play and made a valiant leap toward the opposite corner…but the ball simply grazed the tips of their fingers as it continued on its way and hit the net.

"*Fuck.*" Elena wanted to punch something. Better yet, she wanted to kick something. She wanted to kick the ball so goddamn hard that it would burn a hole through the back of the net on the other end of the field.

The Atlanta players went insane, screaming and hugging.

Dee gestured for Elena and Annie to huddle, and they did, quickly. She gave some instructions, then looked each of them in the eye in turn. Her gaze was flinty hard with focus, and Elena felt her energy lifting just watching her. "Ten minutes left. We've got this!" she shouted, and Elena nodded. It was Dee's final game. Elena would not fail her.

Play resumed, and one minute passed. Then five. Then eight.

With two minutes of regular time remaining, it finally happened. The play was all happening at the opposite end of the pitch, and everyone was there, vying for the ball.

Elena managed to snag an interception from an Atlanta midfielder. She tapped it around one defender, and then she turned on every single bit of energy she had left. She bolted down the field, legs flying, keeping the ball tidily in front of her, scanning the defenders. Only two between her and the goal. She could do this.

She neared the goal as if in slow motion. One yard closer, then two. Two more yards, and she could take the shot.

She saw Annie out of the corner of her eye, near the other side of the field. She was in a great position for a cross, signaling for the ball, wide open because the defenders were focused on Elena.

Elena had a split second to make the decision. Cross to the newbie, or take the slightly more difficult shot herself?

She couldn't trust a newbie, not with this. Elena would do it.

She would score for Dee. For the team. They were going all the way to the finals. She would make it happen.

She had this.

She had this.

Elena lined up, squared her hips, and took her shot. It was a strong kick, and the ball sailed straight and true, right through the tiny space between the two defenders…and directly into the gloves of the keeper.

A groan wrenched itself from deep down in her chest. She hissed out a string of curses that had the defender nearest her raising her eyebrows.

She didn't care.

That was it. It was over.

She could feel it in her gut; there wouldn't be another chance.

And she was right.

They didn't get another opportunity. Regulation ended, then two minutes of extra time passed as the Defiant fought for the ball, but Atlanta evaded them. Elena ran until she could barely feel her legs, but all the while the rock hard mass sat low in her stomach. She knew they had already lost.

The final whistle blew, and Atlanta exploded.

Elena sank to the ground.

It was over. They had lost.

Then she saw Annie, shoulders slumped, looking back toward the goal she had been right in front of only a few minutes ago. The defenders and the keeper on the opposite side of the goal, focused on Elena. Leaving the goal wide open for a shot from Annie, who had a stellar record and a reputation as a finisher, despite the fact that she was young and new to the Defiant.

And that was when Elena knew.

The Defiant had not only lost the semifinals.

She had lost the game for them.

Hours later, Elena stood just inside the doorway of her workshop, her solace.

There were only two places she felt completely at home. The first was on the soccer pitch, the place she'd spent the most cumulative time since she was five years old and introduced to the sport by her well-meaning parents. Practically every other child in the neighborhood had been on that team, but she was the only one who had never left.

The second was here, in her workshop. She had chosen this house because of the large detached garage. It was beautiful and spacious, and she'd had a heater installed for the harsh Colorado winters. Her lathe sat in the far corner, the work bench all along the east-facing wall. Windows all along the top of the sides let in tons of natural sunlight. She'd even had a company come in last summer and put in two sizable sunlights in the roof. There was nothing like natural sunlight when she was working on a piece. The grains of the wood showed up differently in the natural glow.

Now the workshop was her only place of comfort. Just looking at a ball made her stomach twist. She kept flashing back to that moment this afternoon, the one when she could have passed to Annie. It was, in hindsight, the obvious decision. She had been selfish and stupid and made a mistake that no experienced player should have made. And all because she didn't know Annie yet. She didn't trust her.

But Annie was a part of the team. And it wasn't only about trusting Annie herself, but about trusting Coach for putting her on the field to begin with. There were multiple levels that should have made her choose the right decision, but she hadn't.

If she had even the slightest intention of taking the role of captain Dee wanted to pass onto her, she needed to be an example. This had been the exact opposite: brash and selfish. So now, not only did she not want the captain position, she didn't deserve it.

She'd let Dee down. She'd let the whole team down.

Fuck. *Fuck.*

Elena pushed thoughts of soccer from her mind and walked further inside. As she stepped forward, her phone vibrated in her pocket, but she ignored it. It was probably Margot, or possibly another message from one of the two women she'd been talking to on Masked. She didn't want to talk to anyone right now. Even the thought of working on one of her ongoing projects was too much. Instead, she shuffled through a few pieces of scrap wood, then held up a nice piece of oak. She could probably make a simple spice rack from this.

She went to her work bench but didn't pick up any tools. It was like all her energy had drained out when she'd stopped focusing on her anger and disappointment, and all that was left was an empty shell. She just stood there, shifting back and forth, staring at the tiny holes in the pegboard. Time passed, though she wasn't sure how much had ticked by before she finally admitted to herself that she couldn't make anything right now.

She turned around and meandered back to the house, abandoning the oak on the work bench.

Cookie dough ice cream and Netflix were calling her name.

Harper jolted awake to the sound of her phone ringing. She'd set her alarm late today, as a treat for being up at the asscrack of dawn for the past week, and she immediately wanted to punch whomever was on the other end of the line.

A thought entered her mind that something could be wrong, but when she saw **Mom** on the screen, she simultaneously relaxed and tensed up in a completely different way. Her mom had always been an early bird, so the hour wasn't uncommon for her. It had been one of her favorite criticisms of Harper, growing up.

"Why do you need so much more sleep than the rest of us? Margot never did. She was always fine on my schedule."

But that was only one of a mile-long laundry list of subjects where Margot was superior to her in the eyes of their parents.

Harper sighed. She needed to answer the phone. She waged a mental war with herself, finally caving and stabbing at the green circle at the last second.

"Hello?" she answered with her brightest, chipperest, yes-I-am-totally-awake voice.

"Harper. Are you okay? Why did you take so long to answer the phone? Were you asleep? It's almost nine A.M. Are you sick?"

Harper resisted the urge to grind her teeth. "No, Mom, I'm not sick. I was just in the shower, sorry. What's up?"

"Well, your father and I received your invitation for the grand opening of your little *café*." She pronounced it with a crisp French accent, though somehow her tone implied she thought that she was humoring Harper by doing so. "But as you know, your father and I were already planning an autumnal Vermont getaway with the McCormicks. We spoke with the bed-and-breakfast, but they don't have any other openings until December. It's surprising that they even had that available, as the waiting list for this location is quite extensive. They're supposed to have an excellent food selection and quite the wine list."

Because obviously you can't get food and wine anywhere here, Harper thought to herself, closing her eyes and trying to contain her annoyance. She shouldn't be surprised. Her parents had attended the opening of The Playful Pawn, but her father had left early for a meeting with a client, and her mother had spent the whole time typing away on her iPhone in the corner.

While Harper hadn't set the date and time for Bewitched specifically until a few days ago, she had told them last month that she was planning a mid-November launch and to keep the time frame clear if they wanted to attend.

Well, here was her answer to that, apparently.

Harper tuned back into her mother's monologue. "—at which point the amount of snow on the ground would render the visit moot. So I'm truly sorry, dear, but it looks like we simply aren't going to be able to reschedule."

Harper arranged her face into a smile-slash-grimace because she had read somewhere that you could hear facial expressions over the phone. She wasn't sure if it was true, but she never wanted to take chances with her mother. "That's okay, Mom. I understand."

"I knew you would. Oh, I spoke to Margot yesterday! She says the research is going splendidly. We're going to try to swing by Boston on our way back from Vermont. It is an extra layover, but it will be worth it to see her back at Harvard again, don't you think? Such an overachiever, that one."

That article about expressions must have been right, because Harper could hear her mother's prideful beam from here. Or maybe she just implied it from experience. After all, it was the expression that she always used when speaking about Margot, high school valedictorian, graduate of Harvard Medical School. Their parents had always harbored high expectations, but Margot had gone so far as to surpass even them.

Harper, needless to say, had not.

Thus, that beam was not the expression she used when speaking about her other daughter, the artsy one who liked science fiction and "played games for a living."

Yet somehow Harper was still the one who endured comments about giving them grandchildren. Because apparently it was fine that Margot was still single, since her career required a lot of focus. But somehow her parents thought anything Harper did with her life was inherently inferior to the calling of birthing spawn to inhabit a world that had been ruined by their generation's carelessness. (Or at least, that was how she thought of it when she was particularly pissed off.)

Harper didn't feel bad about her accomplishments. She'd been lucky to have the opportunity to go to school, and she'd worked hard to pay for it. She'd been even luckier to have gotten a small loan from her parents for the Pawn, even if it had felt like placation at the time. Not only had the business been successful, but she'd paid back her parents' loan with interest in under a year. Now she was starting another with no fiscal assistance from outside sources only six years later.

It was only when Harper spoke with her parents that she started feeling those hot little tendrils of shame that she hated. She had absolutely nothing to be ashamed of, nor did anyone with more or less education or success than she had. A person's financial situation did not define them, nor did their grades. It was actions and attitude that truly counted.

But somehow she forgot all of this around them.

She couldn't yell. She couldn't argue. She couldn't shout. She just had to grin and bear it.

She was good at that, at least. After all, she had twenty-eight years of experience.

Finally, her mom stopped gushing about Margot and said goodbye, and Harper hung up the phone and tossed it on the other side of the bed. She still had twenty minutes until her alarm, but her sleepiness had long since vanished. It was now replaced by the mixture of shame, guilt, and anger, all swirled together.

Well. Good morning to her.

She needed to think about something good. Harper had the vague feeling that she'd been dreaming about Elena before the interruption, but as much as she wracked her brain, she couldn't summon any specifics.

Damn. Maybe she should go back to bed.

But the thought of Elena brought back the memory of how she'd looked yesterday, slumping off the field in defeat.

She'd looked utterly, completely crushed, and all Harper had wanted to do was shove every single person in the crowd out of the way, run down to the field, and wrap her in her arms.

Which was insane, because that wasn't a thing that they did, and she didn't even know if Elena liked hugs. Not everyone did. Margot hated them.

So of course, she hadn't. In fact, Harper hadn't even texted after the game, because she hadn't known what to say. She'd hoped Elena would reach out, but she hadn't. Harper had guessed that Elena probably wanted to be alone. Or maybe to spend time with Margot or someone else she was actually close to.

But she thought they were friends now, somehow. Maybe not before the painting day, but after the painting day, she felt comfortable saying so. So, why not reach out? She sent a simple text before she could overthink it.

Harper (8:52 A.M.): hey. :)

Harper didn't really know what else to say. She just had the odd urge to let Elena know that she was there.

She watched the phone for a response, but after nothing

happened for a few seconds, she blew out a sigh.

"The day can only go up from here, right?" she asked no one in particular. "God, Margot really needs to get a cat or something."

Then she imagined Margot's confusion upon returning home to find Harper had adopted a pet for her in her absence. Chuckling to herself, Harper climbed to her feet and headed for the shower.

CHAPTER SEVEN

Harper was never going to utter that sentence again in her life.

Her morning had not gone up.

In fact, it had gone very drastically in the opposite direction. It had plummeted spectacularly down to 40,000 leagues below average day level and showed no signs of stopping.

After her mother's call had come an ice-cold shower because the pilot light to the hot water heater had gone out. Then had come her car refusing to start, because the universe was apparently a gigantic asshole.

An hour and an eye-watering down payment later, she received the news that she would be carless for three days, because the mechanic had to wait for the part to arrive.

And now Harper was standing in the middle of Bewitched, surrounded by her gorgeous, brand new shelves, the one thing that she'd been looking forward to today. They were perfect. Just the right height for browsing, just the right cubby size to allow for larger board games, thick enough that they wouldn't bow under the weight.

Her six new shelves.

The problem was, she had ordered eight.

And now the invoice she had been given upon delivery listed them the remaining two as on back-order.

"*Three months?* Are you serious?" Harper clutched her

phone, fighting the urge to hurl it against the wall.

"I'm sorry, ma'am, but like I said, it seems there was an inventory error. Our supplier isn't scheduled to replenish our stock of that model until January."

"I don't have that long. I'm opening my business literally one month from today."

"I can offer you the taller size from that manufacturer for a discounted rate." Harper bit her tongue as he rambled along, offering solutions that weren't solutions at all. That model was 24 inches taller, which was far too big for her needs. She took a deep breath and reminded herself it wasn't his fault. She was desperately trying not to lose it on this guy who was just trying to do his job.

Objectively, she knew this.

Subjectively, she felt like steam was going to start blowing from her ears if she didn't explode, and he had the bad luck to be the only one caught in the path.

Harper used the last shreds of her self-control to keep her voice pleasant. "Can I have your number so I can call you back later once I've thought over the options?"

"Of course, ma'am." He rattled off a string of numbers, and Harper scribbled them down onto the crumpled invoice with shaking fingers.

She hung up, and it provided her with absolutely no sense of satisfaction to quell her anger. Where was a good, old-fashioned, slammable phone when you needed one?

She had come to the conclusion that this day was cursed. Possibly Cursed, with a capital C. Not in a way that implied she actually believed in ghosts, because she didn't. Ninety-nine percent of the time, anyway. Did she fall down the occasional YouTube spiral that caused her to lose an entire night of sleep?

Well, who didn't?

"Is this some kind of joke, Ghosty?" Harper called to the specter that supposedly haunted Bewitched.

Unsurprisingly, there was no answer.

Harper grabbed her laptop and opened the giant spreadsheet that served as her countdown to the grand opening. So far, the shelves were her only major mishap. She'd finished the painting ahead of schedule, thanks to Elena's help. She already had some games, and she had more stock arriving soon. All her other ducks were lined up nicely. Looking at everything all written out like this helped calm the anxiety that had been clawing at her chest. It was just one setback, like any other. She would be fine.

There was really only one thing to do. Shelves were on the schedule for today, so she needed to figure out the shelves today. She would just need to get them from somewhere else and obtain a refund from the first location.

She knew from her initial research that IKEA had a similar model. There was an IKEA 40 minutes away. A quick internet search told her they should have the ones she needed in stock.

The trouble was, she didn't have a car. And when she checked Lyft, she grimaced at the potential price of the ride. After the mechanic had finished with her, she wasn't going to want to pay for a ride across the street, much less a 40-plus-minute drive.

So, that left getting a ride from a friend. Or from family.

But after her call with her mother this morning, her family was out. Thinking about them still made the tips of her ears burn in anger.

She knew Angel would absolutely help out, but it was two A.M. in Angel Time, and she didn't want to wake her up. Nor did she want her to drive all the way to get her.

There was, of course, one obvious alternative. She wasn't exactly sure what the protocol was when asking one's old crush slash new friend for a ride to an interior design superstore.

But helping each other out had sort of become their thing these past couple of weeks.

Of course, with the way today was going, Elena would

ignore her call because she and Dee had run away to Hawaii together, having finally discovered they were in love after all these years.

Not that it would have bothered her. Much. It didn't matter to her what went on in Elena's love life.

Sure, she found Elena attractive, but she always had. Always would. It was just a fact of Harper's life. She had red hair, she hated seafood, and she was irrevocably attracted to Elena Torres.

Elena hadn't responded to her text this morning, but she decided to just buck up and call anyway before she could think about it any more. The worst Elena could do was say no.

Elena picked up after only the second ring.

"Harper? What's up? Is something wrong?"

"No. Well, sort of. But not like *wrong*, wrong." Great. The conversation was off to a smooth start.

Elena paused for a moment, probably a bit confused. "I mean, just normal levels of wrong is also not good. What's going on?"

"I have an IKEA emergency."

Elena emitted a startled laugh. Harper could picture it, the way she would be cradling the phone to her ear and making that adorable, confused expression. "I'm sorry, I thought you said 'IKEA emergency.'"

"I did."

"Uh, that's not a thing."

"It is when your shelf order for your store comes in missing two of the shelves you ordered, saying the others are on back-order until January, and all furniture stores are having major delays right now, and your store opens in less than a month."

"Well, fuck. I stand corrected."

"And to make it worse, my car died this morning. Something about the carburetor? Or maybe the alternator? I honestly don't remember. Something with 'ator' in the name.

But I won't get it back for another three days."

"Damn."

"Yeah. It's not my day."

Elena made a sound that was sort of like the world's least amused laugh. "I feel that."

Harper paused, not sure how to respond. After a second, she just decided to simply say, "I'm sorry about the game."

"It happens. There's always next year," Elena said. It was very clearly a line, but she obviously didn't want to talk about it. Harper would abide by her wishes.

"So. I want to go to IKEA for shelves. But I'm carless."

"So you're just using me for my wheels. I see how it is. And here I thought we were actually becoming friends."

So Elena did think they were friends. Her heart did a little happy dance. "We are! I mean, I think?"

"We are. And of course I'll take you! It'll do me good to get out of my head for a while."

"I promise I won't take long. The website says they have the model I want in stock, but I just want to see these shelves in person before I order them. I don't trust their quality. Like, I mean, I would if I just wanted them for some picture frames or something. But not for—"

"Not for your business. I get it."

"I swear I'll buy you a coffee. Or even some of those Swedish meatballs everyone always raves about. If you're lucky, I'll even share my vegetarian hot dog, because they have the best vegetarian hot dog in the world."

"I didn't even know vegetarian hot dogs existed."

"They do! Though they're usually disgusting. I don't know how IKEA does it, but theirs are magically delicious. Maybe they add, like, Swedish fairy dust or something."

"Okay, you've officially intrigued me. I'll go, but only for the hot dog."

"You're a lifesaver. Thank you so much."

"Yeah, yeah. I'm not kidding about that hot dog. Be there

as soon as I can."

She hung up, and it took Harper several seconds to realize she was smiling. She wasn't sure when she had started, but she was pretty sure it was the first time all day.

"Harper?" Elena called into the apparently empty Bewitched.

"Back here!" Harper's disembodied voice came from a tiny room Elena had assumed was a mop closet when they'd been painting. The door was cracked open, and Elena pushed it in further. The room was tiny, maybe four feet by five feet, and the only light came from a single bulb with a pull cord. Harper was sitting on a lawn chair with a laptop propped on an ancient TV tray in front of her.

"Welcome to my office," she said in a vaguely British accent, waving her hand around as though she were showing off a posh corner office with a skyline view.

"That's, uh, quite the setup you have going on."

"I'm pretty sure it's supposed to be a broom closet, but I like to work with what I've got," Harper said in her normal voice, shrugging a shoulder. "As long as Harrison and I can fit in here, it works."

"Harrison?" Elena peeked around the doorjamb, almost expecting to find a life-size cutout of Han Solo hiding somewhere. Not that there was anywhere to hide.

Harper gestured from Elena to her laptop. "Harrison, Elena. Elena, Harrison."

Elena just stood in place for a second, fighting the urge to laugh. "Uh…"

"Is that how you greet someone? Jeez, just because you become a celebrity doesn't mean you can just shun common decency."

This time Elena did laugh, a short, amused bark. "Sorry, I really don't know what's considered good manners when meeting a computer for the first time. Shake the mouse?"

"Obviously."

Elena felt a grin growing across her face at the absurdity. The whole interaction was a little silly, even for Harper. She also seemed to be avoiding looking Elena in the eye, focusing instead on her electronics. Maybe she was feeling bad for Elena after the game yesterday? Well, Elena would play along. She didn't want any pity, and she certainly didn't want to think about the game. Harper made it easy to forget, with her smiles and her adorable absurdity. As though she could read Elena's thoughts, she held out her hot pink Bluetooth mouse like she expected Elena to take it. So she did, slightly bemused, shaking the item gently a couple of times before returning it to Harper. "Nice to meet you, Harrison."

"Nice to meet you, too," Harper said in a deep tone.

"I'm surprised you didn't name it—him?—after one of the droids."

Harper laughed. "God, am I really that predictable? My first two laptops were, actually. Then I wanted to change it up, and I like the name Harrison, so."

"Not Carrie?"

"Carrie's the name of my car."

Elena laughed so loudly it nearly echoed in the tiny cavern. "You really have a problem."

"I like what I like."

"And I like that." She did. Elena liked a lot of things about Harper. She liked that she was straightforward. That she always seemed to have joy to share. That she was unashamed of her passions. She was similar to Elena in that way.

"So, IKEA?" Elena said, because she wasn't sure what else to say.

"Yes! Great. IKEA. Thank you again. Like, so much."

"Not a problem." Elena moved away from the door frame to let Harper emerge, moving over to inspect the new shelves. There were six of them filling up the lower room.

She eyed the length and height, tested the thickness with

her fingers.

These were totally something she could make.

Elena could already feel the smooth grain of mahogany in her hands. It was the perfect wood for shelves, wouldn't bow under the weight. It would be a shame to cover the natural grain with the black paint to keep it uniform with the others, but she could do that easily.

But she didn't want to overstep or, worse, come off as begging for business. And Harper already had an alternative.

So Elena kept her mouth shut. She just ran her fingers over the shelves and waited for Harper to collect her things.

An hour later, Harper was frowning at a white shelf in the middle of a creepily perfect faux living room inside IKEA.

"What do you think?" Harper asked.

Did she want Elena's actual opinion, or did she just want someone to encourage her? Sometimes it was difficult to tell. Margot and Dee were always the former; she didn't know Harper well enough to know which she preferred. She decided to play it safe. "It depends on what you want." This was true but refrained from giving her actual opinion, which was that the shelves looked nice but probably wouldn't last more than a couple of years.

"Hmm." Harper didn't seem convinced, moving around to inspect the shelf from another angle. She pulled a measuring tape out of her purse, stretching it against the cubby space. "The cubbies aren't quite as tall. But they would still work."

"Why don't you sound convinced?"

"They're just not right."

"If it's the aesthetics you're worried about, it won't stand out, since they'll be in the upper room instead of in the lower with the rest."

"No, it's not that. I'm worried about the durability."

So she did want honesty. Fabulous. "I agree. They would

be a more temporary solution, which makes the price a little steep. Depends on what you want."

"I would really like a more permanent solution. But I looked at some other local hardware stores online, and they don't have anything the right height. Shelves tend to skew a lot into half height and full height, not a lot in between. No one really had anything I was interested in. And I obviously can't afford anything custom."

That was a cue if there ever was one.

"You know that hutch where Margot keeps all her grandmother's antique plates?"

"Our grandmother? Yes, I'm familiar. What about it? Do you know the company that made that? Are they local?"

"Yeah, pretty local. They're standing right here."

"What?"

"It was me. I make furniture sometimes. As a hobby, mostly, though I've done a couple commissioned pieces for friends."

"Wait, seriously?" She was staring, and Elena fought the urge to look away. Something about the way her gray eyes lit up was making something weird happen in Elena's stomach. "I don't know if I'm mad at you for not telling me sooner or elated that something good has finally happened today."

Elena just laughed, but then Harper sobered.

"Wait, shit, I probably can't afford that, though. Startup business and all."

"I'd be happy to do it for just the cost of materials."

"No way, I can't let you do that."

"It'd be no problem at all. I need an off-season project to keep me busy." *Especially since my off-season just started a little earlier than expected.*

Harper sucked on her teeth as she thought about it. "How about cost of materials plus 30%?"

"How about cost of materials plus 10% and you keep my cards in one of those little holder thingies on the shelves?"

"You have business cards?"

"No," Elena admitted.

Harper laughed. "I'm not sure that's a very good deal on your part, then."

"Well, I say it is, and I'm the one offering, so…" Elena shrugged.

"I guess we've got a deal then, partner." Harper started to hold out her hand, then stopped. "Wait, don't you want to come look at the shelves first? Make sure it's something you're, y'know…comfortable doing?"

"You mean something I'm not going to totally fuck up?" Elena asked, raising a brow, and Harper looked abashed.

"Listen, you can't be too careful. I wouldn't trust anyone who wanted me to paint for them without seeing my work first. But I do trust you, to be clear. That was a bad example."

"Don't worry. I was looking at them earlier when I came to pick you up. It's definitely in my wheelhouse. I'll just have to get all the exact measurements before I gather the materials. I already have the wood in mind and everything."

"Why didn't you say anything?"

"I thought you wanted these! I was being a good friend!"

"Okay, okay, I guess you were."

"Now, before we get one of those famous vegetarian hot dogs, would you mind helping me pick out a few things? I have been wanting to decorate my living room a bit, but I don't really know where to start."

Harper perked up. "Good thing you have someone here with excellent taste. It's the least I can do. Quid pro quo and all of that."

"Seems like the theme of our relationship, doesn't it?"

"So far," she said, and Elena felt an odd urge to ask what she meant by that. "What do you have in mind?"

"I was thinking maybe a piece of art for the wall over the fireplace? I don't know. I just feel like the whole room looks empty. I want to give it some life and some color without getting all crazy with the knick-knacks. I don't like clutter. Oh, maybe a throw pillow or two?"

"Are you sure you don't want to just grab a couple of Margot's? She'll never notice."

Elena chuckled.

"And if we don't find anything here, we can always check with Amanda."

It took a split second for Elena to get the reference to the infamous Amanda, who had last occupied the Bewitched space. Elena scoffed and laughed at the same time, resulting in the sort of weird, wheezy squeak somewhat reminiscent of the sounds she made during particularly intense ab days at training.

Harper covered her mouth in what Elena was certain was thinly veiled amusement, and Elena tilted her head toward her. "What? That was funny. I'll keep my eyes peeled for hand-crafted, artisanal candles."

Harper grabbed a couple of deep maroon throw pillows. "These are nice. What color is your couch?"

"Blue." Harper tossed the pillows back down.

They found some a minute later that were white with dark blue geometric patterns. They were beautiful, and would go perfectly with her couch. Elena was overjoyed.

"So, how did you get into woodworking?" Harper asked, breaking the comfortable silence they'd fallen into.

"Well, it started when I took shop in high school—"

"Oh yeah, I remember that."

"Really?"

Was it her imagination, or were Harper's cheeks turning a little pink again? Maybe it was just her complexion. It must be terrible to be so pale.

"I just remember Margot talking about it, because that was, like, the only class that she never wanted to join."

"She's more the master of working with her mind, that's true." Elena laughed, remembering the disasters that had ensued when they'd taken art together.

"She certainly got the brains of the family," Harper said it lightly, almost as a joke, but Elena couldn't help her immediate frown.

"I don't know. I think that art is certainly a product of the mind, too. One is not inherently better than the other. They might be different processes, sure, but they're equally valuable. And besides, you have that fancy business degree, don't you?"

Harper looked surprised but nodded.

"Well, there you have it. Margot may have gotten brains, but you got brains *and* creativity. Don't tell her I said it, but I think you win."

Harper snorted. "Don't tell my parents you said that. They'll have you committed."

"What?"

"Nothing. I'm just…a little mad at them right now. They scheduled a trip in November, even though they knew it meant they couldn't come to Bewitched grand opening."

"What the hell? Seriously?"

"Yeah. Sorry, I know you love them."

"I do, but that's still a total asshole thing to do." It made no sense. She never remembered them having a bad word to say about Margot. Why would they be any different with Harper? "Did you guys have a fight or something? Actually, that's a personal question. Sorry, I didn't mean to pry."

"No fight. We've just never been close. They don't really understand my priorities."

"Is that a way of saying you guys fight?"

"No. We don't fight. We're…cordial. Mostly."

"Ouch. I can't imagine being on that level with my parents." Just thinking about them made Elena miss them.

"Lucky you." But she didn't sound sarcastic. She sounded envious, like she actually meant it.

Elena wasn't sure how to respond, but then she spotted a lamp with a soccer ball on the base. "I'm so getting this."

"Do you want your living room to look like an eight-year-old's bedroom?"

"Who said anything about the living room? This is going in my bedroom."

"Please tell me you're kidding."

"Guess you'll never know," Elena said, putting the lamp back on the shelf.

"How about these?" Harper picked up two bejeweled picture frames that looked like they belonged in the mansion of a millionaire cartoon villain.

"Um, not really my taste."

"Good. That was a test. You passed."

"Oh, thank God," Elena said with a chuckle. "I've liked everything you've suggested so far. I really thought you liked those."

"Please credit me with some taste."

They settled on a throw blanket to match the pillows, a couple of vases, a small, modern glass coffee table, and a kitchen gadget she would probably never use but was too tempting to pass up. They also found a nice painting for Elena's home office.

They grabbed the promised vegetarian hot dogs on the way out of the store. Elena hadn't harbored high hopes, but she was pleasantly surprised.

"Maybe I've had a few too many meals at the Complex, but these are actually delicious."

"See?" Harper said around a mouthful of food. "What did I tell you? Amazing."

"I'll never doubt you again."

"See that you don't."

"Oh! Speaking of you being right, I downloaded Masked. I've been talking to a couple of people. It's actually not bad."

With a mouth full of food, Harper's expression was difficult to interpret. She seemed to take a particularly long time to chew, but when she finished, she shot Elena a bright smile.

"I'm so glad! That's awesome! Have you asked anyone out yet?"

"Not yet. I'm thinking about it, though."

"You should go for it! What do you have to lose? First dates are so much fun!"

"Are you serious?" Elena stared at her.

"Uh, yes?"

"They're literally the exact opposite of fun. That's like saying getting drawn and quartered is fun."

Harper blinked at her. "Where the hell do you go on dates?"

"Doesn't matter. It's awkward. It's terrible. All I want to do is go home."

Elena took another bite of her hot dog as Harper frowned at her. "But I thought you wanted to date, right?"

"I do. In theory. I just want to skip past the first few."

"Well, Matched should help with that, right?"

"Yeah, true." That was the whole point of getting it, after all.

"Do you want to go home now?"

"No," Elena said, surprised that the answer rang true. "No, I don't."

"So, there you go. Just pretend you're going out with a friend. It's less pressure. Just a friend you might kiss."

"A friend I might kiss." Elena repeated the words back to her, mulling.

"Exactly."

"I'll try that. Thanks, Harper."

Her smile was inscrutable. "Any time."

CHAPTER EIGHT

That evening, Elena settled into the couch in her new-and-improved living room, admiring the rectangular glass coffee table Harper had helped her carry inside. She hoped the benefit of fewer drinks accidentally kicked over wouldn't come at the cost of banged-up shins, but if it did, well... bruises healed more easily than red wine stains.

Elena checked her email and found a message from Harper with all the details of the shelves already in her inbox. She grabbed a spare notebook from the junk drawer in the kitchen and jotted down all the necessary numbers. After checking current prices at her favorite hardware store, Elena whipped through her calculations, double checked her figures, and sent them off for Harper's seal of approval.

Just as she was about to set her phone aside, a notification from Masked popped up, displaying a new message from Trail Runner Girl.

She read the message and smiled before dashing off a quick response. Then, chewing the inside of her cheek, Elena stared at the phone like she might a snake that was threatening to bite her. She'd talked to the woman about several topics over the last few days, from their shared love of hiking—unsurprising—to current events, sports, and movies. Enough to know they would at least be able to carry on a conversation for the length of a meal.

"Just a friend you might kiss," Elena muttered to herself. Holding her breath, she quickly typed out an invitation to dinner and sent it, then stared at the screen, waiting for a response.

She didn't have to wait long.

trailrunner22: Thought you'd never ask. :)

And just like that, she had her first real date in a decade. Weird.

And even weirder, the first person she wanted to text about wasn't Margot or Dee.

It was Harper. So she did.

Elena (7:05 P.M.): I did it! I asked her out!!

Harper (7:21 P.M.): omg, nice! congrats!

Elena (7:23 P.M.): Of course, now I have to go on the actual date, but here's hoping I'll survive.

Harper (7:24 P.M.): you will! I believe in you!

Elena (7:25 P.M.): Thanks! :)

Harper (7:32 P.M.): feel free to text me if you need any help, btw. fake emergency call, liberation from an ax murderer's basement... ;)

Elena (7:32 P.M.): ha ha

Elena felt powerful. She couldn't believe she'd actually done that. She harnessed some of the good energy and decided now was the time to get back on the horse. Donning a fleece-lined jacket to protect against the October evening air, she grabbed her mesh bag of soccer balls from the closet with all her gear and headed out to the backyard. A professional goal was set up there, because no one could ever accuse her of lacking dedication.

Soccer was everything to her.

Yes, she had other hobbies. She had friends. But this was

her true home.

Elena let the bag slip from her shoulder to the ground and dug through it until she found what she wanted.

"There you are," she said, pulling out her lucky ball, once-bright blue with neon yellow lightning emblazoned on the sides, marred by scuff marks. She'd been practicing with it when she'd gotten the phone call with her first ever National Team call up, and ever since then, it had been her favorite. Elena used it any time she needed a bit of extra luck, and she needed all of that she could get right now.

She placed the ball on the ground, right across from the old oak tree, which she knew marked exactly twelve yards from the goal. She lined up, took five steps back, then ran forward and let loose a strong kick that sent the ball sailing into the upper right corner.

Thwack.

She waited for the satisfaction of a good, solid shot.

Instead, she felt nothing but absence, like someone had carved out an essential part of her and left only a gaping hollow behind.

Elena didn't move for a few seconds, staying frozen in place as though her joy and love of soccer would come flying back into her chest in a few seconds, making her whole again.

Nothing.

Nothing but cold. But disappointment. But guilt. That was the sound Annie could have made.

That was the shot Elena had stolen from her, from their team.

The glow she had felt from the afternoon with Harper and her pride in herself was a distant memory.

Her lucky ball sat square in the middle of the goal, mocking her.

She turned and left it all behind, abandoning her supplies to the dusky evening.

Back in the living room, she flopped down on the couch

and texted Margot.

Elena (8:32 P.M.): I'm hungry. Why aren't you here to microwave us some of your famous gourmet pizza rolls?

Margot (8:33 P.M.): Excuse me for being out of town saving lives.

Elena (8:34 P.M.): Ostensibly

Margot (8:34 P.M.): Also, what's wrong?

Elena (8:35 P.M.): Does something have to be wrong for me to want your company?

Margot (8:36 P.M.): No, but pizza rolls are your angry food.

Elena started typing, then backspaced everything she had written. She repeated this a couple of times before finally sending a message.

Elena (8:39 P.M.): Not angry. Just a lot going on. Are you up for a call later tonight?

Margot (8:41 P.M.): I figured. And of course! I'm still at work now, but I should be home in about an hour.

Elena (8:42 P.M.): Great. Ttyl

Margot didn't respond, but that was just as typical as the fact that she was still at work even though it was nearly eleven at night in her time zone. Elena pulled up a food delivery app and ordered a large veggie pizza, which wasn't quite what she really wanted, but it would do.

Her pizza arrived in half an hour later. She sat alone in her breakfast nook and at a few slices while Shakira sang about *ladrones* on her phone. She didn't like to eat in silence, and this album was a nostalgic pleasure for her. In high school, she and her mom had worn out the CD over hours spent driving all over the state for games. The memory reminded that needed to call her parents soon; she'd skipped out on their planned call on Saturday.

Saturday.

Everything came back to Saturday.

She'd had losses before, but nothing like this. Nothing that she couldn't bounce back from.

Just as she had the thought, her phone rang. She picked it up and saw the request for a video call coming in from Margot.

"Thank God you called. I'm about to spiral," Elena said the second Margot's face appeared. Her hair was in its usual straight, no-nonsense bob, and she was wearing her new wire-frame glasses.

"Spiral all you want. I'm here. What's going on?"

"It's still the game."

Margot nodded.

"It just...it really fucked me up. It's been five days, but I don't even want to look at a ball. I hate the idea of playing." Elena paused, then reconsidered. "No, it's not even that. It's like I'm just...empty. There's nothing there. And I'm freaking out, because that has literally never happened to me. Not once. I can't play like this."

"Well, the good thing is that you don't have to play like this. You have time to recover."

"But what if I don't recover?"

"Don't be ridiculous," Margot said, in a brusque fashion that Elena would probably have found rude in anyone else. Somehow, from Margot, it was comforting. "You will. You're just still upset, right? You probably just need to process."

"Maybe."

"So, what happened during the game to make you upset?"

Elena looked away from the tiny screen and stared down at the table. "It's my fault we lost. I was stupid and selfish, and I cost us that goal."

"You had less than a second to make that decision. Professionals make wrong calls all the time. No one is perfect."

"I know that. But Dee keeps talking about handing captain down to me, and I never wanted it. I'm shit at talking to people. And now it's not even just that I don't want it. I don't deserve it. I put myself above my team. End of story."

"Okay, slow down, Miss Martyr. Just because you took a single shot doesn't mean you're subconsciously trying to sabotage your team."

"Of course I wasn't trying to sabotage them. But I should have trusted Coach's choice to put Annie in. I didn't."

"Great. You've already identified the reason why you did what you did. You know what you need to work on: trusting your coach's choices. Trusting your new teammate. That's all there is to it."

Elena huffed out a frustrated breath. "Then, what, am I just not supposed to feel bad about this? For ruining Dee's last game and taking the trophy away from my entire team?"

"That wasn't all on you. The game is ninety minutes long. You weren't the only one on the field."

Elena tapped the tabletop with her finger while she mulled over the words. Slowly, she started to calm down. This was why Margot was the perfect person to call when she was upset. She was somehow always able to cut through to the facts.

"Can I ask your advice?"

"Of course."

"Do you think I should turn it down? The captaincy?"

"Based on one game? Absolutely not. Were you going to turn it down before?"

"I hadn't decided yet."

"And why wouldn't you?"

"Because I believe in this team. Because I think we have what it takes to win next year. Because I like the idea of giving back to everyone and being a good example."

"Those sound like pretty compelling reasons to me."

"I still have to think it over some more."

"Sure." Margot let the subject drop easily. "So, what else is going on? Any updates I've missed?"

Elena laughed. "Actually, yeah. You're not going to believe

this one. Are you sitting down?"

"You can literally see that I am."

"I have a date."

Margot's jaw dropped. "No fucking way! Are you joking?"

"Nope."

"As in, a date with a woman? A woman you might have sex with?"

"Yikes, slow down. But yes. A real date with a real woman. Well, as far as I know, anyway."

A crease appeared in the middle of Margot's forehead. Elena remembered thinking of Margot when Harper made that exact expression. "What do you mean?"

"Well, I haven't actually met her in person yet. I've only talked to her online."

"What? *You* are doing online dating?"

"I know, right? Harper talked me into downloading Masked. It's a dating app. Have you heard of it?"

"My Harper?"

Elena nodded.

"Huh, okay. Have you two been hanging out?"

An image popped into her head: Harper, sitting on her couch and giggling over the fact that Elena already had a soccer lamp very similar to the one she'd threatened to buy at IKEA.

"We have, actually. She's cool. I'm surprised I never talked to her more back when we were younger."

"She's great. I was sort of hoping that we'd get closer now that we'd be in the same city again. But now I'm not even on the same side of the country, so..."

"You know, you could always call her."

"She doesn't want to talk to me. But anyway, we're not talking about me. Back to you! Tell me about the lucky lady."

Elena filled Margot in on all of her interactions with Trail Runner Girl.

"Does she not have an actual name?"

"She does. She told me yesterday, actually. It's Heather.

But I've gotten so used to calling her Trail Runner Girl in my head that it just kind of stuck."

"Well, you might not want to call her that to her face."

Probably a good point. "I'll take that under advisement."

They chatted for a few more minutes, and after Elena hung up, she thought about the name Heather.

It was similar to Harper, and Harper was the one who was really responsible for the date in the first place. Funny.

The familiar aroma of Midnight Vegan greeted Harper as she stepped inside on Friday morning. She ordered a cranberry oat muffin and a Good Morning Green smoothie, which had become her go-to order. The smoothie was surprisingly delicious, and all the vegetables and antioxidants meant she could justify the price.

Well, for now.

Not after tomorrow, though. Please! Harper imagined her checking account begging as she as she tapped her phone against the machine to pay. While the proximity and deliciousness of Vivian's baked goods would still be tempting, the food situation would be much easier once she moved into her new apartment across the street tomorrow.

A minute later, Vivian appeared from the kitchen and slid a blue ceramic plate toward her on the counter, muffin sitting neatly in the middle. "You know, we do serve things other than muffins," Vivian said in a teasing tone.

Harper bit back the tiny surge of annoyance she felt at the words. Vivian was only joking. "Are you implying I have a muffin problem?" she asked, playing along.

"Well, I am pretty sure you've been here ten times in the past week, and I've never seen you order anything else."

"I resent that. I also drink your smoothies sometimes." Harper held up her receipt as proof.

"I'm just saying. If you're going to eat here for every meal, maybe add a black bean burrito sometime. Something with some substance. You're going to waste away."

Harper didn't mention that it was her bank account she was worrying about wasting away.

"Fat chance of that," she said instead, gesturing down at her ample frame and grinning at her own joke.

"Just think about it! Gotta keep those muscles strong to lift all those boxes, right?"

"I do yoga. I think my muscles are okay." Harper started to grab for her plate and then paused. "Actually, speaking of which, do you know a good yoga instructor around here? I've been slacking since I moved, and I can feel it."

"Honey, this is a vegan restaurant. I think we've got about twenty fliers up there for yoga instructors." Vivian gestured toward the cork board on the wall near the front door as she headed back for the kitchen. "Take your pick."

Harper eyed the board and snapped a photo of one flier that mentioned it was open to all body sizes and another that said *fat friendly*. She'd definitely visit that one first. She loved it when people actually used the word "fat" and didn't dance around it like some kind of curse.

Happy with her discovery, Harper popped in her Bluetooth headphones, put on some Janelle Monae, and waited for her smoothie. She had gotten into the habit of taking her food over to Bewitched to eat while she worked, then returning the dishes later.

"Smoothie up!" announced the ghostly brunette, whose name she still didn't actually know.

Harper thanked her, then headed to Bewitched for a day of sorting game pieces into tiny plastic baggies. It was tedious work, and she wasn't looking forward to spending all day alone. She missed painting and shopping with Elena. The name made something turn upside down in her belly, and she internally rolled her eyes at herself.

She had already gone down that road once in her life.

She was not going to be stupid enough to let herself fall for Elena again, especially now that Elena was going out with someone new.

Someone who wasn't Harper.

Someone from the app that Harper had *recommended to her*, like some kind of reverse genie, killing her own wishes before they had even the possibility of coming true.

Her thoughts were interrupted when someone suddenly turned into the hallway directly in front of her, having come in through the back entrance. Before Harper's brain could fully process what was happening, it quickly issued three simultaneous commands:

Scream.

Stop.

Throw up hands to brace for impact, in case you don't stop quickly enough.

Unfortunately, she followed all three.

Although she maintained her grip on the dishes, her muffin went flying, and Harper watched in horror as nearly half of her full-to-the-brim smoothie was flung from the glass, directly onto the person's shirt.

"Shit, I'm so sorry! I wasn't—" Harper finally looked up from the gray Henley that now featured a Wookie-sized bright green stain, including some lovely little chunks of what was possibly kale, only to do a double take. "Elena?" she asked, as though she could possibly be mistaken about that face from two feet away. As though she had never spent hours daydreaming about that face and her own face being a lot closer than this.

"Morning, Harper," Elena said, laughter in her eyes.

"I'm sorry! I didn't mean to dump my smoothie on you."

"I figured," Elena replied, and suddenly Harper had to laugh. Maybe it was a delayed effect of the adrenaline, but the whole situation was suddenly hilarious. The giggles bubbled up in her chest, and she couldn't hold them back. Elena must have felt the same way, because she started laughing, holding her shirt away from her body to inspect the damage. "Oh my god, look at this! I look like I've been in a paintball fight."

"You can pull it off! Just say it's a fashion statement."

"Oh, yes! This is an advertisement, really, if you think about it. For some kind of crunchy, nontoxic dye."

"Or alien vomit."

Elena faux gagged. "Ew! That just made it so much worse," she said, leaning against the wall and gasping with mirth.

"Of all the times to be environmentally responsible!"

"What?"

Harper wiped tears of laughter from her eyes. "If I'd just used a plastic cup with a lid, the smoothie would still be safely contained, and your shirt would have survived."

"Well, the shirt may not have survived, but I did, so I think we'll be okay."

"I really am sorry, by the way. Next time I won't put on headphones while walking."

"Seriously, it's no big deal."

"Are you kidding? You look like an extra from a sci-fi horror movie. If only it was two days from now." She muttered the last sentence under her breath.

"Why would that be any better?"

"I'm moving in across the street tomorrow, so I'd have something you could change into." Then inspiration struck, and Harper stood up straighter. "Wait! I have a spare shirt in my office."

"You really don't have to do that."

"What, you're just going to walk around in your alien vomit shirt?"

Elena looked down, paused for a moment, seeming to consider her words. "Actually, yeah, I was about to head to the hardware store. If you wouldn't mind…" Her words trailed off, that rueful smile doing things to Harper's insides that she very desperately attempted to ignore.

It was getting harder and harder to ignore her reactions to Elena.

And it was getting harder and harder to blame them on some sort of misplaced throwback nostalgia mixed with attraction.

It was starting to feel like something new.

Something real.

"Follow me." She started for Bewitched, and Elena followed her.

Feelings were something she seriously didn't have the time to contemplate right now. She was too busy. And Elena had always belonged to Margot. Much like her parents' adoration, the good hair, and the height gene.

Besides which, Elena had never given any hint that she wanted to be anything other than friends. But that was okay. Harper was happy to be friends.

She was also happy she was by nature a paranoid person who always kept a spare shirt in her office. Even if her "office" was now the size of a closet. She grabbed her emergency box from the back of her closet-slash-office and dug through it until she found the black t-shirt. She turned back and held it out toward Elena, who was hovering outside the office door.

"Sorry, it might smell like cardboard. And also probably won't fit you very well, since we aren't exactly the same size. But it's stretchy, so it shouldn't be too bad. And I promise it's clean."

Elena took it. "Thank you."

"I'll just let you—" Before Harper had the chance to finish her sentence, Elena had whipped off her shirt and was standing in front of her in a black sports bra.

Harper's breath caught in her throat.

Holy shit.

Holy *shit*.

Somehow, Elena seemed both smaller and larger with her shirt off. Her body was tiny, her hips flaring subtly out from her waist, but every inch of her radiated power. She was all smooth brown skin and lithe muscle. Her abs were defined, all curves and lines and shadows, and Harper's fingers twitched.

She wanted to touch her and draw her at the same time. She wanted to sketch those lean, strong limbs, the jut of her hipbones, the bumps of her ribcage. She wanted to capture the faint tan lines, telltale signs of hours spent on the soccer field. Then she wanted to run her fingers along every single inch.

Distantly, she realized that Elena probably expected her to turn around, but just as she had the thought, Elena tugged the shirt into place.

"Sorry, that was probably rude. I should've, like, used the bathroom or something. One of the downsides of being a professional athlete. I'm way too used to parading around in a sports bra."

You're not going to catch me complaining.

"Oh, no, uh." Harper paused to clear her throat, hoping to any and every deity in existence that her cheeks weren't as red as they felt. "No problem. *Mi casa es tu casa.* Or, you know. *Oficina*, I guess."

Elena just laughed and turned away, but Harper couldn't will her legs to move. Her knees felt like she'd just downed half a dozen shots of tequila. Her shirt was slightly baggy on Elena's athletic frame, and it was also too short, just skimming the tops of her jeans. When she moved, Harper could see a tiny sliver of skin peeking out.

For the love of Leia. Why was the universe doing this to her?

Harper took a shaky breath and blinked to clear her head.

"I'm going to clean up the hall really quickly. And get a replacement muffin. You want one? I owe you for ruining your shirt."

"You don't have to do that. It's my fault for showing up without warning."

"Oh, yeah. Between the smoothie and—" *the sports bra*

"—everything, I didn't even realize. What are you doing here? I'm fresh out of paint jobs. Not that you're not welcome to just drop by, of course." Harper was rambling. She forced herself to stop.

"Well, I was on my way to the hardware store to pick up the materials when it occurred to me that we don't need to copy the shelves you were going to order exactly. Like, we already decided on a different finish. I know you love the height, but I thought maybe you'd want them longer or shorter, depending on the space you had available."

"Huh. That's a great point! Yeah, I'd love to make them a little longer, actually. I'm not sure if we could extend it by a full cubby, though. Let me grab my tape measure."

"I have mine." Elena said, producing a tape measure out from the back pocket of her jeans like some kind of lesbian magician.

"Okay. You measure while I go get the muffins, then?"

"Sure."

Harper pointed out the space in the front room where the shelves would go, one on each side of the doorway between the rooms.

"What flavor of muffin do you want?"

"I'm not picky. Surprise me."

There were about a dozen ways Harper could think of to fulfill that request right now, and only a few of them involved muffins.

But she just agreed, turned, and walked away, giving herself a stern mental talking-to.

Harper returned several minutes later with the muffins and set the plates on the edge of the large six-seat table in the back corner of the lower level. It was the only table she'd had delivered so far, and it was covered in a dozen different board game boxes.

"I measured and did the math, and there's definitely enough space there to add another cubby."

"Awesome! That was a really great idea. Thanks for thinking of it."

Harper stacked a couple of the games on the floor and pushed another to the side, clearing enough room for both of them.

"No problem." Elena shrugged, sitting down in the chair Elena indicated. "Jesus, is that all one game?" Harper followed Elena's gaze to the box for Gloomhaven.

"Yep."

"Seriously? That's, like, a whole chest. Does it have giant pieces or something?"

"Nope." Harper held up one of the tiny character pieces she had been sorting out. "Normal size. It's just a really massive game."

"That's crazy. Who would even want to play that?" She pointed to the Terraforming Mars box. "Or this one. It's so intimidating."

"They're not that bad."

Elena grabbed the instructions out of the open box. "Are you kidding? This is..." She paused, counting the pages before continuing, "This is 15 pages long! It's like the board game version of *War and Peace*."

Harper laughed. "The rules are a little much, but once you understand everything, it's fantastic. It's actually one of the most popular games right now."

"Really?"

Harper nodded.

"Well, maybe I need to try it out. *War and Peace* or not, it would be fun to go to Mars." She looked through all the other boxes. "Will you have the classics, too, or just this kind?"

"Of course! Some people just come in because they want to play a simple game of checkers or chess, which I totally get."

"I love chess! I haven't played in forever, though. My mom used to play with me sometimes, but she gets annoyed because I take so long between moves."

"Well, if you come by sometime after we're open, I'll play with you. I'll have to help customers between moves, so you'd have plenty of time."

"Perfect." She took the first bite of her muffin, and her eyes opened wide. "Oh my god," she said around a mouthful, holding her fingers up to her lips while she continued chewing. "This is incredible."

"I'm telling you. Vivian is a culinary goddess."

"There's no way this is vegan."

"I said the same thing, but it is. She's just magic."

"Okay, new plan. I'm going to start playing this crazy chest game. It will take me at least a week, during which you will need to keep bringing me muffins. Deal?"

"Deal. Though I may have to get you to sign a disclaimer, since you'll be all alone with the ghost at night. I can't be held responsible for her actions."

"Oh, I'm so scared. Whatever will she do? Checkmate me to death?"

"I'll have you know this place is very seriously haunted." Harper said, smirking. "It could wreak havoc on your psyche to be in here for too long." She leaned forward dramatically, dropping her voice to slightly above a whisper. "The lights even flicker from time to time."

"How will I ever survive," Elena said, deadpan.

"For real, though," Harper said in her normal voice. "The lights have actually flickered a couple of times."

"Tell me you don't actually think it's haunted."

"Of course not. I just need to call an electrician. I don't believe in ghosts. Do you?" she asked, glancing at Elena curiously.

"Nah, I don't think so. My mom super does, though. She's all into that kind of stuff."

"Ghost hunting?"

"Catholicism."

Harper snorted, which caused Elena to laugh loudly, eyes all crinkled and head thrown back, and that was when Harper knew that it was game over.

She was toast.

CHAPTER NINE

Elena had a date.

That was an incredibly weird thing to think.

She had a date. With a woman who wasn't Claire. For the first time in a decade.

Not that she missed Claire, of course. She had long since gotten over wishing her ex would realize she'd made a mistake. That had been part of what she'd worked out in therapy after the divorce and her diagnosis. She'd wanted Claire back, but only because she craved the familiar. Most of all, because Claire had never given her a chance to fix things. She'd just emerged from their bedroom one day with a packed bag, explaining that she felt like Elena had always put soccer before her and that she couldn't take it anymore. She'd ignored Elena's shocked pleas to let her try to do better. She'd just left.

Elena's cell phone alarm went off, reminding her to get ready for said date, and she shook off the memories. She'd set it that morning just to be safe, having learned over the years that when it came to things that were time-sensitive, it was best to set an alarm. That way, she didn't have to be paranoid the entire day that she would accidentally lose track of time, something she was prone to doing, especially if she was playing soccer or building something. Or watching a particularly good television series. Or reading a particularly good book.

She turned the alarm off and stood, stretching and brushing sawdust off her jeans. Harper's shelves were coming along nicely. There was a not-insignificant part of her that wanted to stay here, keep working, and call the whole thing off. She brushed it aside. This would be good for her.

Half an hour later, she was standing in front of a mirror in black skinny jeans, a white silk blouse, and a black blazer, which she had taken off and put back on again at least six times.

She needed a second opinion, but she wasn't sure whose she wanted. Her finger hovered back and forth between Dee and Margot's text threads before she finally just created a group chat.

Elena (5:42 P.M.): Hello! Sorry for the surprise group chat. In a hurry. How is this outfit? Too austere? Do I look like I'm going for a job interview? Should I switch to a brighter shirt? Lose the blazer?

Elena (5:42 P.M.): [image]

Dee (5:43 P.M.): Hey, Margot. Been a long time ;)

Dee (5:43 P.M.): Elena, you look amazing. Keep the blazer. It's fucking freezing outside, and you'll want it

Dee (5:44 P.M.): Plus you look like a stud

Margot (5:45 P.M.): I agree that there's no need to change the outfit. You look stunning!

Elena (5:44 P.M.): Thank you both!!

Dee (5:46 P.M.): Go get 'em, tiger

Dee (5:47 P.M.): Don't think I didn't notice you ignoring my greeting, Margot

(Margot has left the chat.)

Dee (5:48 P.M.): Wow, she really doesn't like me, huh?
Elena (5:49 P.M.): Maybe she didn't see it?

Dee (5:49 P.M.): Sure

Elena (5:50 P.M.): You take a while to grow on people sometimes. You know that.

Dee (5:51 P.M.): I know. Like mold. I'm interesting that way.

Dee (5:51 P.M.): Now, I won't have you late for your date because you're soothing my wounded ego. Have a great time! Love you!

(Dee has left the chat.)

Elena did not have a great time.

To be fair, though, she also didn't have a bad time.

Heather was a tall brunette with a lovely smile, creamy skin, and large, expressive blue eyes. When Heather had mentioned during their chats that she sometimes had problems dating because of her appearance, Elena had not assumed her problem was that she was too beautiful, but apparently that was what she had meant. It seemed like an odd thing to complain about, but Elena thought it must come with its own set of problems.

They ate Thai food and discussed a few things they had already touched on in their messages, such as Heather's job in healthcare administration, their favorite hiking trails, and the current Broncos season. They also talked about some new things, like Heather's love of learning about queer history. She told Elena some very interesting stories.

It was the least uncomfortable date Elena had ever been on. Masked had been a brilliant idea.

But the strangest thing kept happening.

When Heather mentioned that she liked Star Trek, Elena thought about the fact that Harper preferred Star Wars.

When Heather shared her annoyance with the stereotype that all queer women were vegetarians, Elena wondered how long Harper had been a vegetarian and why.

When Heather said her favorite color was green, Elena remembered Harper and her ridiculous alien vomit comment, and she had to fight to keep a straight face.

When Heather asked permission and they hugged goodnight after the meal, Elena thought about the fact that she and Harper had never done that.

Elena drove back to her house alone, still thinking about the last one.

She couldn't seem to get the image out of her mind. She imagined what it would be like to pull Harper close, to wrap her arms around all her softness.

Elena was not normally a hugging person. She needed to know someone well before she was comfortable enough to do so, and even then, though she might give a hug for the other person's benefit, she would never seek one out. As a rule, she did not enjoy hugging anyone she was not romantically involved with.

But she wanted to hug Harper. It was undeniable. She couldn't stop thinking about it.

Did she want to be romantically involved with Harper?

Elena thought over their interactions over the past weeks. Harper was funny and smart. She was kind, creative, and driven. She hadn't once dismissed or condescended to Elena after learning she was autistic. She was a good listener, and Elena felt comfortable around her.

She was also beautiful.

Elena had had this thought before, in fleeting moments, but she had always shoved the thought aside. It hadn't been how she'd wanted to think about Margot's little sister.

But Harper wasn't "Margot's little sister" anymore. She was Harper. Just Harper, in her own right. Elena's friend. A brave, funny, intelligent woman. The owner of the brightest smile Elena had ever seen.

And she was beautiful.

Elena didn't just think this in an objective way, the way she might about a shampoo model or a movie star. She *felt* it. She felt it in the pleasant tingling that spread throughout her body as she allowed herself to have these thoughts. She imagined Harper's gray-green eyes, her pert nose, her soft, rosy lips.

Lips she very much wanted to kiss.

Elena blinked, realizing that she was sitting in front of her house already, with very little memory of the drive there.

This was a new development.

And it was very not good.

Early Saturday afternoon, Angel pulled the moving truck up to Harper's new apartment, and Harper parked her car in the spot beside it.

"Bless you for living on the first floor," Angel said, climbing down from the cab and gazing up at the four-story brick building. She stretched her hands up above her head, the movement showing off the various colorful tattoos twisting around her forearms. Combined with her messy blue pixie cut, she put off an effortlessly cool artist vibe Harper was forever envious of.

"You're welcome. I requested it just for you."

"Wait, you are living on the first floor, right? There weren't any crazy last-minute switch-ups?"

"No, thank God. That better only happen once." Harper grimaced, remembering the first solo apartment she'd rented after living with Angel while getting her degree. She'd thought she'd rented a first-floor apartment but had somehow wound up on the sixth floor of a building with no working elevator, an experience she had no desire to ever repeat.

"For real. Anyway, I think my arms have finally de-noodleized from loading up. You ready to take it all back out again?"

Harper opened the back of the truck and suppressed a sigh at the mountain of possessions before her. "Nothing to do but start, right?"

"Let's do it."

Harper grabbed the closest box, and Angel followed suit. "So, when will Lover Girl get here?"

"She's not my Lover Girl."

"Yet."

"Ever. It's not like that."

"Not like that, my ass. Y'all went to IKEA together. You're practically U-Haul lesbians already."

"You know I'm bi," Harper sniped as she pushed the front door open with her back.

"Oh, excuse me. Ryder, then? Budget? Two Queers and a Truck?"

Harper snorted. "No, but I think I'm going to dump Bewitched and start a moving business just so I can use that name. You in?"

"Hell no, I only do this for people I love. Or people I owe a massive debt to."

"Pity." Harper nodded toward the door on her right. "It's this one. Apartment four."

"You don't have to go pick up the keys or anything?"

"No. I came by yesterday to get everything worked out. The keys should be waiting inside."

She hefted the box under one arm and twisted the doorknob, revealing a small foyer area with the kitchen directly to the left. It was empty, the bare walls painted a utilitarian eggshell.

Harper set the box down on the kitchen counter and pulled the refrigerator door open. On the top shelf sat an envelope with *Harper* written on it in the landlady's spidery cursive. She grabbed the envelope and checked the back, which was still sealed. "Keys!" Harper said, slipping them out of the envelope and giving them a jingle.

Angel gave her a thumbs up and wandered off to explore the apartment. Harper went with her, showing off the living room just off the kitchen, featuring a sliding glass door that opened out onto a tiny patio.

"And here's the best part."

"The door?" Angel asked, seeming unimpressed.

"No, the view!" Her apartment was at the front of the building, so it looked out at the parking lot and, more importantly, across the street to the long brick building with hunter green awnings. She pointed to the closest one on the corner. "That's Bewitched."

"Oh!" Now she sounded excited. "I know you said it was close, but this is *close*."

"I know!"

"Now you can avoid driving, *and* you won't turn into one of those obnoxious people who brag about biking to work."

"I know. It's the dream."

"Well, for you lame people who have to go somewhere else to work. For me, the dream is working on a couch in my pajama pants at two A.M. Weirdly, I never found an office for that."

"So bizarre how that request never went over well in interviews."

"Their loss."

Since she could see the front of the building and out across the street, she also noticed when a familiar silver car pulled up.

"Oh, that's Elena. We should go greet her."

"I'm not the one she wants to see."

"She doesn't want to see me." At Angel's look, she clarified, "Not like *that*. She's only here because I mentioned yesterday that I was moving, and then at nine P.M., I got a text asking what time she should be here to help. She's just being nice. We're friends."

"I seem to recall you made some friends at the Pawn, too, but I don't see any of them here," Angel said, gesturing around at the empty room as they made their way back toward the door.

"That's because it's noon on a Saturday. They're all at

work. Working for me."

"What about what's-her-face?"

"Gwyn?"

"Yeah, her. Weren't you two a thing?"

"Barely. I should've stuck with my rule of never dating customers. Her entire group meets somewhere else now. Do you know how much they spent every week?"

Harper stepped out of the front door of the apartment building and waved to Elena through her windshield, gesturing toward the moving truck.

She met them there, and Harper desperately tried to ignore the fact that she was wearing red and black flannel rolled up to her forearms, like a sapphic fantasy come to life.

"Elena, this is my friend Angel. Or, well, Cynthia, I guess?" Harper said, looking at Angel to take the lead, but Angel just laughed.

Elena looked perplexed but interested. "You have two names? Interesting."

"Not to anyone else. But we met online a million years ago, and that's what I went by. So we just got used to it."

"Ah, I see."

"When your username is HansAngel, the nickname just kind of picks itself."

Elena chuckled. "Makes sense."

"Yeah. So, Cynthia or Angel, either one works. Also not picky about pronouns. Whatever your heart feels, I'll respond to."

"Angel is my oldest friend and a badass graphic designer who makes my drawings look like a toddler's." Angel scoffed and started to interject, but Harper continued talking, gesturing toward Elena as though Angel didn't know their entire history. "Elena is...an old acquaintance, but probably my newest friend, actually." Harper grinned over at her, and Elena's answering smile made it feel like a hundred microscopic TIE fighters were buzzing around in her stomach. "She plays professional soccer."

"That's awesome. So, how did you and Eva get back in touch?"

"Eva?" Elena asked, her face morphing into a confused frown.

Oh, no.

No, no, no, no, no.

Harper cleared her throat and tried for a casual tone. "Oh, yeah, that was my online name. Like Cynthia's was Angel."

"Where did that come from?"

"You know, it's been so long, I don't even remember," Harper said, pretending she didn't hear the telltale squeakiness in her voice. "Anyway, enough chit-chat. We need to get down to business, or we're going to lose the sun."

She grabbed the first thing she saw on the truck, which unfortunately seemed to be a box packed to the brim with solid iron, judging from the weight.

"It's not even two P.M.," Angel said in a tone that Harper was positive meant she was trying to keep from laughing. Then she turned toward Elena. "And hers came from the same place mine did. From her username. As in, HanNLeia4Eva."

Harper was going to murder her best friend, and she wasn't even going to be sorry.

"Wow." Elena's expression twisted as she clearly held back a laugh, and Harper sighed, accepting the fact that she had just lost any and all possibility of being potentially dateable in Elena's eyes.

"Go ahead. Laugh. You know you want to."

"Not at all," Elena said, doing the absolute worst job possible at not laughing.

Harper adjusted her grip on the box. "Listen, I was 14 when I made it! Bad usernames were a rite of passage in the early internet days."

"Plus she gets stuck in boring canon land," Angel added. "She still hasn't realized it's more fun out here where the sky's the limit."

"It isn't my fault they're the best couple in all of cinematic history."

"You just don't see the potential in what isn't shown on screen," Angel countered playfully, a facsimile of a conversation they'd had a hundred times over the years.

"Then why do I ship Finn and Po, hmm?"

"Who the hell doesn't? Anyone with half a brain cell can see the chemistry."

Angel looked toward Elena as though she expected Elena to back her up, but Elena held up her hands. "I, uh, haven't seen all the movies, so I'm not even sure who that is."

"What!" Angel and Harper exclaimed simultaneously.

"Something I'm willing to fix. Worry, do not," she said, in an adorable Yoda impression.

"I'm going to remember that!" Harper said. "But I'm walking away now, because my arms are about twenty seconds away from falling off."

Thankfully, she made it all the way to the bedroom without losing her grip, and as soon as she placed the box on the floor, she shook out her arms and turned to go back for another load. She passed Angel and Elena on the way back, each carrying one end of her small kitchen table.

The truck emptied more quickly than Harper expected, with the three of them working together. Moving from a studio to a one-bedroom, she didn't exactly have a mountain of possessions, but they had seemed endless when she was packing.

They were nearing the back of the truck when Harper grabbed a particularly large box labeled *books* that she immediately cursed herself for packing so full. It took all her strength to lug it to the bedroom, and once there, she took a few seconds to breathe deeply, flexing her fingers to rid them of the soreness. She heard footsteps and backed away from the door, just in time to see Elena appear in the doorway, holding another box. She had shed the red flannel shirt from earlier, and now she was just as wearing a plain gray tank top. It was exactly the same style she used to wear, ribbed, no frills, and it had exactly the same effect.

Which was to say, it rendered Harper entirely incapable of looking away from her arms.

It just wasn't fair. She got that Elena needed muscular legs due to her career, but there was no reason for her to have such ridiculously mesmerizing arms. Arm strength was not necessary for playing soccer. In fact, there were very strong consequences for purposefully using your arms.

All of which to say, *What the fuck, universe?* How was she supposed to avoid having Feelings when Elena was marching around with biceps like that, muscles flexed, bulging and ropy with the strain of the heavy load.

Why was Elena even wearing a tank top? It was cold outside, for crying out loud.

She needed some water.

"Where do you want this box?" Elena's voice jarred her out of her biceps-induced stupor.

"Here is fine." Harper gestured to the open space in front of the bookshelf. Elena stepped in that direction, but her toe caught on the edge of the long beams from Harper's bed frame, and she stumbled forward with a gasp. Harper reached out uselessly, too far away to be of any help, and the box of books slid from Elena's grasp and landed on the floor. The side of the box, which was definitely too thin to have been chosen as a book box in hindsight, ripped open with the force, sending a cascade of hardcovers and paperbacks onto the floor.

Elena caught herself with a hand on the wall, and Harper paused with her hands extended out toward Elena.

"Are you okay?"

"I'm fine." She looked down at the mess and grimaced. "Sorry about your books."

"No worries at all. I've got it." Harper knelt and started grabbing the books, placing them in a stack against the wall.

"Here, let me help you get them."

"It's really no big deal."

Elena bent down despite her protests, and Harper couldn't help but be painfully aware of her proximity. Her skin felt like it was vibrating with the need for Elena to come closer, to touch her. Everything had gotten so much worse since yesterday, and Harper needed her to not be this close. But she couldn't think of a reason to send Elena from the room, so she just gathered the books as quickly as she could.

Then Elena reached for her worn paperback of *The Color Purple* at the same time she did. Elena's fingers brushed hers, and what felt like an entire bolt of lightning shot up her arm. Harper raised her head, intending to tell Elena she had it... only to find Elena's face inches from hers.

The words died on her lips.

She was so, so close.

Her eyes were so beautiful, a deep brown Harper could get lost in.

And she wasn't looking away.

Harper felt like she couldn't get enough oxygen, her head a swimmy, thoughtless mess. She let her eyes drop to Elena's lips, which were parted. She was breathing hard. From exertion? From adrenaline from the fall?

Because she was having the same difficulty breathing that Harper was?

Elena's eyes flicked to her lips, and Harper's heart stuttered in her chest.

Holy shit.

Elena was going to kiss her.

Her lips tingled in anticipation, and she nearly started to lean in.

Then Elena pulled her hand back and cleared her throat. "Sorry." She grabbed the last couple of books and shoved them back into the mangled box, then climbed to her feet. "Man, we really need to do something about our butterfingers problem, huh?" Her voice gave absolutely no indication that anything was out of the usual.

"Good thing you only need your feet for soccer, I guess," Harper joked inanely, her brain still only functioning at partial capacity, reliving the look in Elena's eyes before she'd moved away.

Elena just laughed and was gone a second later, as though she hadn't just turned Harper's world upside down.

Harper sat on the floor for a few more seconds, unable to move.

That had really just happened.

Harper had kissed a decent number of people. She knew what it looked like when someone wanted to kiss her. And Elena had wanted to.

Elena had wanted to kiss her.

She had absolutely no idea what to do with that information.

"Okay, I'm gotta head out," Angel said, appearing in the door frame. "Elena just grabbed the last box. Sorry for not sticking around, but it's like three A.M. right now in Angel Time." She paused, her head tilting to the side, as though she'd just noticed Harper's position. "Are you okay?"

"Yep, fine. Just resting."

"Valid. I would join you if I weren't concerned I might fall asleep."

"You can stay here if you need to! I can get my bed set up in like five minutes flat."

"Nah, thanks. I appreciate the thought, but I didn't bring my tablet, and I've got a commission due the day after tomorrow."

"You could at least nap here." Harper didn't know why, but she was suddenly desperate for Angel to stay. She needed Angel's presence here, because the idea of being alone with

Elena was both elating and terrifying. She kept running over and over that moment in her mind. The way Elena's eyes had dropped to her lips.

But she also needed to remember that Elena had turned away.

"No can do. I need my own bed. Besides, you two deserve to have the place to yourselves. Order a pizza. Drink some La Croix. Have a good time."

Harper climbed to her feet and wrapped Angel in a long hug. "Thank you so much for all your help."

"Anytime, babe."

Harper protested once more, but Angel didn't budge. Finally, Harper let her go, resulting in an apartment filled with stacks of boxes, an empty refrigerator, and a woman whose eyes she couldn't quite bring herself to meet just yet. Instead, she pulled out her phone and swiped over to her apps before walking out to the living room.

"How do you feel about pizza?" Harper asked, and Elena grinned.

"I always feel great about pizza."

"I'm very glad you feel that way."

Half an hour later, Harper flopped down onto the living room floor, then carefully set the freshly delivered pizza box down next to her.

"I really could move the boxes off the kitchen table," Elena insisted, hovering a couple of feet away. "It would take thirty seconds."

"You've already done enough. This is me paying you back. Sit down. Enjoy."

"Yes, ma'am." Elena mock saluted, then lowered herself to the floor on the other side of the pizza box.

Harper wondered if she should read anything into that. Was Elena intentionally leaving extra space between them because she wanted to send a signal to Harper that she was not interested in whatever had happened in that moment earlier?

Or maybe she just wants to be able to reach the pizza easily. Chill, Harper.

She was definitely overthinking.

She needed to start a conversation so she could get out of her own head.

"Random question of the day: what did you want to be when you were a kid? Other than a soccer player."

Elena leaned her head back against the wall, her face going pensive. "You know, I actually don't know. Give me a sec." She thought about it for a minute. "I think I wanted to be a chef."

"Really?"

"Is that surprising? I do still love to eat."

She pictured Elena in a chef's costume and nodded. "Okay, yeah, I could see it. You'd rock that chef's hat." Harper tested the waters, casting out a bit of flirting, and…nothing. It sank like a rock. Harper swallowed down her disappointment with a bite of pizza. "It's weird to think of you as anything other than a soccer player, though."

"What about you?"

"At the risk of being a cliché, I wanted to be a singer."

"You sing? I never knew that."

"Unfortunately, Margot informed me quite young that my voice and I were not destined for stardom."

Elena flinched. "Ouch."

"Indeed."

"So now my singing is confined to my car and my shower. I've learned to live with the disappointment."

"It's good that you've been able to carry on."

"I do my best."

Elena finished her slice of pizza and reached for another.

"So, if you ever open another café, which piece will you choose next? Knight? Queen? Rook?"

"I don't plan on opening any more, but I'd probably go with the rook if I did. More alliteration choices."

"Good point." She tilted her head pensively. "What is a rook, anyway? Do you know?"

"No idea. I know the piece is sometimes called a castle, so maybe it's a castle?"

"An interesting question. I'll have to look it up later."

"I wonder how it got the name chess." Maybe it was the beer, but Harper was suddenly curious.

"The name was coined by Sir Aloicious Chesterton in the 14th century. It used to be called something else."

"How on earth do you know that?"

Elena collapsed into laughter. "I don't. I pulled that entirely out of my ass."

An incredulous giggle escaped Harper's lips. "Oh my god. I can't believe you thought of the name Aloicious on the spot."

"It just came to me."

"I can't believe I *believed you*."

"Neither can I, to be honest," Elena said, her face still amused.

"Speaking of chess, I think I saw the box with my games in the bedroom, if you want to stick around for a round? I've done all the productive things I want to today."

"Totally. I'm free for the night. All yours."

Harper's breath caught in her throat, and she watched Elena's face for any sign of a double entendre, but there was nothing.

She said nothing else remotely flirty over the course of their game, but that could be because Harper started with a strong opening, and Elena never recovered. The game ended after half an hour of Elena scowling at the table, and Harper didn't think it was entirely from concentration.

"Best out of three?"

"That sounds familiar," Harper said with a grin, remembering the painting competition. "You're such a sore loser. Can't stand to do lose even once?"

"I'm not a sore loser. I'm a lifelong athlete who realizes that winning is always the desirable outcome."

"And therefore, you hate losing. Thus making you a sore loser."

"Can I help it if I have been financially and career-fully conditioned to prefer winning?"

"Anyone ever tell you that you're annoying?"

"Just Margot. Must be a family trait."

Harper seriously doubted that Margot found Elena annoying in the same way she found Elena annoying. In a way that wasn't really annoyance at all, but really just a thinly veiled desire to kiss her face off.

So, yeah. Probably not the same.

"For once, my sister and I agree on something."

Elena made a noncommittal noise, running her finger around the top of her beer bottle. "Can I ask you something?"

"Sure! What's up?"

"Why do you think you and Margot aren't close?"

"Oh." That was unexpected. "Um. I don't know if we've had enough beer for that one."

"I just think you should know that she wants to be. She really respects you and what you've done. And she wants to be closer to you, but she doesn't think you want to."

"I do. I just…I've spent my whole life in her shadow, you know?"

"I could see how that would be difficult," Elena said carefully. Harper knew this was probably putting her in an awkward position, the middleman between two sisters with a rocky relationship when she was friends with both.

"I would like it, too, for what it's worth. You can tell her I said that. But I'm honestly not sure how it will go. It's not that I resent her, exactly. It's just that I'm not sure how to be her friend. It's difficult to change a relationship that has been a certain way for so long."

"True. But as a counterpoint, we were nearly strangers for a long time, even though we knew each other. But I can't think of anything easier than becoming friends with you."

Harper felt a warmth spread throughout her body as the words settled in deep. She deflected, because otherwise she thought she might tear up from the sincerity in Elena's eyes. There was something else there, too. Something she didn't know how to interpret.

She cleared her throat. "Well, that's different. We were starting from zero. It's easier to write a new story than to change one that has already been written."

Elena nodded. "Very good point."

"Anytime. You should learn that I'm very wise. Margot isn't the only smart one in the family."

She said it as a joke, but Elena's face was serious when she answered. "I know she isn't. You're brilliant."

A pressure that started somewhere deep in her chest and spiraled outward.

It felt dangerous and stupid and wonderful, and she let herself feel it, all the way to the tips of her toes.

She couldn't have stopped it if she'd wanted to.

CHAPTER TEN

On Friday afternoon, Elena stood beside the newly constructed shelf in her workshop. The bridge of her nose pinched from the heavy mask she wore to keep from breathing in the varnish fumes, and her arms ached from the odd angles she'd contorted herself into to reach every square millimeter. She tilted her head to one side and then another, working out the kinks in her muscles before she took a step back and eyed her work.

She moved to one side, stood on tiptoe, climbed on top of her step stool, then crouched down to the ground. She didn't spot a single area that needed touching up. In fact, the shelf looked fantastic. As long as there were no problems once everything was fully dry, she was done.

The wood was going to look perfect in Bewitched, the natural grain of the mahogany showing through with extra sparkle from the varnish. The first shelf already sat in the corner of her workshop, a testament to how nice this one would look in a day or so.

Also a testament to just how much she had worked on them in this past week.

Not that she'd really been doing anything else. She'd read a book. She'd called Margot. She'd sent an RSVP for Dee's retirement party.

But other than that, she'd spent most of her time in here with her tools and her thoughts.

It had been seven days since Elena's realization about her feelings. Six days since she'd seen Harper, and they'd had that moment.

The moment in which she'd very nearly done something monumentally stupid.

She'd just been so mesmerized by Harper's eyes, the delicate curve of her cheeks. She'd wanted to pull her closer, feel those pillowy lips with her own, place her hands on the curves of Harper's hips.

In the days since, she had alternated between thinking about Harper and forcing herself to think about anything else.

It was a vicious cycle.

Eventually, Elena had concluded three things:

One, she liked Harper as more than a friend. Once she had allowed herself to think of Harper in that way, that had become very clear.

Two, for various reasons, she didn't think asking Harper out would be a good idea. Not the least of which was that Elena was looking for something casual, and she knew from their first night at the gala that Harper wanted a serious relationship.

Three, she would keep going out with Heather, at least temporarily, to show her brain this was who she wanted. After all, feelings might not be controlled by the mind, but actions were, and sometimes, feelings followed actions. She would try for two more dates. If she still wasn't feeling it after that, she would put an end to things. She didn't want to be unfair to Heather.

She felt like these conclusions were solid, her reasoning logical. She felt good about them.

Mostly.

Except for the part where she didn't get to kiss Harper. But she could move past that.

All she needed to do was show herself that they were friends and nothing more.

She missed many things about Harper, yes, but you could miss a friend. Elena missed Margot, too.

But Margot wasn't the one she couldn't get out of her head.

The funny thing was, most of her thoughts weren't even connected with her newly realized feelings. She wasn't fantasizing. She was just remembering all the things they'd done together as friends. Thinking about laughing over chess on the living room floor and being covered in green slime and making up goofy stories in IKEA about pretend families who lived in all the tiny fake rooms.

As Elena thought, she walked around her workshop, hammering lids on tins of varnish and putting everything away. Underneath the movement, she started to feel a sensation almost like tickling all throughout her calves, spreading down to her feet and up to her chest. It was a restlessness she hadn't felt in too long. But it had been a part of her for her entire life; she didn't need to think about what it meant.

She wanted to play soccer again.

She *needed* to play soccer again.

Elena almost held her breath, letting the desire grow, hoping the sensation wouldn't go away.

It didn't. It built. It built as she wiped down her tools and hung them on the pegboard. It built as she texted Harper with a picture, saying she would likely be able to deliver the shelves tomorrow.

It built as she shivered her way across the yard to her house, goosebumps pricking up on her flesh due to the unseasonably early cold snap.

She was nearly shaking from emotion when she pulled on her heavy jacket and grabbed the balls she had finally put away in the closet a few days after her last disastrous attempt.

When she went out to the back yard and kicked the ball for the first time, the contact sent a sensation of absolute *rightness* up her leg, through her hips, and directly into her heart, where soccer had always lived.

It had been hidden for the past two weeks, ensconced in grief and shame.

But it had still been there. Elena felt her love of the game begin to pump into her blood, circulate through her veins, as she kicked another ball straight into the net, then the next. One after another, until only one ball remained in her bag.

She didn't miss once.

Elena grabbed her cones and used the final ball to run drills for the next ten minutes, her lungs stinging from the cold air when she upped the intensity.

She could have cried.

This was it. Soccer was back. *Elena* was back.

Elena (4:22 P.M.): GUESS WHO PLAYED SOCCER TODAY!!!

She sent the same text to Margot and Dee, though separately this time.

Dee responded immediately with a barrage of GIFs and emojis.

Margot didn't respond at all, but Elena never expected a reply from her any sooner than two hours after a text was sent, especially during work hours.

Elena thought about texting Harper, but she decided to tell her about it in person tomorrow instead.

The thought of seeing Harper tomorrow and giving her the shelves and seeing the things she had made sitting inside a place of business, alongside the Harper's mural, gave her a feeling of satisfaction she couldn't explain. Combined with the high she felt from playing soccer, she felt on top of the world.

Harper pulled her hair up off her neck and fanned the sweat-covered skin there.

"Think I may have gotten a little enthusiastic with the

thermostat."

"You can say that again. God, it's a furnace in here." Elena lifted up her tank top to wipe the sweat off of her forehead, and Harper didn't even pretend to herself that she didn't stare at her abs.

She was only human, and Elena's abs would make Michelangelo want to come back from the dead just to sculpt them.

She swallowed against her dry throat and looked away when Elena lowered her shirt down again.

Elena had come over in the early afternoon with the shelves—or rather, she'd driven beside the local moving company whose truck she'd apparently rented to deliver the shelves. They'd just gotten them in place when the truck with all her tables had arrived, an hour before the scheduled window.

Elena had stayed—after refusing payment for the delivery truck, of course, though Harper would try to figure out a way to pay her back later—and they had been moving chairs and tables around the rooms ever since, trying to determine which setup had the best combination of ease of movement and utilization of space. Harper already had a map she'd drawn to scale, but she hadn't liked the way it had looked in person.

Now, Harper stared at the configuration of the tables throughout the two rooms.

It still didn't seem right.

"What if we shifted this one to the corner..." Elena trailed off, her thumb tapping thoughtfully against her chin.

"Yeah, I like that, but then that one doesn't work anymore, and we're back to the—"

"The last layout, yeah."

"But what if—" Inspiration struck suddenly, and Harper stood up straighter. "I know what we need to do."

"No explanation?"

"Just trust me."

Elena gestured ahead with her hand. "Lead on."

Ten minutes later, they had shifted one of the larger tables from the front room to the back room, reshuffled the layout, and moved two of the smaller tables to the front room.

"This is it," Harper said. She felt it in her gut. This was perfect.

"Agreed. Looks fantastic."

"Now, just one final touch." Harper moved to the table nearest her, pulled out a chair, and climbed up on it.

"What the hell are you doing?" Elena asked, rushing to her side, one hand grasping the back of the chair, the other hovering right beside Harper's upper thigh.

Harper was wearing jeans, but she swore she could feel the heat from Elena's fingers through the material.

"Something I did at the Pawn the night before it opened. I stood on a chair to look to see how it would be from a tall person's perspective. Sometimes that changes a lot, you know. Like, it didn't occur to me for so long that some people can see on top of cabinets and shelves I can't. But that aside, it's just a whole different perspective."

"If you say so," Elena said, her tone implying that she wasn't fully buying it.

"Listen, you don't get it. You're tallish already. But not tall enough. And I'm short. I don't even have that advantage. Anyway, the point is that I need to see it from a different perspective, to make sure the tables look even and that everything makes sense. Which it does," she noted, with a cursory glance around the room.

"Terrific. Ready to get down now, Shaq?" Elena asked, extending the arm that had been hovering near her leg.

"Yes, thank you," Harper answered, deliberately ignoring the sarcasm in her tone. She grasped Elena's hand, surprised at the heat of it and the strength of her grip. She knew Elena wouldn't let her fall.

Still, she had a fantasy for half a second, wondering what might happen if she did fall. Maybe her toe would catch on the edge of the table. Or she would have a sudden muscle cramp. Whatever it was, she would lose her balance, everything would be a blur, and then she and Elena would land on the floor in a heap. No one would be hurt, of course. But their bodies would be pressed together, awareness coursing through them. If this were a movie, that's what would happen.

But her life wasn't a movie.

Harper blinked back to reality and squeezed Elena's hand as a signal she was ready to descend. She arrived back on solid ground without incident, and she was almost disappointed for a moment before she realized the movement had brought her so close to Elena that they were almost touching.

She wasn't letting go of Elena's hand. Or maybe Elena wasn't letting go of hers. She wasn't sure.

"You've never started to see something from a different perspective?" Harper asked, and she thought Elena understood what she was truly asking.

Something flashed in Elena's eyes, and she stayed where she was, directly in front of Harper. Closer than she'd ever been before.

Harper wanted to kiss her.

This was not a new feeling. She'd wanted to kiss Elena Torres for nearly half of her life. But this was the first time she thought she might do it.

Because she knew that look. It was the same look Elena had given her in the bedroom a week ago.

Elena wanted to kiss her, too.

She stared into those eyes, deep pools of melted chocolate, and her breathing hitched at the intensity of Elena's gaze. She felt like she noticed everything in that moment. The few stray wisps of hair that had escaped Elena's ponytail and fallen down to frame her face. Those high cheekbones, the soft eyelashes, that tiny divot in her top lip. The way her lips were slightly parted, and how soft they looked. So soft. She could imagine touching them with her own.

But imagination wasn't enough. Not anymore.

Harper could barely breathe as she inched forward just a bit, then paused, eyes flicking back up to Elena's. Just to check. Just to make sure she wasn't imagining things. She couldn't bear to get this wrong.

She lifted her eyebrows just a bit, because she couldn't seem to get words past the tightness in her throat, and she hoped Elena could interpret the question.

Elena nodded, just a tiny, infinitesimal movement.

Harper drew close and tilted her head up, and Elena leaned down, their lips pressing together in a whisper of movement.

Elena's lips against hers felt exactly like she had always dreamed and yet like something entirely new, too. Something her mind never could have conjured up. They were soft but firm, and they parted slightly as Harper's skimmed over them. Harper brought her hands up to rest on Elena's shoulders, feeling the warmth and strength of her. The kiss was a soft thing, quiet, tentative. Harper didn't want to overstep, and at the same time, she couldn't imagine going more quickly. Her entire system already felt like it was on overload, her heart thumping a wild rhythm inside her chest.

After a few seconds, Harper pulled away slowly, her hands still resting on Elena's shoulders. She opened her eyes to meet Elena's gaze, hoping against hope that what she found there would match what Harper was feeling.

It did. Her eyes were wide and dark, and her expression was so warm Harper could have melted into it.

Elena's hands came down to rest on her waist. Then she leaned down, and this time it was *more*. At the first contact of their lips, Harper gasped. She couldn't help it. It was only a small thing, only a bit of air, but the shock of Elena's lips against hers was too much. It wasn't slow or questioning this time, but incendiary, like a flame that had started as a tiny spark but gradually built into a wild conflagration.

Harper kissed her back with every bit of the passion she

had been trying to ignore. She kissed her like she couldn't bear to stop, like she couldn't get close enough, no matter how hard she tried. Elena made a sound in the back of her throat and then her hands were wrapping around to the small of Harper's back beneath her shirt, the trail of Elena's fingers against her skin sending a shiver all through her.

Harper never wanted this kiss to end. She wanted to keep kissing Elena forever, exploring her mouth and finding new ways to touch her, new ways to make her feel even half of what Harper was feeling.

As though she had read her thoughts, Elena questioningly slid just the tip of her tongue inside Harper's lips. Harper gladly opened for her, and Elena deepened the kiss, her tongue meeting Harper's own. The sensation sent an instant wave of white-hot heat straight down her body and between her legs.

And that feeling startled enough that she realized what was happening.

She was kissing Elena.

She was kissing Elena.

The revelation made her pull back, as though her eyes simply had to see this for themselves before she could fully convince herself that it was the truth.

It was.

Elena's hair was askew, her lips pink and damp and kiss-swollen.

She looked incredible.

And Harper was dying to know what was going on behind those dark, enigmatic eyes.

"What are you thinking?" she asked, because apparently being kissed by Elena left her with absolutely no filter. "I mean, you don't have to tell me. I know that's, like, the uncool thing to do. To ask. I don't know. I'm rambling."

Elena's lips curled up into a smile. "You are. And honestly, right now, I'm thinking that you're really cute when you ramble."

Harper blinked, certain for a moment that she had been hallucinating. Maybe she had hallucinated this whole thing.

But no, as crazy as it was, this was reality.

"Is that okay?"

Harper swallowed. "Only if it's okay that I think you're cute, too. But full disclosure, I think that all the time. Not just when you kiss me."

Elena flushed. "It's very okay."

Harper moved in to kiss her again. It was soft again this time, almost shy, and for some reason, Harper felt the oddest urge to smile.

Then her phone started ringing.

Harper was very happy to ignore it and continue their current activities, but Elena broke away and cleared her throat. "Um, that's you, I think."

"Let it go to voicemail." She reached for Elena's hands but then jerked away. "Shit!" Harper shook her head quickly, trying to clear away her kiss-induced haze. "What time is it?"

Elena stared at her. "No idea. Around eight, maybe?"

"*Shit*," Harper said again. "That's Angel. We have plans."

"Is she back in town?"

"No, online. We have a movie night. I'm sorry."

"It's okay. I totally understand."

Every single molecule in Harper's body was crying out to kiss Elena again.

But she hated it when her friends started dating someone and then disappeared, completely dropping her in favor for their new romantic partner. It sucked. She wouldn't do that to Angel, even if Angel would understand when she explained it later.

"Rain check?"

"Of course. No problem at all." Elena smiled, and there was something in her expression Harper didn't know how to interpret. It made her want to stay, made her doubt that they would be able to pick up where they'd left off the next time they saw each other. But she'd already said it, and Elena was already gathering her things. "I'll just head out and let you get to your movie."

"Okay. See you soon."

They had no plans to hang out anytime soon, but Harper thought that the kiss implied Elena might want that, too.

"See you. Have fun." Elena seemed to hesitate for a moment, looking to the door and then back to Harper again. Then she bent down and pressed a quick kiss to Harper's lips before she walked out without another word.

Harper walked back to her apartment in a daze, only ninety-eight percent sure she hadn't hallucinated the past twenty minutes.

But no, her lips still tingled. It had been real.

Harper's text tone went off just as she shut the apartment door behind her.

Angel (8:07 P.M.): You ready?

Harper (8:08 P.M.): HI ELENA AND I JUST KISSED AND I'M HAVING A SLIGHT MELTDOWN SORRY

Harper (8:08 P.M.):BUT YES MOVIE NIGHT IS ON

Harper (8:09 P.M.):AS LONG AS I CAN YELL A BIT FIRST

Angel (8:09 P.M.):O
Angel (8:09 P.M.):M
Angel (8:09 P.M.):G
Angel (8:10 P.M.):Yell away. My ears are ready.

Harper locked the door behind her, pressed the call button, and spilled everything to her best friend, grinning so hard her cheeks hurt.

CHAPTER ELEVEN

This was a bad idea.

No, scratch that.

This was a terrible idea.

Elena watched her reflection in the mirror, dabbing some night cream on her face and rubbing absently. She had known this already, had decided as much during all the hours spent mulling while working on Harper's shelves. But it had been a fairly simple process before. The cons had outweighed the pros, and thus she'd decided not to ask Harper out, as much as she'd wanted to.

But she hadn't accounted for the way Harper kissed.

She hadn't accounted for the way her body had seemed to come alive under Harper's touch.

Elena felt her entire being warm at the memory of the way Harper had made little sounds into her mouth. The way her hands had grasped Elena's hips. The way she'd looked when they'd pulled away from each other, her lips puffy, her eyes dazed and happy and inviting Elena to kiss her again.

The memory of how Harper had smiled against her lips during that last, short kiss was the worst. At the time, it had felt like a gift, like something to be cherished. But now it only served to confuse her.

It wasn't something to be cherished, the logical side of her brain knew. It was something to be ignored.

Feelings weren't facts, and she needed to focus on the facts, as much as something deep inside her was fighting against the idea.

It was a good thing Angel had interrupted them when she had.

Elena flipped out the bathroom light and padded into her bedroom, burrowing down underneath her comforter. She stared up at her ceiling in the dark and thought about facts.

The main fact was that Harper wanted to settle down while Elena did not. That was the most glaring, the most impossible to overcome. If Elena abandoned her plans and dove into a relationship, where would it lead? Soccer was still her first priority. She didn't want to go through another Claire situation again, never wanted to hurt someone the way she had unintentionally hurt Claire.

That by itself was enough to keep from pursuing things. In addition, she and Harper had just become friends. She didn't want to mess that up. Why change a good thing and risk it going bad?

It was clear they were both attracted to each other, but plenty of people were attracted to each other. That didn't make acting on the attraction a good idea, or the right thing to do. In fact, sometimes it was exactly the opposite. Elena could be an adult about the situation and simply ignore it. She was not going to throw away a friendship by making an impulsive decision based on being hormonal and lonely.

And, if Elena were being honest, those were definitely factors.

She hadn't had sex with anyone since Claire. One time, a few months after her divorce had been made official, she'd tried to have a one-night stand with a woman she'd met at a bar, but she had failed spectacularly.

As a matter of principle, Elena believed that people could have sex with each other as soon as they both wanted it, but her brain seemed to have its own timeline she didn't entirely understand. The night of the one-night-stand attempt, she'd gone home with the woman after only half an hour, thinking maybe if she powered through the initial discomfort, she'd enjoy herself.

She hadn't.

Instead, she'd frozen, then left in a hurry, embarrassed and certain she didn't want to try anything like that again.

And she hadn't. The closest thing she'd had to a sexual partner since was her vibrator. They were underrated, vibrators. Loyal, satisfying, and uncomplicated.

Unlike people.

But Elena knew that if she were being honest with herself, while hormones and loneliness were factors, she couldn't blame everything on them. If that were the case, she would want Heather. She was stunning, Elena had known her for long enough to warm up to her, and they had a lot in common.

But Elena didn't.

She wanted Harper with a stubborn specificity that made no sense.

She couldn't make herself want Heather because her heart was already engaged elsewhere.

That thought made her flip over onto her stomach and pull her pillow over her head. It was ridiculous. Her heart wasn't involved, and she had no desire to let it become so, not when there was nowhere this could go but downhill.

She and Harper wouldn't be a good idea. Period.

Elena would tell her as much tomorrow.

With a decisive nod, Elena stuffed her pillow back under her head, turned onto her side, and closed her eyes, ignoring the way her heart felt like it had plummeted into her stomach.

Harper hummed to herself as she pulled open the door to Midnight Vegan. The late Sunday morning line did nothing to dampen her mood, and she swayed slightly to the music in her head while she waited her turn to place her order. When she got to the front of the line, she ordered a black bean breakfast burrito and an orange juice, feeling an urge to go with something different.

She snagged a small round table near the window, enjoying the bustling sounds of a busy café.

"Someone's cheerful this morning," Vivian said, shimmying up to her table. She was wearing a flour-smudged black apron over a patterned chartreuse dress, and a matching headscarf tied her braids back.

"Just having one of those mornings, I guess." Harper tried not to smile and failed completely.

"Care to share what's got you all smiley?"

"Yes, but also I don't want to jinx it." Harper contemplated staying silent for a few seconds before blurting, "It's Elena. You met her the other day, remember?" Elena had come with her to return their plates after the smoothie fiasco, and she'd met Vivian and bought a second muffin to go.

"Of course. You two totally had a vibe going. I actually thought she might be your girlfriend."

Harper felt the smile she'd been trying to hold back break out full force at the thought. "I've been into her for a while, honestly." Understatement of the century, but she wasn't going to go into all the details right now. "But I didn't know if she felt the same. Apparently she does. We got interrupted, though, so we didn't get a chance to talk about it. But I swear to god, I didn't stop smiling all the way home. And yes, it's across the street, so it's not like it was a long trip. But still."

Vivian held up a hand. "Wait, you live at Pine Ridge, too?"

"Yeah. Just moved in last week. Wait, are we neighbors?"

"We are! I'm on the third floor."

"I'm on the first!"

"I'm surprised we haven't run into each other yet."

Harper raised her eyebrows. "That's because you're

always here."

Vivian blew out a breath. "Don't I know it. Speaking of being a workaholic, it's not like I'm the only one at this table who's here every day. How's everything going?"

"Great! I'm right on schedule. We've had a few snags, but nothing I haven't been able to fix."

"Good for you. Fingers crossed it stays that way. I can't believe we're less than three weeks out."

"Don't remind me."

"You have anyone special coming for the big day?"

"Well, Elena will be there, if that's what you're asking."

"Family?"

"My sister is going to fly back into town for it. My parents have decided that's the optimal time to go on vacation, though, so they won't be there."

Vivian frowned. "Seriously? Vacation?"

"Yeah. Something about not being able to get another spot at that bed-and-breakfast? I don't know. Apparently, it was a big deal."

"What assholes."

"It's just kind of what they do. I know I shouldn't let it bother me, but—"

"So don't."

"Don't what?"

"Don't let it bother you."

Harper scoffed. "Easier said than done."

"Listen. You have to think about yourself first." Vivian tapped her own chest with her fingers. "What is concentrating on their expectations getting you? Nothing. Because they're not *your* expectations. They're not your dreams. You're the only one who gets to set those. If they can't let go of their own expectations and embrace yours, then fuck them. You have to learn to measure by your own stick and yours alone."

Harper stared at her, and Vivian ducked her head a little.

"Sorry, I can get a little intense about this."

"No, you're totally and completely right. I always get so tied up in their expectations that I wind up feeling like an underachieving piece of garbage. Then I get mad at myself for feeling like that, because it makes no sense. But that's just it. It's because I'm judging myself based on their ideas."

"Exactly."

It couldn't be that simple, though.

Could it?

She remembered time after time of her parents—and even Margot, sometimes—had made her feel inferior.

She remembered Elena calling her brilliant, saying she was just as smart and successful as Margot in her own way. About how much sense that had made, about how it had felt like something starting to click in place.

And now it clicked fully. She could practically feel the *clunk* inside her head.

It was exactly what she'd started doing several years ago when it came to her weight. She'd come to realize she needed to stop measuring herself by society's standards and forever trying to make herself smaller. Just because her body took up more space didn't mean she should feel bad about it. Over time, she'd learned not to care about the opinions of people she didn't know. For some reason, she'd had it in her head that it was different for people who mattered to her.

But it really wasn't.

There was still one problem, though.

"Okay, so I should let go of their expectations. How do I get them to do that, though? They're the ones who always pull me back into it."

"First, you have to show them your stick. They've been measuring you by this other one for your whole life, and they don't realize it's wrong. Sometimes people are just oblivious, or stubborn."

Harper nodded slowly. "And if they don't know, they're not going to change."

"Precisely. Once they do know, that's when they start showing their true colors. Hopefully for the better."

What would it be like to start standing up for herself like that? Not only with her parents, but with everyone. Being honest and saying what she wanted and how she felt?

It sounded a little bit terrifying, but also freeing.

A thought occurred to her, and Harper chewed her lip. "Vivian?"

"Hmm?"

"I want to tell you that it bothers me when you criticize the food I order."

Vivian's face dropped, and Harper hastened to add. "I know that it comes from a good place! And I promise I'm not offended or anything. But I'm fat. And when you're fat, people are always trying to police your food. My mom makes comments about it on holidays. My doctor acts like I eat Big Macs with a side of pizza and ice cream at every single meal. I've had literal strangers in the grocery store bring up diets to me. So it just really bothers me when people tell me what to eat."

"Shit, I'm so sorry. I never thought about it like that. It won't happen again."

"Thank you. I appreciate it."

"May I also say: well done!"

Harper felt a small glow of pride in her belly. "Thank you."

Now, she just needed to do the same thing with Elena. She'd been silently waiting for Elena to message her, to take the lead with their situation. She'd been too scared to do otherwise.

But maybe it was time to take a step forward.

Vivian disappeared back into the kitchen, and Harper tapped out a message.

Harper (9:32 A.M.): we should talk

The little dots on the bottom appeared almost immediately.

Elena (9:33 A.M.): I agree.

Elena (9:33 A.M.): Will you be at Bewitched all day? I can come by later.

Harper (9:34 A.M.): perfect

Elena held firmly onto her resolve as she stepped into Bewitched just after lunch. She knew she would need it, and when she spotted Harper, she realized she'd underestimated just how much.

Harper was wearing an olive green v-neck that made her eyes look especially bright, and they lit up as Elena walked closer, a smile unfolding across her face that looked both shy and cautiously hopeful. The sight stole Elena's breath away. She was so beautiful, so kind. Elena wanted to gather her into her arms and kiss her. The temptation was so strong that for a single moment, she almost yielded to it.

But she wouldn't. She couldn't, no matter how much she wanted to.

Goals. Soccer. Friendship. She repeated the words in her head like a mantra, but they barely had any effect. She still wanted to do anything other than destroy that fledgling hope she saw in Harper's eyes.

Then she saw Claire's face in her mind, twisted in anger, broken with sadness. She imagined Harper making those same expressions. Would a few months of happiness be worth it when all Elena would do was hurt her?

No.

Harper deserved to find someone who could give her what she wanted, and that wasn't Elena.

Elena steeled herself and stepped forward.

"Hey."

"Hey."

"I wanted to talk about last night."

"Me, too."

Elena shuffled awkwardly from foot to foot. She couldn't seem to get words to emerge from her throat. Harper must have sensed something from her expression, because her smile hesitated and wilted like week-old flowers, and it felt like someone had just kicked Elena in the stomach.

"I need to apologize. I shouldn't have kissed you. I'm sorry."

Elena watched as the light in Harper's eyes dimmed. "I don't understand. I promise you didn't make me uncomfortable. I wanted it, too."

Elena wanted to step forward and make her feel anything-but-uncomfortable again, but she held back.

"I do like you. I want to make that clear." Harper's eyebrows drew together in confusion. "But I know you're looking for something serious, and I'm not. It isn't where my priorities are right now, and it wouldn't be fair to lead you on like that. I sincerely apologize for kissing you and for sending mixed signals. I promise I won't do it again."

Harper just kept looking at her, expression unreadable, and Elena stumbled on through the speech she had planned.

"I know things might be awkward for a while, but I would really like to keep you in my life as a friend. If you want me here, of course. I know it's totally a jerk move to kiss you and then take it back, but—"

"Can I say something?" Harper interrupted.

Yes, please. "Of course."

Elena waited for several seconds while Harper appeared to gather her thoughts. "Yesterday, I probably would have just said okay and moved on, but I'm trying this new thing where I stand up for myself and communicate what I want. So bear with me, because I'm not very good at it yet."

Elena nodded. "I'm listening."

"First of all, when did I say I wanted something serious?"

"At the gala."

"I don't remember that."

"You said you wanted someone to spend the rest of

your life with."

Harper nodded slowly, as though it was coming back to her. "That's true. I do want that, eventually. But I'm not dying for it right this very second. And I don't appreciate you making a decision based on how you assume I feel, rather than actually asking me."

Thoughts swirled around Elena's brain, the first and foremost being just how much she had messed up. "You're right. I'm sorry. That was shitty of me."

"Apology accepted."

Elena didn't know what to say, and she bit back the urge to apologize again.

"You really got yourself worked over this, didn't you? I promise I didn't think you were about to drop down to one knee just because we made out."

Harper's voice was lightly teasing, and Elena felt her cheeks heat. "I know." She paused, considering. "So, then… what did you think? What were you going to say before I started talking and messed everything up?"

"That I liked kissing you. And I would be okay with keeping things casual if it's what you want."

Elena's mind spun in circles. How had she not considered this as a possibility last night? She'd let a throwaway sentence define everything, without actually knowing how Harper felt. But apparently Harper wanted the same thing she did.

She pondered this, going over her reasons to see how many of them still applied.

They didn't.

Not a single one.

Seeking out an arrangement like this was why she'd downloaded Masked in the first place. Now here was the woman she couldn't stop thinking about, proposing the exact thing she'd wanted.

They were adults. They could be friends who also had a physical relationship. Elena may not have ever done that before, but there was a first time for everything.

"If you're interested, of course," Harper added, and Elena realized she hadn't spoken in an uncomfortably long time.

"I am." The words jumped out of her mouth without a single further thought. "Most definitely. What exactly did you have in mind?"

She wanted Harper to spell it out, so she could be sure they were on the same page this time.

"Casual. As in, we go on dates, we do whatever feels good. No messy emotions, no commitment."

"And that's something you'd be into?"

"Yeah. All the cool kids are doing it." Harper winked, then pulled a face. "Sorry, that was supposed to be a joke, but kind of came out as pressuring. It's totally up to you. No hard feelings either way, for real."

"So, basically, we stay friends but with, you know…the colloquial benefits."

"Exactly."

Heat flared in her stomach at the idea. She just had one more question. "This wouldn't keep you from going for something serious with someone else, right? I wouldn't want to get in the way."

"No. And besides, I'll be too busy with the store until spring, probably."

"So you just need someone to keep you warm through the bitter Colorado winter. I see how it is." Elena dared to tease a little, and she was rewarded with a throaty laugh.

"Something like that."

"Well, I would be interested. Very much so."

"Good." Harper smiled. "Me, too."

Elena stepped closer, and Harper matched her movement until they were standing together in the middle of Bewitched, an echo of last night.

But this time, Elena wasn't going to mess it up.

She shifted even closer, until her hands rested on Harper's

waist. Her auburn locks fell messily around her shoulders, and Elena brought up one hand and twirled her finger around a curl. Her hair was so soft. Everything about her was so soft. Elena loved it, wanted to spend hours upon hours with their bodies pressed together just like this, inhaling the scent of her. "So, benefits, huh?"

"Mm-hmm. Feel free to apply for them anytime."

Harper's hands slid up her arms and wrapped around her neck, and Elena's knees grew a little wobbly. "Back at you."

With that, Harper cupped her hand around the back of Elena's neck and tugged gently. The feel of her cool fingers there sent a shiver through Elena's body, and she leaned down and pressed their lips together.

CHAPTER TWELVE

This new arrangement should have been everything Elena was looking for. And it was, hypothetically.

The problem was, she had never done anything like this before. She wasn't sure of the protocol. Did any time they were together now count as a date? How often was too often to spend time together? Was it possible to get clingy in a no-strings situation like it was in a relationship?

Leave it to her brain to turn something easy into something complicated.

Thankfully, there were a surprising number of articles that turned up when she Googled "how to have a no-strings relationship." Sometimes the internet really was great.

She spent a while perusing those, then texted a list of her remaining questions to Dee, who first responded with a very long list of emojis Elena wasn't entirely certain how to interpret—why was she sending pictures of nail polish? Did she think Harper and Elena were going to go get manicures together?

Thankfully, though, Dee followed it up with some calming words and answers that made sense.

Armed with her new knowledge, Elena felt confident enough to send Harper a text.

Elena (10:54 A.M.): I was thinking of checking out that new

Italian restaurant down the street from Bewitched tonight. Would you be interested in joining me?

    Harper (10:59 A.M.): totally. i'm free as a slightly overworked but pasta-loving bird :)

    Elena (11:00 A.M.): Great! What time works best for you?

    Harper (11:00 A.M.): 7?

    Elena (11:01 A.M.): Sounds good! I'll see you then.

    Elena (11:01 A.M.): Looking forward to it. :)

    Harper (11:02 A.M.): me, too :)

And, oddly, it was that simple. She confirmed a few more details, then went about her day. Elena had several errands to run and an ungodly amount of laundry to do. She made her way through her to-do list with efficiency, feeling strangely buoyant as she checked off one task after another. She even caught herself smiling while folding laundry, which was her least favorite chore and one she habitually avoided like the plague.

It didn't even dampen her mood when she texted Heather to let her know they could stay friends, but Elena wasn't interested in anything more. Heather responded politely but briefly, and Elena had a feeling that would probably be the last time she would hear from her. And that was okay.

Before she knew it, it was seven o'clock, and Harper was buzzing Elena into her apartment building.

When Harper opened the door wearing black jeans and a deep purple top that showed off more than a hint of cleavage, Elena's mouth went dry. Her eyes looked wide and smoky, and maybe the makeup she'd used had some kind of magical effects, because Elena couldn't seem to tear her eyes away. Harper's curls were tumbling down around her shoulders in a way that begged Elena to spear her fingers through them.

She had to swallow before she was able to produce words. "Wow. You look…wow."

Harper bit her lip and smiled the cutest smile. "Thanks. You look *wow*, too."

Elena huffed out a chuckle. "Good to know the puffy winter coat look works for you."

Harper reached over to a hook beside the door and pulled on her own black pea coat, and the movement sent a waft of floral-scented perfume toward Elena. Her breath stuck in her chest, and she had to fight off the urge to cough at the cloying sweetness. She cursed her oversensitive nose and schooled her expression, watching Harper lock the door and then following her down the hall.

"Well, you always look *wow*, but I guess I'll have to wait until we get to the restaurant to pass judgment on your outfit."

"White button down with black slacks. Does that pass inspection?" They stepped outside. The night air was clean and bright, and Elena took grateful breaths, annoyed at her nose for not letting her enjoy something most people would probably find pleasant.

"Hmm. I'm sure it'll look nice, but it's certainly a brave choice."

"Brave?" Of all the adjectives Harper could have used for the world's most utilitarian and standard shirt, Elena would not have expected that one. "How so?"

"Well, you'll be facing down its greatest enemy..." She paused dramatically. "Marinara sauce."

Elena laughed as they turned onto the sidewalk and started in the direction of the restaurant. "I guess I'll just have to stick with alfredo."

They'd decided to brave the cold and walk, since it was only a few minutes away, and while the weather was chilly, it wasn't yet the biting cold that would probably arrive in a few weeks. There was only the slightest breeze, and while the city lights prevented her from seeing the stars, she could see the crescent moon clearly. As they walked through the historic downtown district, the brick buildings rose on each side of them, giving the feeling that they were walking backwards through time.

Elena hadn't been sure how tonight would be, if things would suddenly feel more awkward between them. But they didn't at all. Somehow, the additional flirtation just felt like a natural extension of their friendship. It was like she had been subconsciously suppressing these thoughts and comments for the past several weeks.

And while she didn't think that was really the case, she couldn't help but marvel at the ease with which they'd added this new facet to their relationship.

They were seated at the restaurant immediately, and Harper ordered a mushroom pasta while Elena went with the aforementioned fettuccine alfredo. They decided on a bottle of red wine to share, since neither of them were driving.

Conversation flowed easily, jumping from topic to topic.

Elena had something on her mind that she hadn't been able to ask Dee or the internet, though, something that had been niggling at her since their conversation yesterday. She brought it up when a brief lull in the conversation arose.

"So, I have a question. Are you comfortable with me mentioning this to Margot? Would you prefer that I didn't?"

"Good question. I was thinking about this morning, actually."

"I'm fine either way, and I don't particularly plan to tell her, but on the other hand, it seems weird not to? I don't want to hide or act like you're some kind of secret. But I also get that what we're doing is our business. Not that we're doing anything official. I'm just not sure about the protocol." Elena took a breath. "And I'm rambling. So I'll stop. Thoughts?"

"It's okay. I mean, you can tell her if it comes up. Just don't mention any details."

"Obviously."

"It's not obvious! I don't know what you guys talk about."

"Believe it or not, your sister and I don't sit around talking about our sexual exploits."

"Well, I'm not actually your sexual exploit yet."

Yet. Elena swallowed.

"We don't really talk about anything like that. Not sure if it's because we're not really 'talk about our feelings' people or because we don't have anything to discuss. The closest thing she has to a partner is her job. Or that stupid espresso machine."

Harper snorted. "She does love that thing. I wonder how much it cost."

"Trust me, you don't want to know."

"You're probably right." Harper took a bite and then toyed with her wine glass. "Can I ask you a question?"

"Sure."

"Did you ever have a thing for my sister?"

Elena choked on her wine and let out an incredulous laugh. "For Margot? God, no. I mean, I love her with my whole heart. She's basically my sister. But, you know. People don't want to sleep with their sisters."

Harper opened her mouth, but Elena held up a finger. "And don't make an Alabama joke. It's too easy."

"I wasn't going to, but glad you think my level of humor is that low."

"Margot would have."

"Well, she has a fucked up sense of humor."

"That is true. One of the ways you guys are different."

"There are a lot. Our sense of humor. Our hair. Our ability to pick out throw pillows that don't make other want to gouge out their own eyes."

Elena snorted out a laugh. "She does have terrible taste in pillows."

"The list is endless, really. But out of the two of us, I'm glad you chose me to be attracted to."

"Me, too."

"Works out well for you, too. Because she may be straight

enough not to want to sleep with you, but I am not."

Elena nearly choked again. Instead, she painfully gulped down her water, secretly glad for the excuse to have a moment to compose herself.

"You okay there?" Harper said with an expression that clearly meant she was holding back laughter at Elena's predicament. A predicament she had caused with her flirty comment.

Okay, maybe Elena had been wrong. Maybe she wasn't quite prepared for the full force Harper-on-a-date version of Harper.

But she loved it. It was the best kind of surprise.

Harper didn't seem to expect a response and instead asked a question before biting into a bread stick. "Did you ever fall for a straight woman?"

Elena shook her head. "Never. Thankfully, I dodged the whole lesbian falling for a straight woman thing. I did have a huge crush on my married Gender Studies professor in college, though."

"No!"

Elena laughed. "Yeah. I skipped past one cliché and went straight for another."

"I'm so disappointed. I thought you were going to be a rebel lesbian."

"Alas, that's not me. Not a rebel at all."

"Well, you still look pretty damn good in a leather jacket, though. Which, let's face it, is the best part about being a rebel."

"If you say so."

"So, dessert?"

They wound up sharing a warm brownie with vanilla ice cream that made Elena want to weep from the perfect blend of sweet flavors on her tongue. Then she wanted to hide because Harper let out a moan that was downright sinful, and it made Elena's face flame. She had to shift in her seat from the immediate bolt of lightning that had struck directly between her thighs.

Mercifully, she didn't make the sound again. It would have led to some thoughts that were definitely not thoughts she wanted to have in public.

Finally, the server appeared with the check, which they split before bundling up in their coats and heading out back into the late autumn night.

When they made it back to Harper's apartment, they stood in the doorway, hesitating.

"So..." Harper said, but then she trailed off before saying anything further. She looked up at Elena, her eyes wide in the dark, and Elena did exactly what she'd wanted to do since Harper had opened the door two hours before.

Elena stepped forward and kissed her, and it was just as magical as it had been before. It felt like someone had grabbed her by the ribcage and dragged her forward until she was pressed against Harper again. She didn't believe in soulmates or anything of the sort, but perfume or not, the way their bodies fit together felt so natural, so right that something in her chest warmed.

And that thought startled her enough that she pulled back.

This wasn't supposed to be anything like that. She just wanted to have some fun with Harper, for as long as they both wanted it. She mentally shook her head against the stray idea, relegating it to the ether where it belonged, and then leaned in for another kiss.

They kissed for so long Elena lost all concept of time. Long enough that her lips started to feel sore and her nipples were hard underneath her shirt and her panties were damp.

She backed away slowly, breathing through her nose to calm herself. She didn't want to rush things. It just seemed like a better idea to take things slow, both so Elena could know for sure she was ready, and so she and Harper both had a little more time to think things over.

But at the moment, it was difficult to remember anything

more than how good Harper's body felt against her palms, how her pupils were blown wide with want.

"Well, I should head out." Elena's voice was husky.

"Oh." Harper's smile seemed a little smaller than usual, but genuine. "Okay. I'll see you soon."

"Definitely."

While she was walking away, all she could think was that she wanted to lick Harper's nipples and bite her shoulder and feel her slickness under her fingers. The thought of it had Elena so turned on that she nearly turned the car around again.

But at the same time, something in her was telling her to wait. It wasn't right yet.

So instead, she went home and took a cold shower, then fell asleep texting Harper with a smile on her face.

CHAPTER THIRTEEN

Harper still couldn't believe it was happening.

It had been a week, and there hadn't been a single forty-eight-hour period without Elena kissing her. Or her kissing Elena. Or both of them kissing each other.

Either way, her lips had been in contact with Elena's lips every single goddamn day, and Harper's inner teenage self was screaming. Thirteen years ago, Harper had thought Elena would only ever see her as Margot's artsy, nerdy little sister. More recently, "friend" had been added to her résumé. But now...

Well, now there was nothing else to add by way of official titles, but there was a hell of a lot more under "other duties as assigned." She had lusted after Elena almost since she knew what lust was, but now she didn't just gaze from afar. Those arms that had driven her absolutely wild? Now she got to run her lips along them, taste the salty-soft skin, bite gently into the muscle.

Well, she hadn't actually done that yet. She was working up to it.

In fact, their interactions had stayed strictly in the PG-13 category.

"You're kidding me," said Angel, when Harper told her as much.

"I'm going crazy, Angel." Harper was pacing around Bewitched, unpacking some of the drink supplies that had come in earlier in the week. "Like, on one hand, it's totally okay, you know? If she doesn't want things going that far yet, it's totally her prerogative. I don't want to rush her. But on the other hand, I just really want to know what's going through her head."

"Do you think there's something she's not telling you?"

"Honestly? I'm wondering if it might be Margot."

Angel made a doubtful noise. "I don't know. She didn't really seem to care. And you guys talked about that, right? You said you didn't think she'd have a problem with it."

"She wouldn't. My sister is very practical, and she would realize that who I sleep with—or don't sleep with, as the current case may be—is absolutely none of her business, blood relative or not."

"So, if it's not Margot, do you have any other ideas? Has she said anything at all?"

"Nothing. I don't know. Maybe she thinks she's just being respectful? Or maybe she's worried I won't be into what she's into?"

Angel snorted. "Clearly she never heard you going at it with that hot French girl. She'd know you're into all kinds of dirty—"

Harper slammed down the large plastic bottle of vanilla syrup onto the counter with more force than necessary. "You promised to stop bringing that up! I swear to god, I didn't know you were home."

"My ears will literally never recover."

"It's been five years. I think you've had time."

"Remind me to bill you for the therapy you caused one day."

"Oh, yeah, I'm writing it down right now."

"But anyway, in all seriousness, I know you don't want to hear this, but you're just gonna to have to talk to her."

"I know. You're right." Harper blew out a breath and

checked her phone for the time. "Shit, I've got the first interview in fifteen. I should probably go change and get all professional."

"Good luck. Hope it's not a dud."

"Thanks. Go draw something awesome."

"Always."

Harper hung up and went to take the now-empty box out to the recycling bin behind the building.

She had two interviews this afternoon, and another one scheduled on Monday. Since she was only hiring for one part-time position, she was hoping that one of the three would be enough. She'd gotten decent at interviewing people in the past few years, but it was still one of her least favorite parts of the job.

Besides which, she was really just counting down the hours until tonight. Elena had invited her over to her house for the first time since their IKEA outing. It was ostensibly to show Harper her workshop, which Harper actually was looking forward to seeing. She felt privileged to do so, because she knew Elena didn't let just anyone in there.

But she also wondered if Elena might have something else in mind involving her bedroom.

Though, really, the workshop would be up for discussion, too.

At this point, she wasn't picky.

Sadly, her first interview had, indeed, been a dud. The man had showed up fifteen minutes late without so much as an apology, and could barely name a single board game other than Monopoly.

Thankfully, the second candidate had been much more promising, and Harper had nearly offered her the job on the spot. She was going to interview the person on Monday just to be sure, but she already had a feeling that Ayumi would be the first official Bewitcher.

Now here she was, looking at the unassuming single-story ranch with a detached garage, which, if she hadn't been here before, would have had her questioning if she'd put Elena's address into her maps app correctly.

She wondered how tonight would go, if Elena was on the same page she was about tonight's potential plan of events.

She'd been on fire since the last time they'd been together on Wednesday night.

But that was the hormones talking. She needed to chill. Just because she was in that place now didn't mean Elena was quite there yet.

In other words, she was okay with it, but she just wanted to know where Elena stood. It was a simple solution, just as Angel had said. They needed to talk. And honestly, Harper was extremely happy with what they had been doing. If she needed to wait longer, she would wait longer. She was no stranger to self-administered orgasms. She was actually quite excellent at them.

Harper rang the doorbell and tried to think about kittens and unicorns and other random, cute things, so her face wouldn't give the impression that she was ready to tear off Elena's clothes the second she opened the door.

Then Elena answered the door in her typical uniform of jeans and a tank top, and the first thing Harper did was laugh and give a rueful shake of the head. "You do realize it's freezing."

"Not inside, it's not. Come on in." Elena beckoned her inside and stepped back from the door.

"You know, they do make other shirts."

"They don't, actually. Even this brand doesn't make this style anymore. But lucky for me, I bought twenty."

Before Harper could comment on that, she continued, "I can go put on a flannel if that would make you happy?"

"God, you're such a lesbian."

"I'm from Colorado."

Harper raised a brow, and Elena huffed in amusement. "And also a lesbian. But I was wearing flannel before it was a whole thing."

"Sure, trendsetter."

"Okay, before I *realized* it was a whole thing."

It still felt wild to be able to flirt with her like this, to see the way Elena's mouth turned up with the cutest little tilt on the right side when she was being flirty.

Now Elena bit her lip and looked down at Harper's mouth.

Before she could decide whether or not that was an invitation, Elena cleared her throat and backed away.

"So I have a veggie lasagna going in the oven. It'll be about another twenty minutes if you want to go ahead and go see the workshop now?"

"Sounds great."

Before they stepped outside, Elena did, indeed, don a flannel, for which Harper was sure to toss a smirk her way. It shouldn't be allowed for women to look this good in flannel. Honestly, anyone looked damn good in flannel, because it was just one of those magical things. But somehow, Elena looked better in it than anyone Harper had ever seen, including the models for Duluth Trading Company, which was saying something.

Elena, entirely unaware of the effect, continued walking across the yard, and Harper hurried to catch up.

"I had it converted. It's heated and everything," Elena was saying, punching a long code into a keypad on the side of the garage door.

"Fancy."

As the door slid open, Harper's eyes widened. She had no idea the sheer number of tools that would greet her. Plus large workbenches lining each side, and a big, open space in the middle—presumably so she would be able to work on larger pieces like Harper's bookshelves or Margot's dining room hutch.

"Wow, I love the light," she said, looking up at the skylights.

"Yeah, I had those installed a while ago. Nice, right?"

"Beautiful."

She walked around and admired everything, including the two pieces Elena had in progress.

"This one's a rocking chair. One of my old teammates is pregnant, and she wanted one for when the baby comes."

"And what's that?"

"That's...an experiment," Elena said, laughing. "Don't look at it too closely. I'm pretty sure it's going to wind up as saw dust."

"Don't say that. The wood is gorgeous."

Elena just shrugged and moved on, showing her the lathe and a couple of other intimidating-looking contraptions.

"I don't know why I mostly imagined carpentry as, like... you with a piece of sandpaper and a saw, working with your bare hands."

"Ha!" Elena barked. "Not quite. Can you imagine trying to get these grooves by hand?" She pointed at the arms of the rocking chair.

"I'll admit, I never really thought it through." She had certainly thought about Elena in her carpentry gear more than once since she found out about this hobby, but generally her fantasy Elena hadn't exactly been focused on work.

Harper instructed her thoughts to move right along before they traveled down that path again.

Elena showed her a few more small pieces. She even demonstrated how the lathe worked, which Harper found more than mildly terrifying.

"How is it that you managed to find both a career and a hobby that are life-threatening?"

"You don't choose the special interest. The special interest chooses you." Elena said it in a joking tone, as though she were quoting something Harper wasn't familiar with. "Plus, it's really not that dangerous. You just have to be careful. And you can't be stupid. I have a rule that I never come out here if I've had more than one drink. Which I rarely do anyway, but still, it never hurts to be safe."

Hearing that did make Harper feel slightly better, but the sheer number of blades and other sharp objects in the room still made her a little nervous.

"There are just so many different ways to injure yourself."

"Don't worry. I know how to handle myself, and I'm very good with my hands."

Harper didn't know if Elena had meant the words as a double entendre, but she felt a heat pool low in her belly anyway. Elena had been incredible with her hands so far, and Harper was looking forward to finding out just how good those hands were in all situations. But she forced herself to keep it light. "Good for you. Just being in here is like tempting fate for me."

Elena guffawed, but before she could reply, the timer on her phone dinged.

"Ope, that's the lasagna. You ready?"

"Absolutely. Let's go. I'm starving." *For more things than one.*

The lasagna was delicious, and Harper was amazed by how quickly the time flew by while they ate. Before she knew it, she'd finished both helpings, and was breaking into her slice of the small *tres leches* cake Elena had made.

"This is incredible! You really made this?"

Elena looked like she wanted to blush, staring down at her plate. "Thanks. I like cooking. And baking."

"This is amazing. I've never actually had *tres leches* before, but even if I had, I think this would be the best one I'd ever tasted."

Elena stared at her, open-mouthed, and completely ignored her compliment. "Never?"

Harper shook her head, her mouth full of the moist, sugary, gooey deliciousness.

"That's tragic. Well, I'll send you the recipe, so you can make it any time you want." Elena pulled out her phone like she was going to send it then and there, but Harper held up a hand.

"Don't bother. If I try to make it, it'll probably just turn into something horrible."

"Well, just text me when you want one, then, and I'll make it for you."

Harper smiled, and something deep inside her chest clinched at the idea of Elena baking her a cake one day, just because Harper had asked for it.

But that was relationship stuff. She wouldn't ask something like that from Angel, so she shouldn't ask it of Elena.

"On second thought, could you send it to me, anyway? I might give it a shot."

"Absolutely. Everyone should have more *tres leches* in their life."

"Thanks."

"So, do you not cook?"

"Hmm?"

"You said that thing a second ago, about ruining the cake if you tried to make it."

"I was exaggerating a little, but no, I don't really like to cook. It's like, I step into a kitchen, and nothing ever works out right. Obviously, I have to cook; I'm not rich enough to live on take out all the time. But it rarely turns out as great unless I follow a good recipe. Sometimes not even then."

"In my experience, you can never go wrong with a little more salt and garlic. Or oregano. Or cumin. And don't be afraid to put your own flare on things."

"See, but when I stray from the recipe, it never turns out right. A few days before I moved, I tried putting apple cider vinegar in this seitan stew dish, instead of the regular vinegar it called for, and my entire apartment literally smelled like vomit for two hours."

"Oh, no!"

"I had to take the whole pan out to the dumpster and dump it straight in."

"Okay, well, my next rule is: never cook with apple cider vinegar."

"That's definitely my new rule, too. Along with 'Demand that Elena make me a cake every single week.'"

"Demand, huh?" Elena asked, and that little quirk at the edge of her mouth was back.

Harper wanted to kiss it.

"Definitely." She took one last bite and drew the fork out of her mouth slowly, watching as Elena's eyes followed the movement.

"You've got a crumb…" Elena stretched over the table, reached out and brushed where her cheek met her chin. Harper swallowed, feeling her eyelids getting heavy.

Elena looked at her for several long seconds, then sat back down, and Harper couldn't help the disappointed *pang* in her midsection.

"Wanna go watch a movie?"

"Sure!"

After they'd rinsed the plates and placed them in the dishwasher, Harper excused herself to the bathroom, where she brushed her teeth with the toothbrush she had smuggled over in her purse. Whether or not they strayed beyond PG-13 territory tonight, she had no desire to subject Elena to her garlic breath.

Finally, they met in the living room, settling down into the couch together. Elena brought up Netflix, and Harper watched as she flicked through a few categories.

"So. Before we watch, I just want to mention something."

"Yeah?"

"I got tested on Monday, and I'm clean."

"Great. I went yesterday. Shockingly, the socially awkward monk lifestyle approach has also left me in the clear."

"Good."

"Good."

Harper was deciding how to delicately ask about the sex situation, but Elena spoke first.

"On that subject. I wanted to mention…it's probably a little weird to you that I agreed to a friends-with-benefits thing but then didn't, um, apply for the benefits. So to speak." Elena stared at the television, but she wasn't scrolling anymore.

"I had wondered. But it's no problem at all. I promise, I'm good with however slow you want to go."

"I may have been sending mixed signals before, but those signals are only pointing one direction tonight. If it's a direction you're interested in."

"Honestly?" Harper swallowed, and Elena turned to look at her. "I can't stop thinking about it."

Elena didn't respond, just sat looking at her, her chest rising and falling. The tension descended and thickened so that Harper could barely breathe. She wanted to move forward. She wanted to touch her.

She still hadn't seen Elena's bedroom.

"Still want to watch a movie?" Elena's voice was soft and husky.

Harper shook her head slowly back and forth.

"Thank god," Elena said, and dove for Harper's mouth.

Harper met her halfway, noting the taste of mint on Elena's tongue and realizing she wasn't the only one who'd thought ahead. But beneath everything, Elena simply tasted of *Elena*, a taste Harper had come to recognize and grown to crave over the past week.

Harper pulled her closer, her fingers grappling at the edge of Elena's tank top.

Elena groaned into her mouth, running hands up and down her sides.

"You're so fucking soft. I love your body."

Her words, her voice ragged with want, stoked a fire deep

in Harper's belly. She felt herself growing bolder, sucking Elena's tongue into her mouth until she moaned. Her fingers ran through the long, dark tresses, loving the feel of the strands between her fingers.

"I can't get enough of you," she said, moving her mouth to Elena's ear and flicking her earlobe with her tongue. Elena gasped and wrapped her hands around Harper's ass.

They ended up in the bedroom down the hall, after a brief period of distraction in the hallway during which Elena's mouth found Harper's neck, and Harper very nearly begged Elena to fuck her against the wall. She'd managed to get herself under control, at least long enough to make it to the bed.

And now they were in bed, and Elena was lying on top of her, and it was just as incredible as she had always imagined.

She placed her hands on either side of Elena's head and pulled her closer, capturing Elena's lips with her own.

Elena reached down and started tugging at her shirt, running her fingers up and down her stomach, and Harper had to break away to giggle.

"Hey, not fair."

"You're ticklish." Elena grinned, like it was the best thing she had ever discovered.

"Fuck off."

"Sure you wouldn't rather I do that to you?"

"At the moment? No." Elena laughed, and Harper belied her own words by tugging Elena back toward her. Harper grasped her tank top and pulled it over her head, and Elena did the same thing with Harper's—far more sensible, she might add—sweater.

"Holy fuck," Elena breathed, staring down at the burgundy lace balconette bra she'd revealed. She swallowed audibly. "Did you put this on for me?"

"No, I just like wearing sexy lingerie around the house. It's fun."

Elena stared at her like she wasn't quite sure if Harper was insane or joking.

"I'm kidding."

"Oh, thank god. I was going to start doubting your sanity. Though you should most definitely start wearing this as a regular outfit when I'm around. I won't complain."

"Perv."

"For you." With that, Elena captured her lips again, and Harper melted.

Elena couldn't believe she was finally here. In her bed. With Harper. And everything felt so completely, unbelievably, wonderfully *good*.

Elena pressed her mouth to Harper's neck the way that had driven Harper crazier earlier in the hallway. She couldn't seem to get enough of her taste. Her skin was salty-sweet, and Elena wanted to lick every inch of it. She let her fingers drift in between Harper's thighs and was rewarded with a gasp and a buck of the hips.

"Yes. Fuck. Touch me."

Elena wanted to do more than that. She wanted to taste her. She wanted to lick her slowly, thrust her tongue inside, circle her clit, find out exactly what would make Harper come the hardest.

She would hold off, though. Not yet.

Instead, she let her fingers gently tease up and down against her underwear. She pulled down Harper's skirt to reveal the thin silk and lace panties that matched the outrageously sexy bra that Elena was going to be seeing behind her eyes every time she blinked for the next week. Harper's skin was creamy perfection, her breasts begging to be freed from their beautiful cage and worshipped. Elena pressed a kiss to each in turn, right where the fabric ended. She gently ran her teeth along the shape of a nipple beneath the fabric, and Harper keened.

Then she looked up, and the way Harper was gazing at her, biting her lip, her pupils blown, her cheeks flushed, made Elena's own panties go damp.

"Can I?" she asked, running her fingers around the bra to the back fastener.

"Please."

But before Elena could progress, Harper said, "Wait."

Elena removed her hands immediately.

Harper reached for the hem of Elena's shirt. "I don't want to get too far ahead."

Elena aided her in removing her own shirt, and then she resumed taking off Harper's bra.

Luckily, muscle memory came into play, and she didn't struggle with the bra, despite the fact that it had been so long since she had taken off someone else's.

But she didn't even have a moment to celebrate her victory, because all she could see was the pale pink nipples, already tight with want. She leaned forward and captured one with her lips. Harper sucked in a breath, grasping her head and holding her in place. Elena swirled her tongue around and then sucked once more.

"Jesus. You're going to make me come just by doing that."

"Sounds good to me."

Elena moved to her other nipple and simultaneously ran her hands down Harper's sides. She broke away just long enough to look up at Harper, who nodded enthusiastically and lifted her hips. Then Elena tugged the panties down, revealing a tidy thatch of curls.

Harper's fingers ran over her body, finding Elena's nipples through her black sports bra, twisting gently through the fabric. Elena groaned and tugged the garment off, flinging it somewhere over her shoulder. She could not have cared less where it ended up; the only thing she needed was to keep touching Harper.

Harper guided Elena's hand down where she needed her,

and Elena teased at her entrance with her fingers, feeling the wetness there.

"Christ. You're so wet."

"Fuck me."

She didn't have to ask twice.

Slowly, Elena slid a single finger inside of her, feeling the warm, tight rightness of it. Harper let out a long, slow breath and closed her eyes, stretching her body like she wanted the moment to last forever.

"Another finger?"

Harper nodded enthusiastically, and Elena slipped a second finger inside of her. After a couple of attempts and readjusting to find a good angle, the change was almost immediate. She moved in and out slowly, Harper's breathing growing erratic. Elena could already feel her tightening around her fingers.

She withdrew, and Harper made a disappointed noise, grasping at Elena's shoulders. Elena teased her clit for a moment, watching Harper squirm in impatience, before thrusting her fingers inside again.

Harper squeaked in a way Elena thought meant she'd hurt her, and she immediately withdrew her fingers. "No, no, that was good. Again." Harper panted around the words.

Elena obeyed, moving her fingers inside at the same angle slowly, watching for confirmation. Harper's moan of approval gave it enthusiastically, and Elena thrust again and again. Less than a minute later, she felt Harper's orgasm grip her fingers, and Harper cried out, her body taut. She shook and shook, but when Elena thought she might be done, she said, "Keep going. Please. Fuck. Oh my god."

Elena obeyed, and Harper leaned up from the bed, her mouth in an O, her eyes squeezed shut. Then she collapsed, panting, before pulling Elena forward for a long, slow kiss. She pulled back. "Can I ride you?"

"Be my guest."

They maneuvered until Elena was lying down and Harper was straddling her thighs. Elena propped her hand against her leg, palm up, and Harper slid down, taking two fingers inside. It was incredible. Elena watched her move, her hips working in a rhythm of her own design, and she reached up and toyed with one of Harper's nipples.

Elena had never been one for talking during sex, but for some reason, she felt the need to today. "You're so amazing. You feel so good."

Harper's answer was to stretch her head back and bow her spine, grinding down onto Elena's fingers.

It was the single sexiest thing Elena had ever seen. She felt like she was on fire between her thighs, the pressure so close to release, and Harper had barely touched her.

She'd always been one for touching more than the other way around, but she wanted Harper's fingers on her.

Harper came with a yell, slumping down onto Elena, their sticky skin pressed together. She rested for only a few moments before she rolled to the side, then ran her finger up to Elena's chest and pinched gently at a nipple. Elena arched into her touch, her head pressing back into the pillow.

Harper's head followed her fingers, and she licked and kissed Elena's skin until Elena was nearly begging her to move lower.

Finally, Harper caressed her clit for a few moments before sliding two fingers slowly inside, and it felt so good, Elena couldn't help a groan. Harper fucked her slowly, carefully, before speeding up at Elena's request.

It was incredible. Harper was incredible. The pressure in her core built and built until it was almost unbearable, and Elena was gasping, straining for that final tiny thing that would give her release.

Finally, she ground out, "Touch my clit. Please."

Harper did, her rhythm faltering slightly as she sat so she could touch the bundle of nerves while still fucking Elena with her other hand.

She ran her fingers over Elena's clit two times. Three.

Elena exploded. She had no concept of reality as her muscles contracted and expanded, her senses rioting. She felt like she was riding a roller coaster to the end of the universe, where gravity was a lie and her entire body was filled with spirals of stars and comets. The orgasm was unending, her body shaking and shuddering, until the sensations finally faded and died, and she collapsed onto the mattress, spent.

After they had been lying down for a few seconds in silence, Harper said, "Holy shit."

"I can't believe we didn't do this sooner."

"Guess we'll just have to make up for lost time?"

"I think that sounds like the only reasonable course of action."

Elena leaned up to kiss her, something that was becoming increasingly, dangerously natural every single time she did it.

"You up for it?"

"Hell yeah."

CHAPTER FOURTEEN

Elena pulled up to Avery and Meredith's house two minutes before three o'clock, which was when Dee's retirement party was due to start.

The majority of the Defiant players lived in team-provided apartments, but Avery and Meredith rented the two-bedroom bungalow together as roommates. They had been so excited about hosting that Elena hadn't even needed to feel guilty about not offering up her own house. As much as Elena loved her teammates, she had been more than happy to leave the hosting duties to others, her main contribution having been sent through Venmo.

It was the perfect house for a party. Even though it was on the small side, it was picturesque, painted canary yellow with spotless white shutters. It fit Avery, who was possibly the most cheerful person in existence. They never failed to have a smile on their face. Unless, of course, they were staring down a player who was trying to score a goal against them (unlikely, given that the Defiant had been second in the league for the least number of goals conceded overall).

Elena pushed the doorbell, and Avery opened it with a wide smile. Their light brown hair was shorn into a buzz cut, which was partially covered by a conical cardboard party hat, of the style Elena didn't think she had worn since her seventh birthday.

"Elena! Welcome! You're the first one here."

There were so many streamers and balloons, Elena thought the house was well on its way to floating off into the sky. "The place looks great! Anything I can do to help?"

"I'm all set up out here. I was in charge of decorations. You can check in the kitchen with Meredith to see if there's anything she needs help with, though."

Elena stepped out from under the huge banner that said *Congratulations, You're Retired!* in large blue letters, with *HR told us we couldn't call you old.* written in a smaller font beneath. Folding chairs were set out along the perimeter of the room, and there was a small gift table in the corner. Elena went over and placed her gift there beside the two others. She'd bought Dee some of her favorite brand of whiskey, along with some sunscreen, because Dee had been talking about the vacation she would take when she was retired for a year. And every time she mentioned it, Elena's only comment was that she should wear sunscreen.

She moseyed into the kitchen, where Meredith was setting down a large plastic platter filled with cut vegetables. It was next to a couple of small pots with dips in them, as well as various other finger foods.

"Are those pigs in a blanket?"

Meredith nodded. "I asked Dee for her favorite snack food, and she wanted these. I was confused as hell. Avery had to explain. But I made a test recipe the other day, and they're delicious."

"I love those! Anyway, what can I do to help? How's the drinks situation?"

There wasn't much left to do, which was good, because soon the house was filling with her teammates. Joana, Priti, and Charlotte were first, having carpooled and arrived together, but Natalie and Min were only a couple minutes behind them. Elena wondered idly if those two ever went anywhere separately. If she didn't know Natalie had a long-term boyfriend, she would have sworn that the two of them were romantically involved.

Elena did harbor her own private suspicions that things weren't entirely platonic from Min's side, though. Min had been Elena's roommate during the Olympics last year, and after their victory, everyone had gotten totally sauced on champagne. Min hadn't been able to stop talking about how much she missed Natalie and how much she wished Natalie were there and how much Natalie deserved a spot on the National Team.

She wasn't wrong. Natalie was a strong midfielder with exceptional pass accuracy and a second sense for exactly when to go in for a slide tackle. Elena could absolutely see her being a part of the National Team, but it wasn't her call. Thinking of the National Team reminded Elena that calls should be going out this weekend for the camp in mid-November, and she felt a tiny jitter of nerves. Even though Elena had been a regular on the team for years and she'd played well in the last several games, it was always a gamble. There could always be someone ready to swoop in and steal her spot.

She shook away the thoughts and paid attention to her teammates, listening to stories about what everyone had done in the off-season so far.

Several players had already moved back to their regular homes out of town for the off-season, but Miriam and Annie were at least able to join via video call to cheer when Dee arrived at three-thirty.

Elena grabbed some food and sat down next to Charlotte, who confessed to a recent obsession with gardening podcasts, even though she had a proven black thumb and no way to plant anything until spring.

When it was time for presents, Dee chose Elena's gift first.

Dee stuck her hand into the bag and emerged with sunscreen. She made a confused face for half a second and then doubled over with laughter. "You're really committed to my skincare routine, huh?"

"Listen, skin cancer kills! Not a joke. You're welcome for saving your life!"

"Great, Mom. Thank you." She pulled out the whiskey and gave a firm nod of approval. "Okay, *now* we're talking."

The room burst into laughter, and Elena looked around the room, soaking up this last moment they would all have together as a team. Elena prayed for minimal trades during the off-season. There had already been a rumor about Priti being sent to Minnesota, but there were often rumors that never came to fruition. Elena desperately hoped that was the case. Priti had only been with them for a year, but she was already an invaluable part of their midfield. The team was so good now. She knew they had the potential to become even better.

It wouldn't be the same without Dee, though. And try as she might to forget it, Dee would never play for the Defiant again. She might stop by at gatherings every once in a while in the future, but it would just be a fun reunion, and soon, there would be players on the team who had never even met her.

She would be gone. And someone else would be captain in her stead.

She knew Dee was waiting for her final answer today. Dee would pass it on to Coach Talia, who would talk to management and ultimately make a selection. But Elena knew that if she accepted, it was a done deal. She'd laid awake last night, thinking about it. She didn't want to be captain. She'd never wanted to be captain. But she owed it to Dee to do this, at least for a season. If it didn't work out, she could pawn it off on someone else next year.

But god, she hated failing at things. And as much as she didn't want to do it, part of the reason was that she didn't think she would be good at it. She thought she would make a lousy captain, if she were honest.

She said as much to Dee when she cornered Elena in the empty kitchen some time later, while the others played Pin the Soccer Ball in the Goal in the living room.

"Why?"

"Why would I make a lousy captain? Where do I even start? It would be faster to make a list of the reasons I would make a good captain. Because that list would be pretty short."

"Is that really how you see yourself?"

Elena shrugged. "Not in, like, a super depressing way or anything. I just know my strengths. Soccer is a strength. People have never been my strength. And being captain is more about the people than it is the soccer. I just think you should give it to Joana. She's been here almost as long, she's older, she's wise, and she'd make a good leader."

"She would."

Elena nodded, glad Dee was seeing sense, but Dee wasn't done talking. "But you'd be better." She held up a finger. "You want a list? Here's a list."

"I wasn't serious—"

"Hush. I'm talking. One. When Avery came out to us as nonbinary, you made them that 'You put the Avery in bravery' card. Did you know it's still hanging up in their cubby?"

Elena shrugged. She did know, and it made her happy to have made someone happy like that. But it didn't mean anything.

Dee raised another finger. "Two. Who remembers the birthday of every single person on the team?"

"That's literally just a Google Calendar with alerts. Anyone can make one. I don't even know when your birthday is."

Dee shook her head. "It doesn't matter. You *care*. You care more than anyone knows. You just don't like to make a big deal out of it, and that's fine. Making big, movie-worthy motivational speeches isn't what makes a captain. It's caring."

"Okay, but what about when someone needs me to talk them down or resolve a dispute or something? You know I'm not good at sugarcoating."

"Everyone loves you *because* you don't bullshit them. They know you're going to tell them the truth. It's never going to be politics and favorites and game-playing like it sometimes is. I know you don't want it. And if you're serious, I'll respect that. Take tonight to think about it one last time. Let me know by noon tomorrow if you've changed your mind. That's when I'll text Talia."

Dee wasn't even calling her "Coach" anymore.

"I'll think about it." Elena had already thought about it, but the way Dee believed in her made her doubt her decision. Harper had, too, last night, when Elena had confessed the reason she'd been distracted and irritable. She'd said Elena would make a great captain.

To be fair, Harper probably had no idea what being a captain entailed. But still. She believed enough in Elena that she'd said so, and that had to count for something.

Dee went back to the other room to join in the game, and Elena stayed in the kitchen, sipping at her water in the tiny party cup.

Maybe she had been so focused on why she would be a bad captain that she hadn't stopped to consider there really might be reasons she'd be a good one. She still didn't *want* to do it. But now, there was a niggling bit of hope alive in her that hadn't been there before. The belief that even if it wasn't something she wanted to do by nature, it was something she *could* do. She wasn't going to fuck it up.

Elena filled her cup with punch and took a long swig. It was fruity and had that slightly too-sweet taste of sweetener, which was unsurprising, as even in the off-season, most of them tried to limit their sugar.

Thanking about sugar made her think of baking, which she'd been having the urge to do more of, now that it was colder. She wondered what Harper's favorite cookies were and made a note to text her about it later.

But she was getting distracted. She wasn't supposed to be thinking about Harper right now.

She thought about her dilemma. She once more saw Harper in her mind's eye, staring at her, smiling, believing in her. She thought of Dee's words.

Elena did care. She cared so much. The Defiant meant everything to her. There were parts of the job that wouldn't be easy for her, but she wasn't afraid of a challenge.

Most of all, there were many parts of the job she would be good at. She was a loyal player who believed in a drama-free team where everyone had a voice. She was an excellent play tactician. She could lead by example. She could even show that people made mistakes, but after those mistakes, they learned from them. Like she had learned from hers.

And just like that, she made a decision.

She rinsed the plastic cup and tossed it in the bright blue recycling bin and went to find Dee.

"I did it! I'm going to be captain!" Elena announced as she flung open the door to Bewitched early Saturday evening.

Harper looked up from the floor, where she was looking for the transparent card sleeve she'd dropped.

"Congratulations!"

"And I got the call ten minutes ago! I'm officially going to camp!"

"Yay!" She'd known Elena had been a little worried about getting called up to National Team camp, but Harper had assumed she was just being paranoid. She'd been right. No one in their right mind would leave Elena Torres off their team.

"I don't know why I was so nervous. But it's official now, so I can calm down!"

She didn't sound calm at all, but Harper didn't point that out.

"Amazing! When do you go?"

"The twelfth."

Suddenly, Harper felt like someone had kicked her in the stomach, and she looked back down at the ground, pretending she was still searching for the sleeve, even though she had just spotted it near the chair leg. She took a few seconds to breathe through the feeling, wondering why she was having such a dramatic reaction. There was no reason for it. So Elena couldn't come to the Grand Opening. So, what? They were still friends. They could still have sex. Elena still cared about her. It literally changed nothing.

But she still couldn't help flashing back to earlier that afternoon, when she'd taken Vivian's advice and called her mom.

"I don't know what you expect this information to change, Harper. It's nice that you're happy with your accomplishments, but I don't think your father and I should apologize for wanting what's best for you. And we certainly aren't paying a fortune to change our tickets just to come to a little party."

She should have known better than to get her hopes up. Either about her parents, or about Elena.

That wasn't fair. She knew it. This wasn't Elena deliberately choosing to do something fun over supporting Harper. This was her job, and perhaps even more than that, it was a privilege that only a select few players were chosen for.

But it still hurt.

It hurt more than Harper wanted to think about, but she couldn't ignore it. The deep ache meant only one thing: that she cared far more about Elena than she should. That she'd fallen for her, like some stupid clichéd teenager who didn't know how to separate the physical from the emotional.

But Harper didn't have time to think about this revelation right now. So she steeled herself, took a deep breath, and made a big show of "finding" the card sleeve and standing up again.

"I'm happy for you," she said, but her smile must not have been convincing enough, because Elena's face turned worried.

"Shit, you're upset about the opening. I'm sorry. I was

bummed about it, too. I really wanted to be here for your special night."

"It's okay." Harper tried to force that to be true.

"It's not! I wanted to be here to support you. And to tell everyone that I helped paint, of course. So they can assume I'm a brilliant mural artist, not just the world's slowest bathroom painter."

At that, Harper couldn't help but crack a real smile.

"That's better."

Elena pulled her into her arms and pressed a quick kiss to her forehead. "I'm sorry I'm not going to be able to come. For real."

"Don't worry about it. We'll survive without you." Harper moved back to the table where she'd been working. "Give me a couple minutes to finish getting this one sorted, and we can go?"

"Okay."

Elena wondered off toward the back. Harper finished putting the last cards into their sleeves, then carefully placed everything back inside the box. She headed toward the back room, where she found Elena looking through the games and muttering to herself.

"Having an interesting conversation?"

Elena blushed and set the box back on the shelf. "Sorry, I was talking to myself."

"No worries. I do that all the time. Angel told me I should get a cat, so it seems less crazy. But she has two of them, so that's really her answer for everything."

Elena laughed.

"Would you ever get a pet?" Harper asked, suddenly curious.

"Yeah, definitely. I would love to get a cat, but my schedule doesn't really allow it. Y'know, since I'm alone and everything."

"Not a dog person?"

"Uh…no. Not really. Like, at all. Sorry."

"Nothing to apologize for!"

"Glad you think so. The internet doesn't seem to agree with you. Nor did my ex, who called me a monster on more than one occasion."

"What the hell?"

Elena nodded. "I never realized that feelings on dogs would be something that could cause fights. But she wanted to adopt a dog, and I didn't. At the time, I didn't know about sensory sensitivities. I just knew that a lot of things about dogs made me feel literally sick to my stomach, and I didn't know why, and I didn't know how to explain it other than to just say that I didn't like them. Hence, monster comments. But anyway!" Elena waved both of her hands, like she was brushing the subject aside. "Back to cats. Love cats. Why were you asking?"

"I was just wondering. I used to have a cat."

"I know. Leia."

"You remember her name?"

Elena shot her a look.

"Okay, so maybe I'm a little predictable."

"Just a bit. Plus, I'm pretty sure she spent more time in Margot's room than she did in yours."

"Only when you were there. You lured her away from me."

"I did not lure her!" She was so cute when she protested.

"Maybe not, but I swear, she had some sort of Elena-dar that let her know when you were in the house. She would abandon me for you in two seconds flat. But I guess I can't blame her. I wanted to be around you all the time, too."

"Huh?"

"Um." Harper stared, her mouth agape. She could not believe she'd just said that. She'd meant to tell Elena at some point, but not like this. But it wasn't like she could take it back now.

"It's a good thing we're talking about cats, because the cat's out of the bag!" she joked, but Elena still looked confused. "Uh, I guess now's a good time to tell you I had a super massive crush on you in high school. Surprise!"

"Really? On me?"

Harper nodded.

"Huh. I had no idea."

"Well, that was sort of on purpose. I knew you weren't interested, so I didn't tell you."

"I might have been. You should have said something."

"Can't believe my cat had more guts than I did." Harper shook her head ruefully, mostly to get the attention off of her teenage self with her serious lack of self-esteem.

"She was a pretty fierce cat."

Elena said nothing for a few seconds, then smirked a bit. "So, you liked being around me, huh?"

"I did."

"What about now?"

Harper tilted her head, pretending to consider. "Eh. It's okay."

"Just okay, huh?" Elena drew closer. "Anything I can do to improve that assessment?"

"Well, you could give me a massage."

"Hmm, what kind of massage?"

"A naked massage?"

"That can most definitely be arranged." Elena took her hand and pulled her gently toward the door. "Let's go back to your place."

"Lead the way."

Harper did, trying her very best to keep up a pretense that everything was fine, when it most definitively was not. Feeling Elena's hand warm in hers was all it took for those flimsy internal walls to come crumbling down, to remember the realization she'd had earlier.

She'd promised to keep things casual. She'd said she only wanted to be friends with benefits.

And now she'd gone and done the one thing she'd

promised herself she wouldn't do.
    She'd fallen for Elena.

CHAPTER FIFTEEN

Harper hung up the phone and breathed a sigh of relief. Her interview from today had gone better than the first one, but Ayumi was still the clear winner. Thankfully, she had been overjoyed to receive Harper's phone call. They talked about a time for Ayumi to come in and fill out some paperwork, and Harper checked one more item off her to-do list.

Now, she just had to finish getting everything ready for tonight. She'd printed fliers and shelled out for Reese's and Snickers to tape to them (because people were more likely to pay attention when you gave them the good candy). They had a QR code that went directly to her website, which was primed and ready to go with all the information about the grand opening, their hours, and a couple of special events Harper was already planning.

Since the historic downtown district was cute and foot-traffic friendly and a very popular destination for Halloween, it was a great place for good, old-fashioned, face-to-face marketing. Of course, nowadays, social media did most of the heavy lifting, but sitting around crafting Instagram posts wasn't ever going to be her favorite thing to do. She'd outsourced that responsibility to Shawn for the Pawn, and after a while, she was hoping she might be able to do the same for Bewitched. But for now, that responsibility, like everything else, fell on her, so she got to work.

After an hour on social media, she was looking forward to handing out fliers. That was what those damn websites did to her. But at least they were a decent distraction.

Now all she had left to do was tape her fliers. The work was tedious, which normally wasn't a problem for her. She didn't mind tedious tasks. However, today she did, because they allowed her way too much time to think.

To think about what a fucking idiot she was, primarily.

She had decided to jump head first into a casual, no-strings situation with Elena.

In hindsight, it had been the stupidest, *stupidest* idea she could have come up with.

But she'd been so desperate for some part of Elena, any part that she could have, as much as she would give her. She had taken something she'd known, deep down, she should not have, because she simply wasn't prepared for it.

On the other hand, it made no sense. She'd had sex without emotional entanglements before. She'd had a long series of booty calls with Ben from her Accounting for Small Business Owners class throughout most of her second year at PPCC. Between her classes, her job, and the plans for the Pawn that she'd already started, she had been far too busy for anything else. Eventually, he'd put a stop to it after he'd found someone he wanted to get serious with, and Harper had wished him well and sent him on his merry way.

But, as in many other ways, Elena seemed to be the exception. Her exception. Which was great, except for the fact that now Harper had set herself up for a mountain of heartache, for absolutely no reason. She could have just stayed friends, and she could have dealt with this with some therapy and some wine, but no. Instead, she had gotten too close to the fire, and now she was getting burnt.

For a wild second, she wondered what it might be like to tell Elena how she felt. She imagined Elena's eyes going all soft, leaning forward, and whispering in Harper's ear, "I think I'm falling for you, too."

Whereas in reality, Harper knew exactly the opposite would happen. Elena had been completely upfront about what she had been looking for. In fact, Harper had been the one to propose this type of relationship in the first place. Elena had been the one smart enough to think it was a bad idea, but Harper had gone ahead with it, anyway.

Stupid.

Elena sat alone on an exercise bike in the Complex, sweat dripping down her forehead, pedaling away while she mulled over her thoughts.

It was a new experience for her, having her feelings accepted for what they were, instead of being fought over. Claire had never been like Harper. Though, to be fair, Elena understood herself more now, with the benefit of context and some therapy. She hadn't had that when she'd been with Claire. She'd been diagnosed after their divorce, when she and Dee had gotten closer, and Dee had observed that Elena shared many traits with her autistic older sister.

The dog conversation from a few nights before was a prime example. She'd had that fight with Claire periodically for years. Claire had always called her unnatural or heartless or a monstrous bitch. At the time, it had been hard not to believe her. She knew other people didn't have the same reactions she did, but it was difficult to explain. Because it was hard to describe the bone-deep revulsion. The way her stomach twisted in nausea when she heard certain sounds. The way the sensation of a cold, wet nose made her want to crawl out of her own skin. She didn't *want* to have these feelings, but she did anyway. It wasn't a matter of choice.

But Harper hadn't said any of those things. She'd simply accepted Elena's feelings for what they were: feelings. Not an indication of her morality or her status as a decent human being. And she didn't treat Elena any differently because of it, which was one of Elena's deepest fears and the reason she preferred not to tell most people. She didn't want special treatment. She didn't want to be treated with kid gloves or like someone incapable of making her own choices. She just wanted to live her life, and she wanted the people closest to her to be able to respect her preferences, just as she would respect theirs.

Surprisingly, Harper had climbed onto that list more quickly than anyone in Elena's life. There were very few people she cared about to that level. She had her parents, Dee, and Margot. That was it. But now Harper was there, too.

She thought back to the way Harper had fallen asleep with her head on Elena's shoulder on Saturday night, how Elena hadn't wanted to move her. She'd sat there, even though *Bend It Like Beckham* had ended and the movie channel had moved onto some annoying comedy, but the remote had been on the other side of Harper, so she couldn't change it. She'd just stayed. But she hadn't been annoyed or impatient. She'd simply felt a deep sense of contentment. Thinking about how nice it felt, thinking about how natural it was to spend so much time with Harper.

Now she couldn't stop thinking about that moment. She'd stayed there for half an hour, unmoving, until Harper had woken up on her own and apologized profusely for falling asleep on top of her.

She wasn't sure exactly how these casual relationships were supposed to go. But she was fairly certain they weren't supposed to feel like this. And she didn't know what to do about it. She didn't know how to keep Harper at arm's length romantically while simultaneously staying close to her as a friend and doing what they were doing.

Elena contemplated calling Margot, but that seemed a little too complicated. It would be way too awkward to talk to her about Harper, and leaving Harper's name out would feel too dishonest. Plus, the truth would come out eventually, and Margot would realize Elena had been talking about Harper, thus putting her in the same position as telling her outright now.

Plus, she hadn't been lying when she'd told Harper they didn't really talk about relationship things very often. Margot wasn't a touchy-feely person, which usually suited Elena quite well.

This left Dee, who probably wouldn't be awake, but Elena called her anyway.

Surprisingly, Dee picked up on the second ring, sounding fully awake and cheerful.

"'yello?" She always answered the phone in a way that sounded like a seventy-year-old man from Texas, and it never failed to amuse Elena.

"I need advice."

"You called me at eight A.M. on a Monday because you needed advice?"

"I did. Sorry if I woke you."

"You didn't. I've been trying this whole early riser thing to see what all the fuss is about."

"You?" Elena felt her own eyebrows raise of their own volition.

"Yes, me. But I don't think it's going to stick. There's literally nothing special about it; you can do the same things at ten A.M. as at six A.M. More, actually. I've been getting into this online game lately, and I wanted to go to Best Buy this morning to get a new mouse. So I drove all the way over there, and guess what? They weren't even open! It's all marketing bullshit, is what I'm saying."

"Marketing by whom, exactly?"

"Breakfast cereal companies, probably."

"I'm sure that's exactly what's happening," Elena said.

"Anyway, didn't mean to ramble. I'm now ready to dispense

advice. What can I do you for?"

"It's about Harper."

"I assumed as much."

"Thanks for the vote of confidence."

"I just mean, you don't usually come to me for non-relationship advice. Presumably that's what your other best friend is for. You should be glad you have me, though, since I doubt a heartless ice queen is going to be a great personal cupid."

"She isn't heartless. And she's not that bad."

"Maybe not to you."

"Well, I didn't try to hit on her the first time we met."

"Didn't you meet when you were like twelve?"

"Fifteen."

"Still. Now stop talking about what's-her-name and tell me about her little sister instead."

"You know full well her name is Margot, and you're the one who brought her up." Elena wasn't sure why she was still going on about this, except that maybe subconsciously she was evading what she had actually called about. She didn't want to say it out loud.

"Stop changing the subject."

"Okay, so, Harper. This whole 'casual' thing we're doing."

"What about it?"

"It doesn't feel casual."

"How so?"

"Nothing specific. Just…the feel of it. It doesn't feel like being just friends who have sex. It feels like a relationship."

"And that's bad?"

"Yes!" Elena exclaimed. "I want no-strings. I want casual. But I've never done this before, and I don't know if maybe I'm doing something wrong."

"Are you doing anything that feels bad?"

"No."

"Anything she's asked you not to?"

"No, of course not."

"Then I don't see the problem."

"The problem is that it isn't casual!"

"I hear you. But I'm just going to ask this once, and feel free to consider not biting my head off for suggesting it." She paused, and Elena readied herself for whatever she had to say. "Are you sure casual is really what you want? Or do you just not want to get hurt again?"

Elena felt the words like a punch to the gut, but she didn't want to analyze the feeling. Besides, it was all wrong. She shook her head emphatically, even though Dee couldn't see her.

"That's not it. It's that I don't want to be the one *doing* the hurting."

"It's okay to admit you were hurt by what Claire did."

It was weird to hear Dee actually call Elena's ex by her real name. It made the question hold too much weight, suddenly. Like it was too real. Like her problems with Harper might be related to what Dee was suggesting.

"Of course it hurt. My marriage fucking ended. I lost the person I thought I was going to spend the rest of my life with."

"And you don't think part of the reason you want to avoid relationships is that you don't want to get hurt like that again?"

"No." Elena's answer was immediate. "It isn't about me. I do want to try the relationship thing with someone, eventually, but only after I retire, so my focus isn't on my career. It's about protecting the other person. Not me."

Dee didn't respond immediately, and Elena barely kept from grinding her teeth in annoyance. This conversation had not gone at all how she'd wanted. She'd wanted something simple she could fix, advice on how to stop something she was doing to accidentally give off relationship vibes. Maybe she shouldn't have made cake. Or maybe she shouldn't have let Harper sleep on her shoulder.

"Well, it sounds like you have everything figured out already. I'm not sure what you want me to do here."

"Sorry. I don't, either, I guess. Maybe I just needed to talk some things out."

"Well, my ears are always here for you."

"Thanks for your help."

"Don't mention it."

She certainly wouldn't be.

Elena hung up the phone and headed toward the locker room showers. She needed to go shopping to finish her costume for tonight, when she would be handing out fliers with Harper. They were spending a lot of nights together. To be fair, some of it was because Elena was helping out at Bewitched, but now that Harper had hired someone, she wouldn't need to do that anymore.

A small flame of guilt flared up in her stomach when she thought about Bewitched. She couldn't believe, of all days, that the National Team camp was going to overlap with the grand opening. She'd seen how upset Harper had been about it, even though she'd tried to cover it.

But at the same time, maybe it would help establish a sense of boundaries. After all, a friend would be nice to have at a big life event, but certainly wasn't a requirement. Elena hadn't begrudged Margot for not being there for her college graduation or on the day she'd been drafted. So, maybe it was a good thing, objectively.

She couldn't seem to quite convince herself of it, though.

They were back in Harper's apartment after two hours of handing out fliers.

Two hours of trying not to stare at Harper's cleavage in her bright pink, distractingly low-cut dress. She'd dressed as Daphne to Elena's Velma, and they'd drawn plenty of attention with the giant, inflatable Scooby that Elena still wasn't sure why Harper owned. It had worked perfectly, leaning into the ghost-hunting theme and drawing in both families and nostalgic adults.

Overall, Harper had seemed very happy with the results.

Elena was happy, too. Most of all, she was happy that she was finally going to get to take that dress off of Harper. Maybe it was a side effect of thinking too hard in the morning, so her brain had shut off and just let her enjoy things tonight. Maybe it was just the fact that she was a weak lesbian and Harper had cleavage to die for. But Elena couldn't stop thinking about it, couldn't stop wondering what underwear she had on underneath the dress. If she was hiding another one of those silky bras that made Elena lose her goddamn mind.

Harper seemed to have the same idea, because she'd pulled Elena close as soon as the apartment door had closed behind them.

She touched Harper all over, warmed her frozen fingers in between her own. She kissed the curve of her cheek, her neck, her clavicle. She pressed kisses along the neckline of her dress and cupped Harper's breasts through the fabric, finding her nipples already achingly hard.

Elena peeled off the dress and found that Harper wasn't wearing anything special, just a regular bra, but it didn't matter. Elena wanted her with a wildness that she couldn't explain. Harper removed her own clothes, including the glasses Harper had teasingly said she should keep for a later date.

But it wasn't the time for that right now. She didn't want to play games, and neither did Harper.

Elena wanted to fuck her. She wanted to taste her. She wanted Harper to come undone around her tongue. She whispered those things into Harper's ear, and Harper grabbed her hair and nodded, and Elena pushed her into on the bed and slid down her body. She ran her fingers around the sensitive insides of Harper's thighs, tracing lightly, inhaling the scent of her. She pressed her mouth against Harper clit through her underwear, and Harper swore, grabbing at her head and pulling her closer.

Elena pulled off her underwear until Harper was bare in front of her, and Elena leaned forward, licking slowly, starting at her center and moving all the way up. Harper gasped, and Elena found her clit, moving her tongue in slow, careful circles. She followed Harper's instructions, fucking her the way she liked, moving her tongue deep inside.

Harper came undone with a cry, her body taut and shaking, drenching Elena's mouth as she came.

Elena nearly came from the sensation alone.

But she wasn't done.

She climbed up the bed, spooned Harper from behind, both of them on their sides. Elena reached around to play with her nipples and then her clit from the new angle, simultaneously kissing her neck and biting gently in a way that had Harper keening with the need for release. Elena pulled back, not granting it, once, twice. When Harper was begging, she placed her knee in between Harper's legs to create space, then reached through to fuck her with two fingers. Harper was soaking wet, to the point where Elena slipped in like her fingers had been crafted specifically for Harper's pleasure. Harper moved her hips in time with Elena's thrusts, slowly becoming faster, more desperate. Then Elena curled her fingers forward slightly, and Harper cried out, her insides tightening around Elena's fingers.

Then Harper turned around and reached out to touch her.

And suddenly everything was wrong.

Fuck.

Fuck.

Elena had hoped that she had gotten over this, the way her body sometimes just decided it didn't want to be touched. Harper's lips on her neck, which normally caused her so much pleasure, suddenly turned her stomach cold and slithery, like a snake was moving around her insides. Even though she was throbbing with want, when Harper's fingers came up to find her nipples in a way Elena normally enjoyed, she shifted away unconsciously. She clenched her teeth, hoping Harper wouldn't notice the movement, that maybe the sensation would fade. But Harper stopped, lifting her head in confusion.

"Is something wrong?"

"Sorry. It's not you. Shit. I'm sorry." Elena ran a hand through her hair.

"What is it?"

"I don't know how to explain it. I just…I don't really want to be touched right now."

Harper drew back. "Did I do something?"

Elena shook her head emphatically. "No, no, not at all. This is a me thing. It just happens sometimes, randomly."

"Oh. Okay. No worries. I kind of wish you would have told me, though. I feel a little selfish." Harper laughed awkwardly. "I promise I wouldn't have made you do that if I had known I couldn't return the favor. I'm no pillow princess."

Elena moved forward and dropped a quick kiss to her lips.

"Hey, you can be a pillow princess for me anytime. I promise that was good for me, too, okay? Really fucking good. Like, I am incredibly turned on right now. You wouldn't believe how much." It wasn't a lie. She was still hot and empty and aching, and she wanted more than anything for her body to cooperate and enjoy Harper's touch right now. "I wish you could touch me. I really, really want it. I want you. I always want you."

Harper bit her lip, then opened her mouth like she was going to speak, but then she didn't say anything.

"What?"

"I was just wondering…"

"Yes?"

"If you're interested…I could watch." Harper bit her lip again and looked up at Elena through her eyelashes.

"Watch me?"

Harper nodded. "Watch you touch yourself. And I could touch myself at the same time."

Elena felt her nipples tighten at the words, immediately having a vision of Harper fucking herself.

"Yes, please."

She couldn't believe this was happening. They shifted around a bit until they found the perfect setup. Harper's bed was in the corner of the room, and Elena propped herself up on pillows against one wall while Harper did the same along the other. She watched as Harper reached into her nightstand to pull out a tiny purple vibrator.

"Do you mind?" Harper asked as she held the object up.

"Go right ahead." Elena answered, already caressing her own clit in slow, soft circles. She felt shy at first, but the way Harper's eyes honed in on the movement, darkening, made her lose her inhibitions.

Harper flicked the switch, and the tiny object came to life with a barely discernible hum. Harper touched it to her clit and immediately gasped slightly, her hips twitching.

"Fuck, it's insanely hot to watch you do that," Elena said, picking up the pace a bit with her own movements.

Harper's eyes were hooded and dark, and she moved the vibrator slowly up and down through her folds. Her legs were spread wide, and Elena could smell the dampness, could see her curls, could smell the moisture, could see her thighs trembling.

Elena moved her other hand down and slid one finger inside herself. She watched Harper's eyes follow the gesture and saw her chest heave. Fuck, Elena wanted to touch her nipples, wanted to suck them in her mouth and hear the way Harper gasped.

Instead, she withdrew the finger she had just used to fuck herself, slipped it into her mouth, and sucked the moisture off. Harper groaned. "Oh my god."

Elena wet another finger, then used them both to twist her own nipples. The sensation shot like lightning down to her core, and she felt herself grow instantly wetter. She kept playing, first with one nipple, then another, the pressure growing inside her like a balloon ready to pop.

She slid her finger back down her body and slid one finger inside. This time, it slipped in even more easily. "I'm so wet."

Harper watched, her own movements continuing. "So am I. I need something inside."

"Fuck yourself for me. Slow."

Harper set the vibrator aside, then slipped two fingers inside herself and groaned again. Elena mirrored the movement, even though she wanted it hard and deep.

Slowly, she picked up the pace until she was thrusting in and out of herself quickly. *Yes.* This was exactly what she needed. She watched Harper do the exact same, and it was almost too much. She felt her breathing increase, desperately trying to hold off but praying for the orgasm to come all the same, because she was in ecstasy that was almost too great to bear.

Elena watched Harper's fingers disappear inside of herself and thought about what it was like to be buried deep inside her, to fuck her hard, to hit just the right angle that made her come all over Elena's fingers.

Orgasm hit Elena like a wave, and a second later, she watched as Harper came, her head thumping back against the wall, her mouth open and eyes squeezed shut.

Afterward, they cuddled close, buried in Harper's soft comforter, facing each other, with Elena's arm draped over Harper's hip. The contact was nice, calming. She loved the way Harper's skin smelled, could spend hours there, inhaling her, enjoying the silence.

If she did that, though, she would fall asleep, and she shouldn't do that.

She would just stay for a few more minutes.

Just as Elena was thinking she should leave, Harper's breathing started to slow. She nestled into the crook between Elena's arm and her shoulder and mumbled, "I love you."

Then Harper turned over, faced the other direction, and almost immediately began snoring. They were tiny, delicate snores Elena would have found endearing at any other time. Instead, she was frozen to the spot, and the sound blended together with the buzzing in her ears.

Elena stared at the mess of curls splayed across the pillow, as though Harper's hair would have any answer for what her lips had just said.

Because there was no mistaking those words. Her voice might have been slurred from drowsiness, but they had been clear as day.

Shit.

CHAPTER SIXTEEN

I love you.

The words echoed a steady beat as Elena drove home, went to bed, and stared at the ceiling for an hour before finally drifting off to sleep. They were the first thing she heard when she woke up, and they accompanied her as she went through one of her standard off-season workouts, her post-workout shower, and all of her morning errands.

She hooked up the aux cord in her car and put on Fleetwood Mac, blasting the volume as she drove back home.

A notification for a text from Harper popped up on her phone while she was making the quinoa for her salad, and she read it on the lock screen and swiped it away, so it wouldn't show as read.

Elena had no idea what she was supposed to do.

That was all she knew. She knew that she *didn't know* what to do. She didn't know if Harper was aware of what she had said. Elena assumed she probably wasn't. But whether Harper was aware of it or not, she still felt the emotion. Harper was an honest person. She wouldn't say something she didn't mean.

Elena didn't want to think about it anymore, but it seemed to be the only thing she could think about. But even though she couldn't stop thinking about it, she didn't seem to have any feelings in response. Only thoughts. It was like all her emotions, everything deep down, had suddenly been covered in deep, impenetrable ice.

But that was okay. It was easier. She didn't want to go digging and explore whatever was happening below the surface. Whatever it was, it was bound to be a mess. It was easier to live with the ice.

It was better to stay objective, and she could stay more objective without feelings. And objectively, she knew this was a disaster.

The problem was that they had been spending too much time together. Elena had barely spent more than forty-eight hours away from her at a time, even before they started their arrangement. It had clearly created some sort of false, deep intimacy, and that was why Harper felt the way she did. Or, thought she felt the way she did. It wasn't likely that she was truly in love with Elena. Even if she'd had a crush when Elena was younger, they'd really only known each other for a month.

She was thinking about it again. Elena shoveled the first few bites of her salad into her mouth. It was a delicious salad, with fresh green romaine and arugula, quinoa, grilled chicken, cucumbers, shredded carrots, and her favorite lemon ginger dressing.

She could barely taste it. She shoveled it down so she could get done with eating and back on the move.

Elena kept herself as distracted as possible. She grabbed the magnetic notepad off her refrigerator and wrote down every tiny thing she could think of that she'd been meaning to do, from vacuuming out her car to looking into possible destinations for a vacation after their World Cup victory the following year (she knocked on wood mentally). She'd always wanted to go somewhere tropical. It was about time she did. She'd thought about inviting Dee and Margot, to see if maybe spending some time together could force them to get along.

But then again, maybe she should just let things stay the way they were and keep them apart until they forgot all about each other. It wasn't good to mix different parts of her world. Things got too messy that way. It was easier when everyone stayed in their assigned boxes.

And now she was back to thinking about Harper.

Elena groaned aloud, and she moved onto the next item on her list.

She needed to go shoe shopping, which she absolutely hated to do.

Before she left, she responded to Harper's text, which had been an invitation to get together the following day. Elena declined, stating that she needed to concentrate on practicing and getting into prime shape for camp in a couple of weeks.

She didn't wait for the guilt to kick in. She just kept moving.

Just as she was opening the door to leave, her phone dinged with a notification from her dad, asking if she was free to chat. For the first time all day, Elena smiled.

"Mba'ëichapa nde asaje?" Elena greeted her father a few minutes later when he answered her FaceTime call. She curled up on the couch, propping her iPad up on her knees. Her mom was from Columbia and had made sure Elena grew up speaking both Spanish and English, but Elena liked to greet her dad in Guarani, even though those few phrases were basically all she knew how to say, because it made him smile.

The picture was grainy at first but then cleared. Somehow, she was still surprised every time she saw him and his hair was more gray than black. She was so accustomed to it being dark that it took her aback, even though they called at least once a month.

He took a sip from a metal straw, and Elena smiled, because some things would never change. Eduardo Torres loved his *tereré* and hardly ever went anywhere without it. Elena had gotten him a custom thermos a few years ago with a Cerro Porteño logo, and he'd acted like she'd just announced she was pregnant with the grandchild he and her mother were always pestering her about.

"Missing my favorite daughter."

"Missing your only daughter," Elena said with a smile, knowing that he enjoyed the exchange every time they called, regardless of how many times it had occurred.

"What, just because you're my only daughter, I can't miss you? Why did you abandon us down here in this land of godforsaken humidity?"

"I think I heard you say that more about ice when we were growing up than I ever heard you complain about the humidity."

"True enough. So, are you crawling the walls yet?"

"What?"

"With boredom. Ready to get back to *fútbol*."

"Always. You know me."

For once, soccer wasn't the first thing on her mind. It was second, behind Harper. Harper always seemed to occupy so much space in her mind these days. It made it difficult not to think about her.

"When is your next game?"

"November! Not too far." Elena perked up even more. "Actually, I was going to call you and mom! The camp is in Florida, so I can spend a few days with you after it's over."

"Wonderful! Your mother will be glad to hear it. She doesn't stop talking about how much she misses you. If the weather there wasn't so bad for her arthritis, we'd go back in a heartbeat to be near you."

"You know there's no reason for that. I can come see you any time. And who would keep those mahjong players on their toes? And the shuffleboard? Plus, I know you'd miss Bill and Marge. Don't deny it."

Elena said it with a straight face. She was teasing, but he fell for it, falling into a rant in Spanish about their annoying neighbors who lived in the other half of the duplex. They had a running rivalry with them in their different events in the senior community. She knew her father secretly enjoyed the competition, even though he pretended otherwise.

Her mother, she wasn't entirely sure of. She'd always been harder to read.

"Where is Mom, by the way?"

"Oh, Soledad got one of those machines that can cut out tiny little paper shapes," he said, referring to her mother's best friend. "So they're over at her house cutting out tiny Virgin Marys or something for their Christmas cards. That's their new favorite thing to do. So she left your old dad here all alone."

"Well, I'm glad to see you. I've missed you."

"So, tell me what you've been up to now that you're not on the pitch all the time."

"Oh, I'm still on the pitch plenty." Not as much as she would usually be, though. She'd been spending most of her time with Harper. But she didn't want to talk about that. "Don't worry, I haven't lost my touch. I could still get a PK past you on the first try."

He scoffed. "You fly down here and just try."

She laughed, loud and throaty, and it felt good.

Somehow, talking to her dad about *fútbol* and food and the retirement community gossip, she felt better than she had all day.

Harper stared at her phone, rereading Elena's text. She was saying no to hanging out because she needed to train for camp? Elena already practiced every day. She had nothing else to do now besides hang around. She had camp in two weeks, and she'd mentioned having a photo shoot for some National Team sponsor at some point soon? Harper didn't remember when.

The point was, it certainly wasn't soccer that was keeping her away from Harper.

No, Harper knew entirely what it was that was keeping Elena away.

Harper had told her.

Had it been stupid? Possibly.

Had it been true? Yes.

Was she sorry? Unclear as of yet.

Elena clearly needed some time to process. She wasn't by nature a deceitful person; she'd told Harper on multiple occasions that she hated lying. The fact that she'd lied about this meant that she didn't want to talk to Harper about the real reason. Really, really didn't want to.

Harper couldn't blame her. She had gone directly against what she had promised. She'd promised not to feel anything, not to rope Elena into anything serious. She'd known the conditions from the beginning.

But everything had changed for her. Yet nothing at all had, at the same time.

Being around Elena so often had simply highlighted everything Harper loved about her. Her generosity, her sense of humor, her ability to laugh at herself. How serious she got when she talked about soccer, and how she wasn't only in it for the glory. The way she truly cared about everyone on her team.

Harper felt like if she had the same opportunity Elena had, she would probably want a little more of the glory for herself. She wouldn't blame Elena in the slightest.

But that simply wasn't Elena. It wasn't her nature. She didn't like the spotlight in any way, shape, or form.

And Harper loved that about her.

She loved everything about her.

Hence, the problem.

"So, what are you going to do?" Angel asked, her words fuzzy with the yawn she let out. She'd just woken up when Harper had called, even though it was evening. Harper was in the back room of Bewitched, printing out shelf labels with her label maker and putting them on the shelves.

"I'm going to wait it out, I think. Give her some space.

I'm the one who did what I wasn't supposed to. She's not in the wrong here."

"I mean, I'd argue she's a little in the wrong. You shouldn't just freeze someone out."

"It hasn't even been a day. Give her some time."

"I guess."

"I just…kind of wish she'd talk to me. Tell me why it is that she doesn't want a serious relationship."

"She didn't tell you?"

"She did. She said it's because soccer is her top priority, and she knows she can't be fully committed and everything someone needs in a relationship until she is retired."

"So, you already know why."

"I just don't know if that's the whole story. Surely there's a compromise that could be worked out, you know? I don't know what her ex expected, but being with a professional athlete, obviously you've got to know they're not going to be able to put you first all the time. They have important commitments, the same as anyone in a high-stakes career."

"Remind me again how you feel about her not getting to come to your grand opening?"

Harper sighed and moved to the other side of the shelf, putting on the sticker that said *Two-Player Games*. "Yeah, yeah. Listen, it's easier said than done." It just rankled a bit.

"Let's hypothetically say she does agree. She's into you, and she wants to try the relationship thing. You're okay knowing you'll always come second to a sport? You've already come second your whole damn life."

"It's different, though."

"I just don't want you doing some weird, unhealthy thing where you get into a relationship where you feel inferior, just because it's what you're used to."

"Okay, one, stop trying to use that one psych class you took against me. And two, it's completely different."

"Are you sure?"

"Absolutely. The biggest thing is that Elena is honest about it. She's not pretending to love me and soccer equally, but then ignoring me or making me feel like shit with crappy comments."

"To be fair, she's not pretending to love you at all."

"Um, ouch?"

"Sorry, babe. I just don't want you to get too far into this in your head, you know? I agree that giving her some space is a good idea. Then you should talk to her. Ask her how she's feeling, and if she'd be up for something with you. Assuming that's what you want?"

"Duh. That's what I was thinking, too. Something like that. I just really think we should give this a shot. I don't want her to shoot me down just because she's scared I might be like her ex."

"You just have to remember it's not only about you. You're only half of the equation. Less, if we're counting the baggage her ex probably left her with."

"I don't know. She's mentioned a therapist. And she seems pretty well-adjusted."

"So do I at first glance, and yet you are fully aware of my fully unhinged self."

"I wouldn't have you any other way," Harper said with a smile.

"Okay, I've got to go shower and get my morning coffee going."

"Draw lots of pretty things for me!"

Harper hung up and went back to her job. She had just finished the shelf and was about to start the next one when there was a knock at the door, and a voice said, "Hello?"

Harper walked to the front room and found Ayumi standing just inside the door. She waved her in.

"Ayumi! You made it!" Harper cringed internally at herself, since this was, in fact, Ayumi's first time showing up as a hired employee. It wasn't like Harper would expect her to blow it off.

"I do try to do that sometimes when I'm working," she said with a smile.

"An excellent work ethic. I knew I liked you."

"So, what are we doing tonight?"

Over the next two hours, Harper walked Ayumi through how the café worked, from the simple drinks they would serve in-house to the food items they would be teaming up with Midnight Vegan to serve. They went down the hall, and Harper introduced Ayumi to Vivian.

"I'll introduce you to Meg and Sappho, too, sometime," she said as they walked back through the corridor. "They're kind of like the real ghosts of the building. You never know when they'll appear."

They walked back into Bewitched, and Harper showed her around the different sections. Ayumi talked about her friends at college who were excited to come check Bewitched out once it opened. It was a productive shift, and they got a lot done.

Even though she wanted to, Harper didn't check her phone. She only looked at it after Ayumi had left.

Elena hadn't texted once.

Harper tried to swallow down her disappointment as she walked back to her apartment alone.

CHAPTER SEVENTEEN

I don't think we should do this anymore.

Elena backspaced until the text field in front of her was blank again, the cursor blinking at her mockingly. The thread of texts above the empty box beckoned her, with their jokes and their deeper conversations and, most of all, the memory of how much simpler everything had been when they were sent.

Not like now.

Elena sighed and looked up to the ceiling of her home office, as though the blank white space would be of any assistance.

She felt a little bad about the idea of sending a text. But this wasn't like last time, when Elena had made a plan based on an assumption, without knowing how Harper felt. This time, she knew how Harper felt.

That was the problem.

Hey. I'm sorry to do this over text, but I don't think the casual thing is going to work out.

No. She cleared everything again, closed her eyes tightly, and pressed her phone to her forehead, feeling the cool screen against her skin.

What the hell was she supposed to do? If she did this in

person, Harper would very likely ask why. And Elena didn't want to say it. She didn't want to put Harper in that position, because Harper probably didn't know, and Elena didn't want to embarrass her like that. *Oh, yeah, I don't want to have amazing sex with you anymore. I know that you're in love with me, and I can't deal with that right now.*

What an asshole move that would be.

And yes, logically, she was still doing that. But she would at least spare Harper the humiliation of knowing that Elena knew her secret.

It had been two days since Elena had blown off Harper's text about hanging out, and Harper hadn't said anything else. She obviously knew something was wrong.

Elena had run out of the tasks she'd made for herself around noon today. There was nothing else for her to do. The laundry was done, she'd meal prepped, she'd bought cleaning supplies for approximately the next decade. She'd even started planning a vacation, just to give her brain something else to focus on.

But then she found that every time she tried to imagine going somewhere new, she imagined Harper by her side. She'd found herself considering what Harper would like, whether she would prefer the beach or the mountains, if she would want to go somewhere cold or hot.

And everything about that was wrong.

Instead, Elena closed out the browser and brought up the folder with the video files of all her games. She navigated to the folder for last month and clicked to start the video, grabbing the bright blue dollar store notebook that lived in her desk drawer. She watched the game at a quick speed, pausing, backing up, and taking notes every so often. Dee was right. Her passing game had improved. She knew it from the stats that the coaching staff always read off to them, but it was another thing to see it played back in front of her.

Her passes were tighter, more concise. Of course, they'd

never been bad. Pretty much all of soccer involved passing, and with her position as a winger, the skill was especially important. But it was good to see her hard work paying off. Still, she found small things to work on. She'd scored once in this game with three more shots on goal, and she studied each failed shot closely, watching for tells or ways she could have improved her footwork.

She was one of the best in the country, but that didn't mean she ever stopped striving to be better. The best players never did.

An incoming FaceTime call interrupted her, and Elena paused the game before swiping to accept the call.

"Hey, stranger," Elena said, holding up her phone.

"Hey, stranger, yourself. How are you?"

Not great, thanks to your sister falling in love with me, but thanks for asking.

"I'm okay. Just watching some tape."

"You know you're on vacation, right?"

Elena frowned. "Off-season isn't vacation. There's always work to be done. The players who take the whole time off are the ones who—"

"Elena, I know. I was just messing with you."

"Sorry, I'm still deep in the zone. What's up?"

"Just wanted to see if you wanted to get together at some point around the thirteenth? I'm coming back for Harper's grand opening for a couple of days."

Elena gritted her teeth. Of course Margot would want to talk about it. "I can't go to that, actually. I have a National Team photo shoot the day before and then go straight to camp."

"Oh, damn."

"I know, it sucks." Well, that's what she had thought before, anyway. Now she was grateful for the excuse to avoid Harper.

"Weird that they would schedule a photo shoot right before camp."

"Well, it's not the whole team, just some veterans. It's for

Dee's retirement."

"She's retiring?"

Elena nodded. "This is her last camp with the National Team. She'll be fully retired at the end of the year."

"How exciting for her. Now she can spend all her time sitting in bars, hitting on women."

Elena felt a stir of annoyance. "That's not all she does. I don't get why you hate her so much."

"She's annoying. And she hit on me the first time we met."

"Everyone hits on you. You're gorgeous."

Margot just shrugged and sipped her wine.

"I was wondering something, actually," Elena said. "Speaking of vacations."

"Were we speaking of vacations?"

"Yeah. I was thinking of taking one next year."

Margot's eyebrows shot up. "Really?"

"And I was thinking you could come with me?"

"Me?" Her eyebrows jumped right back down, and she was staring at Elena like she'd grown a second head. "You know I don't do vacations."

"Not every trip we take together is going to wind up like the camping fiasco of '13."

Margot visibly shuddered. "Why in god's name did we think going camping was a good idea?"

"It seemed like it at the time!"

"Not to me. I still can't believe I let you talk me into it."

"Listen. How was I supposed to know the wind turned into a fucking hurricane at night up there? And the bear we really couldn't have foreseen."

"There were literally lockers to keep your shit away from the bears. That was the first sign."

"Hey, you didn't turn around and leave. We were both in that tent."

"Explain that to my pillow. Oh, wait, you can't, because it *blew away*."

"At least we learned from our mistakes?"

"One would think. I do still have the equipment in my garage, though."

"Why, exactly?"

"I don't know. You like nature and shit; I thought you might want it again."

"Excuse me for enjoying nature, unlike some people."

"Listen, I like to stay in a firmly climate-controlled environment, as the gods of science and innovation intended, and I will not be shamed for that."

Elena chuckled.

"Okay. Well, I'm going to go if you don't mind. I still have a few things to finish up here. I just wanted to give you a heads-up about me being in town, but I guess you'll be off being a big-shot."

"You're a big-shot, too, y'know. Otherwise you'd be here now."

"Fair enough."

They said goodbye, and Elena hung up. She hadn't noticed the notification she'd had sitting there before. It was a text from Harper, from twenty minutes ago.

Elena opened it out of curiosity. It was just a meme about something they'd discussed a few days before. It was meant to make her laugh.

She didn't laugh.

Instead, she tossed her phone onto the plushly carpeted floor. Between talking to Margot and the meme, too many things were reminding her of Harper now. She needed to think about something else.

She grabbed her notebook and twisted her desk chair back toward the computer.

Her inner therapist was screaming at her (or, rather, Elena could imagine her staring at her in a slightly reproving manner and waiting for her to fix her own mistake), but she didn't care. It was what she needed to do. She could process things later.

Elena pressed play. She scribbled notes and watched every move closely, and didn't let herself think about Harper at all.

When she found herself looking at the art frame, which Harper had helped her pick out at IKEA, she took it off the wall and carried it down to the basement.

There it was, in black and white. It was officially over. Harper stared down at her phone, and she only realized she'd started crying when the words started to go blurry. Shit. She couldn't cry here, on full display behind the main counter. Ayumi was in the next room, sorting endless pieces into tiny plastic baggies, but she was barely out of Harper's sight line and could easily walk in with no notice.

Harper swiped the tears away roughly, then slammed her phone onto the bar with more force than she meant to. Her screen had dimmed but still hadn't locked, so the message was still visible. She read it again.

Elena (7:22 P.M.): Hey. I just wanted to let you know that I don't think we should continue with the whole "casual" thing. I don't think it's the right call for us. But I really hope we can stay friends! :)

It was the smiley face at the end that killed her. After breaking Harper's entire heart in a single text, she had the audacity to end it in a smiley face.

Harper couldn't breathe.

She wanted to be angry. She wanted to be livid. She wanted to be completely, insensibly enraged.

But she wasn't. She was just sad. Because Elena had every right to end things via text message. It wasn't a relationship; she wasn't breaking up with her. She was simply putting an end to the casual arrangement. Ben had probably done the same, since they'd pretty much only ever texted. She didn't remember. Probably something like, **It's been fun, but I've met someone. Have a great life. Thanks for the awesome sex!**

Not exactly, of course. But something like that. Because it was no big deal. Just like she and Elena weren't supposed to have been a big deal.

But they'd been a big deal to her.

And while she had been okay with giving Elena some time to process, Harper realized now that she hadn't truly believed Elena would end things.

It wasn't like she was delusional; she hadn't believed Elena would burst into Bewitched one day and confess she was in love with Harper, too. It was far too fast. For Elena, this was all new. It had only been a month since the gala, and while Elena had always been special to her, seeing Harper in this different light was brand new for Elena. She understood that.

In short, she hadn't expected a miracle. But she also hadn't expected it to end like this. Not in a single text. Not without at least talking to her.

Harper just prayed that Elena wouldn't cut her out of her life entirely.

She inhaled slowly and let the breath out again.

It was okay. It didn't make a difference. They would still be friends, would just change back to how things had been before the sex.

Harper had absolutely no one to blame but herself. She'd scared Elena away.

"I'm going to Midnight Vegan to grab a smoothie. You want anything?" Harper hollered back to Ayumi. It might be slightly rude, but she didn't want to show her face right now, which probably demonstrated clearly that she had been crying. She didn't want to start their work relationship by showing she was some kind of overly emotional person who couldn't let go of their personal issues during work hours. Or someone who was just generally dramatic. Or, worse, she didn't want to Ayumi to be uncomfortable enough that she quit.

"I'm good, but thanks!" Ayumi replied from the other room immediately, and Harper breathed a sigh of relief.

Harper went to Midnight Vegan and ordered a chocolate chip muffin. She changed her mind on the smoothie and ordered a coconut milk hot chocolate instead, because nothing was more comforting than hot chocolate. She needed all the comfort she could get right now. She just needed to power through the next hour Ayumi would be there, and then she could go home and curl up on her bed.

Vivian brought her order out from the back, and immediately, she frowned.

"What's wrong?"

"Is it that obvious?" Harper asked.

"Yes. You don't need to tell me, though, if you don't want."

"I do, but..." Harper shot a look over at the cashier.

"Here, follow me." Vivian led the way back to the kitchen and closed the door. "Here. There's no one else here."

The whole story came spilling out, from her high school crush, to their arrangement, to Elena's text. Harper told the whole thing quickly, punctuated by tears only once she reached the end.

"Shit, honey, I'm so sorry. Is it okay if I hug you?" Vivian asked, and her warm brown eyes were too much.

Her strong arms wrapped around Harper, and she smelled of sugar and vanilla, and Harper felt a little better immediately. Her chest still felt like someone had stuck an ice pick in the middle of it, but maybe one that was slightly less pointy than before. She took a deep breath, and Vivian stepped back. Harper's head barely came up to her shoulder.

Harper sniffed and wiped a stray tear from her cheek. "Thank you."

"Of course. Need a tissue?"

"Yes, please." Harper looked around, and Vivian handed her a paper towel to wipe her nose. She tossed it in the trash. "Do I look like I've been crying?"

"Maybe just run to the bathroom and splash some cold water on your face."

Harper followed her advice, then came back out. Vivian gave a nod of approval and handed over her hot cocoa and muffin. "That's better."

Harper smiled weakly. "Thanks for your magic hug."

"Anytime."

Harper was startled by the sound of a door banging against the wall, and she turned toward the noise. Ayumi stood there, her eyes wide, phone pressed to her cheek.

"Harper?" Ayumi glanced around and then saw her, rushing forward. "I smelled smoke. I'm not sure where it's coming from, but it's pretty strong. I already called the fire department."

"Shit! It's the ghost!" Harper heard a voice behind her say, and she turned to find the cashier from that first day she'd visited, who couldn't shut up about the ghost and Bewitched being haunted.

It took another second to process everything, and before she even fully realized it, Harper's legs were propelling her down the hall toward the place she had started to think of as her new home.

A thin, hazy layer of smoke was already floating up near the ceiling, and Harper's heart plummeted to the floor.

It was going to burn down. All of this. All of her work. All of her love. All of her savings.

It was all going to burn.

CHAPTER EIGHTEEN

Harper stood at the bar of Bewitched the following Thursday. She looked around at least once an hour now, grateful that she had a building to be looking at.

Everything looked fantastic. It was two days until their grand opening, and you couldn't tell at all that there had been a fire there a week before. A tiny fire, thanks to Ayumi's quick reflexes and their proximity to the fire station, due entirely to the faulty electrical wiring that had caused the occasional light flickering she'd once mentioned to Elena.

Not a ghost, as she was quick to point out to the Midnight Vegan cashier, whose name, it turned out, was October.

"Sure, that's what you think. Skeptics can always find some way to explain things away."

Harper had barely refrained from rolling her eyes.

She had already had it out with the landlord for not ensuring the wiring was up to code. An electrician had come in the next day to do all the necessary rewiring, and there hadn't been so much as a flicker since.

Weirdly, Harper felt better than ever about the Grand Opening now. She always had the feeling that something major could never happen without one big thing coming along and trying to fuck it up.

And it had happened. The worst had happened.

But she was still here. Bewitched was still here. Ayumi was also still here, and she now possessed an infinite amount of Harper's gratitude, as well as the biggest bonus check Harper had been able to afford.

Oddly, something else had come out of it.

The local news station had covered the fire, and @bewitchedbishop had gained over 500 followers on Instagram in the past week. Harper had taken advantage of the opportunity, posting several times. Once with the damage, once thanking the fire department, and once with a pretty, aesthetic picture of the main room, all fixed up, announcing that everything was okay, but that they were all welcome to say hello to the ghost at the grand opening on Friday.

As for Elena, Harper hadn't heard from her in days.

Harper was being an adult about the whole thing. She'd texted back that she understood and that she also wanted to stay friends.

But Elena hadn't dropped by Bewitched once. She hadn't texted about the fire, so Harper assumed she didn't even know it had happened. Normally, she would have told her immediately, but nothing about their situation was normal. And Harper didn't have time to sit down and think about the situation and decide what to do, because she'd been too busy with repairs, on top of getting everything else ready for the grand opening.

Harper listened to music to drown out her thoughts. She played the new Blackpink album through the overhead speakers, because listening to Taylor Swift now made her think of Elena. And Taylor really had too many sad songs. Harper had never really realized it before.

Everything made her think of Elena, really, but she knew that would pass. She would heal and move on with her life, but it would take time. She just hoped Elena would stay in her life as a friend, not only as someone who happened to exist on the periphery through Margot.

Harper lifted another box onto the counter and sliced it open, taking care not to go too deep with the box cutter, refraining from damaging the smaller box inside. She'd finally received her shipment of the brand new board games she would be selling.

The board games that would be sitting on the shelves Elena had made.

Harper wasn't sure how long it would take to get to the point where she could look at the shelves and not think about Elena, but she really wanted to get there soon. To be frank, it really sucked that they were front and center in the place where she would be spending at least ten hours a day for the next several months, until she had a steady enough stream of income that she would be able to hire a full-time employee.

They were such nice shelves, though. She remembered how Elena had beamed with pride when she'd showed them to Harper.

Harper shook her head to clear it and moved on to thinking about her business. The thing that was most important right now. Everything was nearly perfect. She set out two boxes of Catan on the shelf, right next to Wingspan. Despite not being one of her favorites, Catan was easily one of her top-selling games. She pulled the next game out of the box and smiled. Calico, her favorite game to hand-sell, featuring the adorable sleeping cat on the front.

She mentally ran through her checklist for the day. Most everything was done. Vivian had all the supplies for the food, and they had their communication system set up, so they could easily inform Midnight Vegan when food had been ordered. Then October or one of the other Midnighters would walk the food over to the main counter at Bewitched, where Harper or Ayumi would deliver it to the correct person.

They had received the last of their drink supplies. They had a few teas, dry hot chocolate and masala chai mixes, two types of brewed coffee, and a few syrups to make drinks with their tiny espresso machine.

Of course, all the drinks had fun fandom names, such as Middle Earth Latte and TARDIS Tea (which was always served in a bright blue mug, of course), just to make everything a bit more fun. Ayumi had made an excellent suggestion of taking the blank wall in the back and painting The Bewitched Bishop in Gallifreyan. To be honest, Harper was surprised she hadn't thought of the idea. It was, frankly, brilliant, and would be an excellent addition to their Instagram and the atmosphere.

Everything was ready.

But Elena wasn't here.

Just as Harper was afraid tears might start to emerge, though she was trying very hard not to let them, her phone dinged with a text message.

She looked down to find that it was from her mother. For a split second, she thought it might be a message congratulating her on the opening. She was pleasantly surprised.

But when she unlocked her phone, all she could do was let out a dry laugh that was the opposite of what a laugh should be like.

It was a picture of a beautiful Victorian-style house surrounded by beautiful trees in what was no doubt beautiful Vermont, where her parents were, instead of being here, supporting her.

Harper took a deep breath.

She didn't respond like she might once have. Instead, she just put the phone away and turned back to her games.

She would be okay. Margot's flight would be here in a couple of hours. At least she had one family member who actually seemed to care about her, even if she had an odd way of showing it sometimes.

She was building her own family. She had Angel and Vivian and—

Well, she'd thought she'd had Elena. Not in the way her heart yearned for, but at least as a friend.

It seemed that she might not even have that anymore.

But she would be okay.

She placed another game on the shelf, then another, then another. Eventually, there were no more.

Elena hated flying.

She'd grown accustomed to it after years as a professional athlete, but nearly everything about it was still terrible. The plane was loud, the food was terrible, the movement was unpredictable, and that wasn't even mentioning the people. She'd once gotten stuck next to a woman who'd spend an entire two-hour flight trying to talk to Elena about her relationship with Jesus. Then there were her personal nemeses: people who watched videos on their phones without headphones.

Elena, on the other hand, was a huge fan of headphones. She never got onto a plane without two pairs—her favorite wireless, noise-canceling earbuds along with a backup wired pair, which she didn't have to worry about running out of battery.

The headphones improved things, as did the fact that the higher-ups had started springing for business class in the past couple of years.

Elena stowed her things away and sat in her seat, grateful for the extra leg room and the fact that she had a window. She hated both being climbed over and climbing over others, but given the choice, she preferred to be in control of when it would happen.

And now she was flying in exactly the opposite direction of where she wanted to be. She wanted to be going to Florida for camp, where she could at least distract herself with soccer. Instead, she was flying to California for a photo shoot with a National Team sponsor. She, Dee, and a couple of the other veterans from the National Team would be there. The shoot would last all day tomorrow, and then on Saturday morning, she'd fly directly to Florida for camp.

Elena buckled herself in, adjusted her earbuds, and waited for takeoff.

Elena had everything she needed to make the flight as bearable as possible. She'd worn the high-waisted black yoga pants she liked to wear while flying. She had a fully charged phone with her favorite app for ambient sounds. She had a bottle of her favorite brand of water. At the very least, it was a beautiful day with white, fluffy clouds, which she always enjoyed looking at. But today, even the clouds couldn't cheer her up.

Everything just felt wrong.

It had been that way for days now, so it wasn't something she could blame on the plane.

She knew exactly what it was. It was Harper. The lack of her. The thought of her. The way Elena knew she must be hurting and wondering why.

Elena shut her eyes and breathed through her nose. This was one of the things she'd been worried about. That she wouldn't be able to sit with her thoughts for long enough to make it to California without examining what was going on underneath. She was reaching the end of how long she could ignore whatever it was beneath the ice.

Well, if she couldn't ignore Harper and focus on something else, at least she could focus on the facts.

Was it possible she'd made a mistake?

But that was the thing. She hadn't.

She *knew* she hadn't.

It was time for a pro/con list.

She pulled out her phone and started a new note. She wrote down every single pro and con she could think of. By the end, it was clear. She had made the obviously correct decision.

So why did she still feel *wrong*? Why did being without her feel like the time Elena had been without soccer? Why did she feel like she'd make a mistake, even though she could see in front of her, in black and white, that she hadn't?

Elena wasn't so tied to data that she couldn't see that sometimes life didn't quite match up with a pro/con list.

But this shouldn't be one of those cases.

Maybe she should give a weight to each of her reasons. It would make the process more complicated, but it would also be more accurate. For example, the fact that Harper didn't like country music barely deserved to be on the list. But then there was the fact that talking to her made Elena feel like she was sitting in a warm bath with a plate of her favorite brand of chicken nuggets.

In other words, completely at peace and happy and okay with being herself, even though that might be a little weird.

But it didn't matter how much math she did. At the end of the day, soccer was her priority. The last thing she wanted to do was cause Harper pain.

On the other hand...Elena looked down at the pro list, and at the bottom, she'd written **Harper** with the intention of finishing it with another item for her list. She had forgotten what she'd originally wanted to put there, had probably gone off down a rabbit hole with her thoughts.

But when she went back to backspace it, she couldn't make herself hit the button.

She just sat there, her thumb hovering over the key, staring at that single word.

Harper.

Each letter came together to form a knife that pierced through the protective layer of ice and directly into her heart. Her hand moved to her chest, rubbing at the pain that suddenly blossomed there. The movement didn't soothe the ache. In fact, it got worse by the second as she pictured red hair, fingers stained with paint, a t-shirt with holes and the adorable snort-laugh Harper sometimes did when she was surprised by how funny something was.

The name stared up at her like an accusation.

But of what? All she'd done was what she'd known needed to be done, for the good of them both.

And yes. Yes, she was suffering. Now that the ice had cracked, it was like the wrongness she'd felt before but multiplied by a thousand. She felt like someone had ripped out her intestines and tangled them all up before shoving them back inside.

But she didn't know what to do with that. She didn't know how to reconcile the fact that she was hurting and Harper was hurting, but ultimately, it was still the better choice. It was a short-term hurt.

A future hurt, a long-term hurt, would be so much worse. It was a fact.

Still, she couldn't bring herself to backspace the name.

Instead, Elena closed out her notes app and reached into the pocket of the seat in front of her where she'd stowed her book. It was a Stephen King she'd never read, impulse-bought at the airport twenty minutes before her flight. She'd been overwhelmed by a sudden fear of being trapped on a plane with no drills or errands to run, nowhere to go to escape her own thoughts. She thanked her earlier self for her wisdom and cracked open the cover, hoping it would be scary enough to distract her. She switched her ambient noise to rain sounds and flipped to the first chapter, letting the new words take the place of the one that had blinked up at her from her phone screen.

Elena pushed open her hotel room door at nine P.M. to find Dee already there. Jess and Tamika were probably sharing the room next door. Jess was the goalkeeper, and Tamika was the left winger to counter Elena's right. Of the four of them, Elena was the youngest by a year, but she'd been on the team the same amount of time as Tamika.

"What crawled up your ass?" were the first words Dee

spoke to her.

"'Hi' to you, too."

They talked a bit about their flights, but Dee clearly got the message that Elena didn't really want to talk tonight. Instead, they both headed to bed for an early night. The photo shoot was to take place late-morning the next day, and Elena didn't want to show up looking exhausted.

She tossed and turned most of the night anyway, and when her alarm went off the next morning, she felt like she'd barely even closed her eyes.

She made it through the photo shoot without any issues. Thankfully, with the insane amount of makeup they all had on, Frankenstein would have looked like a Victoria's Secret model. The bags under her eyes after the nearly sleepless night were no match for the power of modern cosmetics.

Elena begged off of dinner with the three others, claiming that she had to call her parents. Dee gave her a knowing look, but Tamika and Jess just waved her off and said they'd see her the next day.

Elena didn't call her parents, though she did text her mom the goofy selfie she'd snagged with the others in-between shots.

Elena read for a while, and then Dee came back from dinner with the others.

Dee flopped down on her bed and gave Elena a pointed look. "Okay, so tell me what the hell's going on with you?"

"Nothing."

"Nothing, my great aunt Franny's arse."

Elena frowned. "What?"

"It's a thing people say to express disbelief."

"It most definitely is not."

"It could be. And you're dodging the point. Tell me what's wrong."

"I don't want to talk about it."

"And I didn't want to skip ordering dessert at dinner.

Sometimes, grown-ups have to do things we don't want to do. I don't want anything messing with your head during the game tomorrow. Do you think whatever this is might do that?"

Elena considered. Usually, she was good at drowning out anything other than the game when she played. She could shove other issues down until the game was over, so all her focus was on the ball, the pitch, and the players.

But…she thought for a few seconds, then eventually gave a nod of agreement.

"Okay. I'm here whenever you're ready."

Elena told her. She paced back and forth as she recapped everything that had happened since she'd last talked to Dee, then read off her main reasons she'd come up with on the plane, simplified to a short bullet-point list.

Finally, she stopped and waited for Dee's reaction.

"Please tell me you didn't read that to her."

"No. Like I said, it was just that text. I haven't talked to her since."

Dee blew out a breath. "Okay." She thought for a few seconds, and Elena sat down on the bed, waiting for what she would say. Maybe she wouldn't say anything. Maybe she would agree that Elena had done the right thing.

Elena didn't know which one she was hoping for.

Finally, after a long minute, she spoke. "Okay, one, don't tell anyone I said this, but are you sure you want soccer to be your number one priority?"

Elena stared at her. "You're the last person I thought would consider that something that was even up for debate."

"Because I'm the same way?"

It felt like a trap, but Elena agreed anyway. "Yeah. I know you are. We've talked about it." At least a dozen times. There weren't many people who were tied to their careers the way Dee and Elena were.

Dee nodded. "Yeah. I was. And now I have exactly one set of friendlies left before I'm officially fully retired. Do you know what I've learned?"

"What?"

"Making soccer your whole life…isn't always the best choice." The normally carefree expression on Dee's face turned to something completely inscrutable to Elena. "I mean, don't get me wrong. I love my life. I love soccer and the endless line of very flexible, very enthusiastic fans."

Elena grimaced.

"But…" Dee continued. "There's something missing. It's like I'm not sure if I took advantage of my life in the way I should have. I'm almost forty, and—"

"You're thirty-six."

"*Exactly*," Dee continued, with an enthusiasm that implied she thought Elena had been agreeing with her instead of arguing. "I'm nearing the second half of my life, and what do I have? Money, sure. Fame? Yep. Opportunities for empty sex? Always. But now I'm going to have more free time than I've had in my entire life, and I have absolutely no one to spend it with."

"You have me."

Dee shot her a look. "You know what I mean. A serious person. A relationship person. For the times when you lie down at night and just want someone there with you. Not for sex, but just to watch a movie or talk about your day. Like, if you see a guy in a really funny hat walking down the street, who are you going to tell? Stupid stuff. I don't know. I'm not making sense, and this is supposed to be about you, not me. The point is, you have that. You have someone who wants that with you, the way you clearly want it with her." Dee pointed at her. "And don't pretend you don't. When you called the other day, I very kindly refrained from pointing out that you sounded like someone panicking because they'd caught feelings, because I thought you weren't ready to hear it. But you're ready now. You wouldn't be all upset like this if you didn't have feelings for her, too. Do you deny it?"

Elena shook her head. Dee was right. "No," she said, her voice small.

"Good. So, what have we established?" She held up a finger. "Harper has feelings for you." She raised another finger. "You have feelings for her. And you're just, what? Throwing it away because of some stupid ball? Because of a game that's going to start trying to throw *you* away in two or three years?"

Elena blinked. "That's not—" she started. "I—" She tried again.

Dee just waited.

It sounded ridiculous when Dee put it that way. But there was no way her solid, well-thought-out logic could have been so flimsy, so full of holes, and she'd never noticed.

Was there?

She thought about it some more. "I don't think that what you said is quite accurate. I don't think I should stop caring so much about soccer just because I'm not at the beginning of my career. I want to end strong. I want to go for as long as I can. You know that."

"I know. I was being dramatic for effect. But it doesn't have to be one or the other, Elena. I understand why you feel that way. I do. The way Claire left really fucked you up. But I'm going to tell you something you probably don't want to hear."

"What is it?" Elena asked warily.

"You're doing the same thing to Harper right now that Claire did to you."

Elena stared at Dee like she had just hit her over the head with a baseball bat.

Holy shit.

Dee was right.

In her quest to avoid hurting someone the way she'd hurt Claire, she'd wound up hurting Harper the way Claire had hurt her.

Of course, it wasn't exactly the same. She was nipping a

fledgling relationship in the bud, whereas Claire had walked out on a marriage.

But the concept was the same. She was freezing Harper out, not even giving her a chance. Not giving *them* a chance.

Why?

Because she was scared. She was scared of doing the hurting, and she was scared of getting hurt again herself. She was scared she wouldn't be able to balance her career and her relationship with Harper at the same time.

But that didn't make any sense. Elena had been so certain after Claire left that she would have been able to fix things, if only Claire had given her the chance. Elena had grown a lot since then. She'd become more self-aware. She was far more equipped now than she had been then. And, perhaps even more importantly, Harper wasn't Claire.

Elena had to have faith in herself. She had to have faith in Harper.

Most of all, she needed to talk to Harper. If they were going to do this, Elena needed to learn to stop trying to make all the decisions herself. To actually ask Harper, and to listen to what she had to say.

That needed to be her first step.

But how to go about it? Should she just call Harper now, and then wait to talk to her in person until next week, once camp was over? In the past, that would have been her obvious choice, even though it was just a couple of easy friendlies.

She remembered how crushed Harper had looked when Elena had told her she couldn't be at the grand opening.

There was no contest.

She was going home.

Elena stood up and realized that at some point, Dee had stopped paying attention to her. She was reclining on the bed, playing on her phone, and only looked up once Elena cleared her throat. Her gaze was questioning. "So?"

"So, that was a lot to think about."

"Do you know what you're going to do?"

"I do." Elena felt a smile growing that she couldn't hold back. She felt everything settle into place inside her body, righting the wrongness that had been bothering her since she'd sent that text. She took a deep breath. "I'm going home."

Dee grinned at her. "Excellent choice."

"Good luck. I'm sorry I won't be there to play with you for your final game."

"Don't worry, I've got this." Dee winked. "Go get your girl."

CHAPTER NINETEEN

The first thing Elena did the next morning was call Coach Brianna, the National Team head coach. She would have called her last night, but it had been midnight by the time she'd had her revelation. And Coach was notorious about her love of the "early to bed, early to rise" philosophy (much to many of the players' dismay).

The good thing was that when Elena woke a little after five-thirty, she knew that Coach Brianna would already be awake. She tiptoed to the bathroom so as not to wake Dee—who had long held the opposite view of the optimal sleeping time and did not appear to have maintained her new early rising habits—and pulled the door closed with a quiet *snick*.

She flicked through her contacts impatiently, then waited while the phone rang. When Coach answered, the words tumbled out before she could stop them.

"I'm sorry, but I can't make it to camp."

There was a surprised silence on the other end of the line. "Elena?"

"Yes. Sorry. It's me. I have...a family emergency. Thing." She added the word to the end like it would make the sudden call less strange, but it only made the whole thing more awkward.

"Okay." She paused for so long that Elena almost started

speaking again before she continued, "This is unexpected. I hope everything is okay."

Elena knew she was looking for more details. She was grateful that they had known each other long enough that they had built a certain level of trust, which was why she could get away with being vague but truthful. "I appreciate that. I think it will be. I promise I wouldn't do this to you last minute without a good reason, and I apologize."

"Understood. Well, looks like Macauley is going to get that spot she wanted after all."

Elena forced a chuckle. She didn't quite understand Coach's reason for bringing that up. It could be a passive-aggressive dig to make Elena feel bad about canceling, but it could also be something to lighten the moment.

Elena didn't care at this particular moment. She went through the social niceties impatiently and then hung up the phone. A quick glance at the time told her she still had six hours before the flight she'd booked from her phone last night. She looked around the bathroom and pursed her lips, clicking her tongue. What was she going to do to kill time?

She was wide awake, so sleep wasn't an option.

She could take a walk and get some breakfast.

Elena did like breakfast.

She dressed quickly and quietly and let herself out of the room. As she stepped outside into the warm southern California morning and started walking, it suddenly hit her.

She wasn't going to camp. She had never turned down a camp, not once in her entire career. She had a sudden flashback to a nasty fight she and Claire had had one time, when camp had overlapped with their second anniversary.

To Elena, it hadn't really mattered. In her mind, she'd thought they could just celebrate a few days early or a few days late. But Claire hadn't seen it that way.

There were a lot of things Claire hadn't seen. Though, to be fair, there were a lot of things Elena hadn't seen.

Things were different now. Elena wasn't perfect. But all she could do was the exact same thing she did in soccer: look objectively for things she should improve and work on making them better.

Clearly, making decisions without talking to Harper was something she needed to work on.

Harper.

Just the thought of seeing her again filled Elena with a plethora of feelings, from elation to terror that she might reject Elena because of the way she'd behaved.

But looking directly at her fears made them seem a little smaller. A little less difficult to handle. Instead of being afraid, she felt ready for the challenge.

All she could do was be honest. So that's what she would do.

Elena enjoyed her breakfast and then took a ride share to a mall near the airport. She still had a couple of hours before she had to be there for her flight, and she wanted to find Harper something special.

The only thing was, she didn't know what that might be.

Clothes seemed weird, gift baskets too impersonal. She thought about getting Harper another yoga mat, but she already had two of those. A game would be an obvious choice, but it wasn't like she had a shortage of those.

As she was walking around, gazing into all the stores that she passed and waiting for inspiration to strike, and colorful storefront caught her eye. It was one of those stores that sold all kinds of random items you might want for gifts. Colorful headphones, glittery tumblers, and miscellaneous things no one really needed.

She stepped inside, and her gaze went directly to the display of fandom-themed chess sets as though pulled by magic. The first was for a popular kid's book series. The second was for something fantasy-looking that she'd never heard of. Then she pulled out the third, and she grinned in triumph.

It was a Star Wars–themed chess set. It had those white

plastic guys instead of pawns—Harper would know their actual name, but Elena didn't—with various villains on the side labeled *Dark Side* and several lightsaber-wielding heroes on the other. The box was heavy, as though maybe the pieces were made of stone or glass, and the hefty price implied it should be nicely made. But she still asked the bored teenager at the cash register if she could open it to look.

A glance inside ensured the quality, and Elena happily handed over her debit card.

It was perfect.

Now, the only problem was that she had no way of getting it to the airport. The rolling suitcase she'd been pulling around the mall was already completely full of supplies to last her a week. After some contemplation, it became clear that the only solution would be to buy another.

So she went to a department store and bought a carry-on bag and placed the game inside. Opening both suitcases to move her practice clothes from one bag to the other got more than a few strange looks from the few people milling about the mall bright and early, but she didn't care. Once she was satisfied that the chess set was properly packed, she zipped everything back up again and looked at her phone. It was time to head to the airport.

She took a ride share again, stood in line through security, and got to her gate…only to discover that she had been plenty early for the original time, and that the flight was now delayed for an hour.

She cursed.

Well, all she could do was wait.

She waited one hour and then another, her leg jiggling impatiently, walking back and forth in front of the gate area so much she practically wore a groove into the linoleum.

Eventually, she got on the plane with enough time that she should still be able to get to the grand opening in time, as long as all went well.

With all of that time to herself, Elena had plenty of time to think. At first, she considered going for a big, public gesture. Elena felt horrible about her actions and knew she needed to do something to make up for them, but upon reflection, she decided that surprising Harper on an extremely important night, especially without knowing how Harper felt about public displays, wouldn't be about making Harper happy. It would be about assuaging Elena's guilt. So she nixed the idea.

Besides, she'd never quite understood the appeal of grand gestures. Not only because they inevitably made her cringe, imagining how she would feel in such a scenario, but because she genuinely didn't understand the concept. Truthfully, grand gestures did not mean anything. Anyone could hold a boom box over their head or get down on one knee in front of a camera at a baseball game. But those things lasted a few minutes. It was the actions performed every day, in the long term, that truly counted.

And Elena was ready for them.

The grand opening of The Bewitched Bishop had kicked off only twenty minutes before, and already they were nearly at capacity. Harper had had high hopes, but even she was surprised by the turnout.

She wasn't grateful for the fire, but it had certainly turned out to have one hell of a silver lining.

For the first time in a week, she felt a deep sense of happiness and satisfaction that not even imagining Elena's face could dull.

Elena was off-limits for the night. She spent enough time thinking about her already; she was going to do her damnedest not to think about her for the next couple of hours. She was going to celebrate herself and her accomplishments instead.

That was easier to do when she looked at Margot and Angel, sitting together at a two-person table in the front room.

It was easier when she gazed around and saw so many people having a good time.

It was easier when she spotted Shawn's small frame coming through the door, when Vivian appeared with three plates of Second Breakfast Potatoes, one right after another, when Harper accepted compliment after compliment on her mural.

Even Meg and her wife made an appearance.

"Where's Sappho?" Harper asked with a grin, and Meg laughed.

"She's not much of a crowd cat."

Meg wasn't much of a crowd person, either, and she and Pearl disappeared after only a few minutes, though they promised to come back at a quieter time.

She wanted to burst from pride, walking around the room, greeting people, answering questions, seeing that this new business was going to be just as successful as she'd hoped. It made her feel like she was walking on air.

Then Harper heard the front door open and turned to greet the newest customer.

She stopped short, her mouth partially open, and gazed at the woman in front of her, almost not believing her own eyes.

Elena was here.

Elena, who was supposed to be at camp, was here.

Elena, who had basically ghosted her, was here. At the grand opening of The Bewitched Bishop. She was surrounded by people, but suddenly Harper heard nothing but a buzzing in her ears. Vaguely, she recognized that she had been looking without words for far too long, but she didn't know what to say.

"Hi." The word emerged rusty and odd, like she hadn't taken a single drink of water in three days. She hoped Elena couldn't tell over the ambient noise.

"Hi." Her expression was inscrutable. "Congratulations on your grand opening."

"Thank you." She couldn't hold back the question. "What are you doing here?"

Elena swallowed visibly. "I skipped camp. You are more important."

Harper stared at her, certain there was no way she had heard correctly. But there was nothing else she could have said to make her presence make any sense.

"You skipped out on camp with the National Team?" *For me?* She bit the words back just in time. "So you could be here?"

Elena nodded. "Yeah."

Harper didn't know what to say to that. Her emotions were all tangled, and she needed to stay professional, and it was so good to see Elena, and she wanted to kiss her but also shout at her. Everything was all mixed up.

"Well. Thank you," she said, and she knew it was awkward and didn't fully convey anything, but Elena just nodded.

"You're welcome. Also, I know now isn't a great time to talk, but I would really like to talk to you, if you would give me the chance. Would tomorrow be okay?"

Harper nodded. "I open at eleven, but you can come by any time before ten-thirty. That's when Ayumi gets here."

"Okay. I'll see you in the morning."

"Okay."

Harper moved on to the next person she saw and greeted them with a smile, as though her entire world hadn't just been rocked to its core. She had the sudden, desperate need to talk to Angel. But she couldn't. She had work to do. Instead, she made her way to a table and greeted the patrons sitting there. She swung by the table where Angel was playing 7 Wonders with Margot. She was surprised by the fact that the two of them seemed to have hit it off. *Probably because they both hate people*, she thought, chuckling to herself. She helped Ayumi mop up a spill. She greeted October when she brought in some friends and explained how to play the game she recommended to them.

In short, she did her job. She did it well, and she did it with a genuine smile, which was a welcome sensation after her past couple of weeks.

All the while, deep down, she wondered what tomorrow might bring.

CHAPTER TWENTY

For the third night in a row, Elena could barely sleep.

She couldn't stop going over their conversation in her head. How Harper had looked. How she had acted. What she had said. Elena had no idea how Harper might react to what she had to say, but at least she had agreed to see her. Elena wouldn't have been surprised if she'd asked her to leave.

But she hadn't, so Elena had ordered tea and lemon cake, and she had stayed tucked away in the corner of the back room for an hour. She'd wanted to stay to show her support, but she also hadn't wanted to take up a table that could be used for paying customers, or worse, be something that made the night harder for Harper. So she left eventually, looking forward to the morning.

She wondered just how early was too early.

She didn't care at all about seeming desperate. She just didn't want to show up before Harper and be sitting there like a weird stalker.

Eventually, she drifted off into an uneasy sleep. She woke up once at three A.M., wide awake, thinking she had overslept and that Ayumi was already there and that she'd have to wait until the end of the day.

She had to put in some wireless earbuds and nature sounds to relax enough to fall back asleep.

This time, when she fell asleep, she finally stayed that way. She slept so deeply that she could barely manage the dexterity necessary to turn her alarm off when it blared a tone at eight o'clock.

Elena took her time getting ready, and she still wound up leaving ten minutes before she'd planned. She grabbed Harper's gift and drove off, stopping along the way to buy a gift bag and tissue paper.

Harper's car was in the lot when she pulled in.

Her stomach churned in a combination of nerves and excitement. She really wanted this. She wanted a future with Harper. She only prayed that Harper still wanted it with her.

Or rather, that she'd wanted it in the first place. One might think they could safely assume, given the feelings she'd declared, but Elena had gotten into too much trouble assuming already. She wasn't going to do it again.

She took a deep breath.

"Here it goes." Her voice sounded unusually loud in the small, silent car, and she climbed out, bracing herself against the cold.

Once inside, she peered into The Gay Agenda to catch a glimpse of Sappho, to hopefully bolster her courage. She did, in fact, see the cat perched up on top of one of the nearby bookshelves. But instead of giving her courage, Sappho looked remarkably like she was judging Elena.

"Maybe you should have considered being not being an asshole in the first place," her gaze seemed to be saying.

"Fair point," Elena muttered.

When she got to the door of Bewitched, she stopped short. It felt wrong to just walk in, like it was a privilege she needed to earn back.

Instead, she stepped forward and knocked. The room on the other side of the door was unlit except by the weak sunlight that filtered in through the front window in the late autumn morning.

As it turned out, she couldn't have entered by herself if she'd wanted to. Harper appeared on the other side of the door and twisted the lock before opening it.

It felt personal, like she had locked Elena out. It felt like a signal that she had lost before she'd even begun to fight, even though she knew that logically, it probably had more to do with the fact that the Bishop was now a functional business. So it would be logical to keep it locked during the hours said business was closed.

Even so, it felt like an omen.

The rabbit trail of her thoughts left Elena so disconcerted that she forgot the line she had planned on opening with. After exchanging a simple, "Hey," she stepped through the door, her mind a complete blank as she racked her memory for what she'd planned to say.

Harper closed the door behind and locked it again. She didn't say anything else. She just stood there, looking at Elena, and her expression was unreadable.

"I got you something." She shoved her arm out, extending the gift between them. Suddenly, the shiny purple bag that had seemed great before looked like something more appropriate for a toddler's birthday party. Harper hesitated a moment before reaching out and taking it.

"Thank you."

"It's a congratulations gift. For your opening. And an apology gift," she added. "Kind of a two-in-one."

Elena could kick herself. She had spent literal hours composing potential speeches in her head, and every single one of them had deserted her.

"Mmm." Harper made a noncommittal sound, still not moving to open the present, and Elena wanted to walk backwards out to the hallway, back to her car, and then start her entrance over again. But that wasn't possible. All she could do was talk.

So, talk she would.

She might not remember her speeches, but she knew the two most important words she needed to say. Words she'd needed so desperately to get out that she'd had to stop herself from texting them multiple times over the past thirty-six hours.

"I'm sorry." Once didn't seem like enough, so she said it again. "I'm sorry."

Harper didn't say anything. She just kept staring.

Elena swallowed. "I'm not good at speeches. I had a whole thing planned, and I haven't been able to stop thinking about it. But now that I'm here, and it's like all my words just went..." She mimed something blowing away in the wind.

"I understand." Harper said, her voice quiet and curiously flat, giving nothing away. "You don't need to make a big speech. Just tell me what you came to tell me."

Elena blew out a breath. "I'm extremely sorry. That's the biggest thing. The most important thing. I messed up. You told me how you felt—actually, did you even know that? I don't know. You said, um—" She cleared her throat. "You said...on Halloween night. You said..."

"I told you I loved you. I know." Harper's tone was matter-of-fact, like she was reciting the weather report for the day, and not something that had changed the entire potential course of Elena's life.

Elena was taken aback for a moment. "Yeah. That." Elena cleared her throat again. "And I did not react well."

"You think?" Now Harper's voice was showing emotion. Anger wasn't the emotion Elena had hoped for, but it was certainly one she deserved.

"I deserve that."

"You do." Harper stepped toward her. "It's okay if you don't feel the same way. I can take it. I know what our agreement was, and I'm the one who went against it. But you disappeared like some kind of asshole. Why couldn't you just talk to me?"

"Honestly? At first, I didn't really know what to say. You

took me completely by surprise. And at the time, I thought it was the opposite of what I wanted. I thought I wanted exactly what we had—the no-strings thing, having fun. All of that. It was great."

"I thought so."

"But when you told me you loved me, I freaked out." Elena fiddled with the string at the end of her jacket sleeve. "See, soccer has always been the most important thing in my life. It's a big reason why my marriage ended. And I had decided that I never wanted to put anyone in that position again. I didn't want to have a serious relationship until I was retired, because I didn't think it would be fair to the other person. It wasn't just you. I didn't want that with anyone."

Harper nodded. Elena knew she'd told Harper the basics of her stance early on, but that had been when she'd been talking about meeting some random woman on the internet. Now that the stakes were a thousand times higher, she wanted to make sure everything was clear.

"But now I see that it doesn't have to be one or the other. I can have more than one important thing in my life. I can choose to prioritize a person over my career, and it wouldn't be the end of the world. In fact, it's the opposite. It's the thing I want to do most in the world."

Harper's fingers came up to press against her mouth, and her eyes filled with tears.

Elena stumbled on, praying that was a good sign. "But it's not just anyone I want that with. It's you. You're so… you're so amazing. You're creative and you're brave and you're brilliant. You say what you feel, and you go for what you want. I admire you so much." Elena gestured toward the bag Harper was still clutching in one hand. "I know a gift really doesn't mean much, in the grand scheme of things, and I know it's not some big grand gesture. But I think you'll love it. I really hope you'll love it. Because you deserve good things, so many more than you've gotten. You're honestly my favorite person in the whole world."

The tears were sliding down Harper's face now, but she still choked out a laugh. "I'm going to tell Margot you said that."

"Go ahead. Tell her." Elena said earnestly. "I don't want to hide the fact that I'm crazy about you. I'm done doing that. From myself, from you, or from anyone else. Whatever you want with me, however you want our future to look, I want to be with you."

"Really?"

Elena nodded. "I am totally and completely serious. You have no idea how much I've thought about this."

"I thought about you a lot, too." Harper stepped closer, reached out, and grabbed both of Elena's hands in hers, and Elena's heart sang.

"I know relationships are complicated and that we have some things to work through." Elena said. "But I'm committed to showing up, and to listening. I know that's a problem for me, and I'm working on it. I'm committing to trying. I want to try. With you. If you want me."

"I do. Very much."

Elena felt tears welling in her own eyes at the words, and she blinked them away. "It's like you say, right? Something big can never happen without one thing coming along and trying to fuck it up. Turns out that for us, it was me." Harper offered her a crooked smile. "And I'm sorry for that. Again. But if it helps, I have a really good feeling about us now."

"I do, too." Harper said, and though her words were blurred by tears, her smile was more radiant than the sun. Elena stepped forward and started to bend down, but Harper pulled away enough that their mouths didn't make contact.

"What is it?"

"I just want to clear a few things up first."

"Okay." Elena stepped back and made sure she was making full eye contact to show how serious she was about listening to Harper now.

Harper straightened her shoulders. "I've been working a few things out. About myself. I want to go after what I want, and what I want is you. But you should know that I'm in this. One hundred percent. So if you want to try, I want your commitment that you will be, too."

Elena nodded several times. "Yes. Absolutely."

"As in a full-fledged, committed relationship?"

"Yes."

"Okay. Good." Harper cast her glance toward the ceiling. "Fuck, okay, that really makes me want to kiss you, but I have to get through this first. The main thing is that I want you to talk to me. I appreciate what you said about listening, and that's definitely important. But I would also like to listen to you, and I can't do that if you don't talk to me. I want to know, especially when it's something big or when there's something that's bothering you, okay?"

"Okay." Elena thought for a few seconds. "Sometimes it takes me a while to work out how I feel about something, or at least how to put it into words. I'm not always great at that. But I promise you I will try my best, and I'll tell you when I need time to think something over. I won't just disappear again."

"I understand. We can come up with a system, and you can always even tell me in writing, if that's easier. That would be totally fine."

Elena tilted her head to the side, and Harper looked down at the floor. "I might have done some reading about autism."

Surprise flooded Elena's body, followed by something warm that she didn't know how to categorize, as she thought about Harper spending time learning about things for her. "I...appreciate that," was all she could manage.

"Now, the last thing I have to say." Harper took a deep breath, and when she met Elena's eyes, her gaze was fierce. "I will not come second. I understand that you have an important career, and that's amazing, and I will always be supportive of it. I understand that sometimes you'll need to miss things because you have responsibilities. But in the times it comes down to me versus soccer, I don't expect to always be the loser."

Elena nodded. "Definitely. That's actually why I came back early. I wanted to show you that it's not all soccer for me, not anymore. Dee and I talked, and she helped me realize just how fucked up my priorities were." Elena paused, gathering her thoughts before continuing. "I get now that it doesn't have to be all one or the other. But like you said, though, it is my job, and it's a lot. Some things will be unavoidable. If this camp had been a tournament, the way I skipped out could've had serious career consequences."

"I promise that I get that. And it's not like it's only you asking things of me. I'm barely going to be able to leave this place for at least the next six months." Harper waved a hand around to indicate their surroundings. "So, there will definitely be things I won't be able to do. Like, I won't be able to go to all your games when the season starts again, like a good girlfriend should."

Elena chuckled. "I promise I can live with that. Besides, the best part about you being here is that I can be here, too. We have a lot of good memories in this building, you know? Painting. Kisses. Alien vomit."

Harper laughed. "I'm glad you see it that way. Now, just one more thing," Harper stepped forward and smiled a little. "But before I say it, you have to promise not to run away."

"I promise."

"I love you."

Elena's breath caught in her chest at the way Harper said the words, so bravely, with so much certainty. But at the same time, she wasn't sure what to say in return, because she didn't want to lie. Not about this.

Before she could reply, Harper continued. "I know you don't feel the same way yet, and that's okay. I wouldn't ever want you to lie to me, especially not about this. But I just wanted you to know."

Elena felt her chest expand until it almost felt like it would no longer fit inside her rib cage. She moved in close to Harper, taking her into her arms. "Thank you. I'm glad you told me, because hearing that… honestly, it scares me a little, although in the absolute best way. But I love hearing it. As for saying it back, I don't want to say those words before I'm absolutely certain they're true. But I will say this: I choose you. I wasn't looking for what happened with us. It was a surprise. You were a surprise. A wonderful one." Elena paused, then added, "Although for future reference, that makes you a major exception, because I usually hate surprises."

"Really? You dealt so well with this one."

"Ha, ha." Elena smiled down at her and brought her hands up to her lips to kiss them once before continuing. "I'm glad you came into my life. I choose to keep you here, for as long as you want to stay. I choose to keep fighting for you, to try my best to make you happy, because making you happy has become my favorite thing. I'd build you a hundred more shelves just to see you smile."

Harper shook her head back and forth, her eyes leaking tears once more. "That won't be necessary."

"So what'll it take?"

"Just you."

Elena felt like her cheeks might break from a smile this big. "So, I have an important question."

"What is it?"

"Can I kiss you now?"

"Yes, please."

So she did. She leaned forward and captured Harper's lips with her own, and it was like floating on a cotton candy cloud, everything bright and happy and warm and perfect. If Elena had to choose only one moment to relive for the rest of her life, she would choose this one, her whole body reverberating with joy, her hands on Harper's cheeks, and Harper's arms wrapped around her.

But she didn't want to stay here forever.

Elena had a feeling they had a million more moments ahead of them, and she was looking forward to each and every one.

EPILOGUE

Harper watched from the VIP section of the stadium as Elena went through a series of warm-ups for the game that was about to start.

Even in a tank top and shorts (and approximately half a bottle of sunscreen), Harper was sweating in the afternoon sunlight.

She watched as Elena slid on the captain's armband, the same way she had every game this season, and Harper's chest swelled with pride. Elena was a wonderful captain, just as Harper had known she would be, and everyone on the team looked up to her.

Today, the armband was striped with the colors of the rainbow for the Defiant's annual June pride game, matching the numbers on the back of their jerseys. Harper had learned over the past months that a stunning number of the team claimed one or more letters of the LGBTQIA+ alphabet, and watching them strut around in their colors gave her a whole different sense of pride. She'd enjoyed getting to know a few of them since the season started. Some had even become regulars at Bewitched—she saw Min and Natalie at least once a week.

Thinking about Bewitched made Harper glance down at her phone to check if she had any missed messages from

Ayumi or Shawn, who was helping out while Harper was here. There was nothing from either of them, but she did have a text from her mom.

Mom (1:54 P.M.): How are things going at The Bewitched Bishop? Have you been able to hire Ayumi full time yet?

Harper allowed herself a small smile. Her relationship with her parents hadn't magically been fixed overnight, but her mom had started to make tentative overtures recently, often asking her about how things were going at her businesses. It was a start.

Harper typed out a response and sent it just as someone sat down in the seat beside her.

"Did I miss it?"

Harper turned to see Margot, who appeared cool and fresh as a daisy, despite the heat.

Typical.

"Nope. You're just in time. Kick-off is in two minutes."

"Thank God. I basically ran here from the airport."

"You ran twenty miles?"

"Well, I asked my Lyft driver to hurry, which yields approximately the same cardiac results."

Harper laughed, then sobered. "I still can't believe you abandoned Denver for Boston."

"Hey, now, I still visit you, don't I?"

"Yeah, but it isn't the same."

"I know. You miss me."

She did. She didn't ask Margot if the feeling was returned, though, because Harper still wasn't quite sure she would believe her if she said otherwise.

"So, where's the blond?"

Harper frowned. That applied to at least three players on the team.

"Who?"

"You know. The annoying one. Tall. Blond. Bastion of

lesbianism. Hits on anything that breathes?"

Harper was confused, both because Margot had an excellent memory for names and because her description matched Dee, who was retired and would thus not be playing, which Harper was pretty sure Margot knew. But before she could answer, the person sitting alone in the row in front of them turned around. It was Dee herself, wearing a Defiant baseball cap and mirrored aviator sunglasses.

"She's talking about me."

Harper felt her cheeks flush in mortification—further than they probably already were from the heat—at being caught saying mean things. Never mind that she herself had not said any of the aforementioned mean things.

But Margot seemed not to care at all. She shrugged. "Are you going to argue?"

"Nope. Was just going to thank you for the compliment, actually. I'm going to add 'bastion of lesbianism' to my résumé. Maybe buy a bumper sticker and some scarves."

"You would be the kind to make merch for yourself, wouldn't you?"

"You're the one who gave me the slogan. It's a pretty high bar to live up to, you know. Being a bastion. Good thing I'm up for the job."

Harper looked back and forth between them as the exchange continued, like the world's most uncomfortable tennis match.

"That's not what your latest conquest told me."

"I don't have 'conquests.' That's disgusting. But haven't had any other complaints. Just you.'

"Glad I'm here to bring you back to earth, then."

"Any time you want me to take you to heaven, just say the word." Harper couldn't tell for sure from behind her mirrored sunglasses, but she had a feeling that Dee winked.

Margot moved her glance, so that she was staring at the other side of the stadium, holding up a hand to shade her eyes, as though she were looking at something far away. "Oh, wow, are those pigs flying? No? Huh. Guess you're just gonna have to wait for that. Another day, maybe. Better luck next time." She clicked her tongue, then pulled her phone out of her pocket and started typing on it, a clear dismissal.

Dee turned back around without another word, and Harper stayed silent, unsure of what the hell had just happened. Margot didn't like people as a whole, but she rarely singled anyone out for her particular dislike. Dee would flirt with a rock that was vaguely shaped like a woman, so her behavior was fairly typical, though there had been an odd edge to her flirting. And why had she been flirting with Margot? She must have known by now that Margot was straight.

…Or is she? Harper realized she didn't actually know. She'd just assumed Margot was straight, since she'd never mentioned otherwise.

But here was definitely not the time or place to discuss it, and regardless of her sexuality, she certainly hadn't been encouraging Dee's advances. There was no doubt about that. Harper was glad when the whistle blew, signaling the beginning of the game, so hopefully she wouldn't have to bear witness to a repeat of whatever that had been.

Instead, Harper watched as Elena passed the ball to Min, who dribbled it down the field and took a shot that ricocheted off the goal post.

She and the rest of the audience groaned, but it was a strong start. Harper had a good feeling about this game.

Harper knew Elena was nervous. It was their first time playing Atlanta since the semifinals last year, where they'd lost. She was nervous it would get into the players' heads. She'd even gone so far as to prepare a speech, which she'd practiced with Harper early this morning. She remembered how shy Elena had been at first, but then how she'd gotten into the words.

We may not be perfect. No one is going to play perfectly all the time.

Give yourself grace. Give yourself forgiveness. Learn. Move forward. And most of all, keep playing. We're a team. Trust each other. Stick together, and we've got this.

She hoped the speech had gone well. Given the energy the team was already showing, it seemed like they'd taken the words to heart. She gasped as an Atlanta defender went in for a tackle, but Elena did some kind of magical footwork that evaded her, taking the ball up the field toward the goal.

"Go, Elena!" she hollered, at exactly the same time as Dee.

She got closer and closer to the goal, all alone with no other Defiant players near her. She gave the ball a solid kick, and it went sailing past the keeper and into the back of the net.

Harper jumped to her feet and screamed until her throat hurt.

"3-0. I can't believe we beat them 3-0!" Min said, climbing into the back seat of Elena's car.

"Hell yeah, we did!" Natalie agreed, sliding into the other front seat. They'd started a tradition where they rode with Elena to Bewitched after all the afternoon home games. They always put on some early 2000s country hits, which Min complained about, but Natalie jammed to, saying they reminded her of her Mom, who still lived in Missouri where Natalie had grown up.

"That last-minute cross for the tap-in, Elena? Chef's kiss." Min made a gesture with her hand like she was an Italian chef tasting some really incredible spaghetti.

Elena shrugged. "It was a great finish. Thank Annie."

"Oh, I will."

Natalie put on the music, and Elena started tapping the steering wheel to the beat as she pulled out of the stadium parking lot.

"What in the ever-loving hell is a badonkadonk?" came Min's voice from the back seat.

Natalie laughed. "Listen, don't pay attention to the lyrics. Just have fun."

"I'll have fun with my headphones, thank you!"

"Says the girl who listens to someone called The Vaselines. What kind of a band name is that?"

"At least they don't make up words about asses. And... slapping their grandmothers? *Aiya*! What is wrong with you people?" Min yanked her ever-present headphones out of her slouchy black backpack and quickly slid them into position over her ears.

"Her loss," Natalie said, and reached forward to turn the volume up.

The music moved from song to song, and Elena enjoyed every single one. Harper still hadn't come around to country music, so Elena enjoyed it when she could.

Elena had started making a concentrated effort to bond a little more at a personal level with some of her teammates. It had come easily with Min and Natalie, especially Natalie, who was quiet and bookish and liked the same type of books Elena did. Min was loud and knew more about music than she did about sports, which Elena found hilarious for a pro athlete.

But most of all, they both loved to play games. They were at Bewitched almost as much as she was, thanks to their team-subsidized apartment being within walking distance.

When Elena pulled in behind Bewitched, she was pleased to find that the small parking lot was mostly full. That boded well for business, and indeed, when the three of them stepped inside, they found only one empty table in the front room. Natalie and Min immediately abandoned her to go stake their claim.

Elena went looking for Harper and smiled as she passed the Star Wars chess set that was carefully displayed on one of the shelves Elena had made. Sitting in front of it was a tiny sign that said *for display only*. She and Harper broke the rule, of course, but Harper had loved it so much she'd wanted everyone to see it.

Elena kept moving and eventually found Harper in the corner of the back room, explaining Scythe to the group at the table. She was getting really into it, with hand gestures and facial expressions. Elena loved watching her like this. She was in her element, surrounded by people who were happy to spend time together. Harper shone when she talked to other people, which was something Elena would never understand. But she loved it about her.

She loved Harper. So much. She couldn't believe it had taken her so long to say the words. Two months after Harper's grand opening, Elena had said the words for the first time. She'd known by then that she meant them with every bit of her heart.

Their relationship was a journey, and perhaps she'd taken one leg a bit slower than others would have taken it. But she had wanted to do everything right. Of course, she hadn't, because she was human, but they'd worked through their mistakes and miscommunications. They'd compromised. They'd loved each other. Their relationship wasn't perfect, but Elena loved every moment of it.

Many of those moments took place here, at Bewitched, because Harper rarely left.

Today, for example, they hadn't driven to the game together. Elena only knew Harper had come because she'd seen her in the crowd and run over to give her a quick kiss right after the game ended. Shawn occasionally came over from Colorado Springs to watch Bewitched for a few hours, which wasn't something they could do every week, but Elena appreciated it when they did. She always seemed to play better when she knew Harper was watching.

But Elena didn't mind how much time Harper spent here. She loved watching Harper in her element, nerding out about nerdy things. And she'd come around on the games, even the complicated ones, often playing with Harper during lulls. She also sometimes helped out when it was busy, since Ayumi was still the only official employee.

After a few minutes, the table seemed satisfied, and Harper was free to be temporarily abducted back to her tiny office.

Harper finally spotted her, and the beam that covered her face made Elena's stomach warm with happiness. She would never tire of seeing that smile.

In fact, she wanted to see that smile much more often. Hence the piece of paper currently folded carefully in her pocket.

Harper threw her arms around Elena, then took her hand and led her to her office, where she proceeded to push her against a wall and kiss her until Elena had other ideas about how they could spend the rest of the afternoon.

Elena emerged from her haze, blinking slowly. "Wow. What did I do to deserve that?"

"I like kissing you. Is that so bad?"

"Not at all. Kiss me like that all you want."

"Oh, I plan to. Tonight."

Elena smiled. "Have plans for me tonight, do you?"

Harper nipped at her bottom lip. "I do."

"Interesting, since I have plans for you, too."

"And what might those entail?" Harper asked, sidling closer and running her hands up Elena's sides.

"I—" Her response was cut off by a loud explosion of sound that sounded like a game of Pictionary gone very wrong.

Harper sighed and stepped back. "I should go. It's like the wild west out there."

"I noticed."

"I'm definitely going to have to hire someone for the summer."

"Oh, really?" Elena asked, surprised. "You'll be okay to afford it?"

"More than okay. I'm actually thinking about making Ayumi full-time. She asked me for more hours the other day.

She has more free time, now that it's summer break."

"Wait, so you can afford both making her full-time *and* hiring someone new?"

Harper nodded. "The other one would be temporary, just for the summer. Our traffic has gone way up now that school is out. I thought about hiring someone in advance, but I didn't want to guess wrong. I wasn't wrong."

"You never are."

"I'm glad you've learned," Harper said with a cheesy grin.

"Actually, speaking of that..." Elena said. "Do you have another second before you have to get back out there?"

"I'll give you thirty." The wink belied the fact that she was teasing.

"You mentioned something last week, and I told you I'd think it over. To that end, I have something for you." Elena removed the folded piece of paper from the pocket of her jeans.

"'Notice of Intent to Vacate?'" Harper read the title aloud. Her voice was a bit confused, but then her eyes widened and flew up to meet Elena's. "Are you sure?"

"That I want you to move in with me? Yes, absolutely. I want your Darth Vader Band-Aids and your plethora of hair products and every single other thing that comes along with you."

Harper pulled her in and squeezed her tightly, and Elena squeezed back, loving the way Harper's body folded softly and perfectly into hers. Elena leaned down and kissed her.

"It's really rude of you to do this when I can't do anything about it."

"Tonight, love. Tonight."

"I'll hold you to that."

"By the way, I forgot to mention there's a gala next week that my agent says I need to go to."

Harper cocked her head, an amused smile covering her face. "Is there, now?"

"Mm-hmm. I was thinking of asking Margot to fly in to be my date."

"Oh, really?"

"Why, did you have another suggestion?"

"I hear she has a hot sister."

"Huh. That's very interesting information. Guess I'll just have to go with the sister instead."

"If she'll go with you."

"True. She might be out of my league."

"Actually, I think she's totally in your league. Maybe you should even form your own league together."

"I think you're right. We can even make hats!"

Harper tossed her head back and laughed, and a sunburst of happiness expanded in Elena's chest. She dropped her hands down onto Harper's hips and pulled her close again.

"So, you'll go with me?" Elena asked, her lips moving against Harper's ear. Harper snuggled deeper into her arms, hiding away from the world for just another moment.

"Always."

Author's Note

Thank you for reading! If you enjoyed *The Game Changer*, please consider leaving a review on Goodreads, The StoryGraph, or wherever you purchased this book.

* * *

Want to stay in touch and hear about future releases?

Sign up for my newsletter at finleychuva.com.

(Coming soon for all subscribers: a bonus scene showing how Margot finds out about Harper and Elena!)

About the Author

When Finley Chuva was twelve years old, she started sneaking 1980s Harlequins out of her aunt's basement, and she hasn't stopped reading romance novels since. Now she writes her own with significantly more queerness and less usage of the word "mousy." She loves tea of any kind and Flamin' Hot Cheetos (preferably not together). She lives with her wife and their assortment of pets in South America. *The Game Changer* is her first novel.

Learn more at finleychuva.com.

Printed in the USA
CPSIA information can be obtained
at www.ICGtesting.com
LVHW040541080824
787702LV00023B/199